TREE GOD
Behind the Iron Curtain

by

Alan Hamer

authorHOUSE®

AuthorHouse™ UK Ltd.
500 Avebury Boulevard
Central Milton Keynes, MK9 2BE
www.authorhouse.co.uk
Phone: 08001974150

© 2007 Alan Hamer. All rights reserved.

No part of this book may be reproduced, stored in a retrieval system, or transmitted by any means without the written permission of the author.

First published by AuthorHouse 8/8/2007

ISBN: 978-1-4343-2265-4 (sc)

Printed in the United States of America
Bloomington, Indiana

This book is printed on acid-free paper.

"To the people of Mogilev, to my family, my friends and my colleagues. You not only lightened my life, you enlightened my life and will remain part of my being forever."

PREFACE

In September 1964 at the behest of Russian Premier Alexey Kosygin, himself a textile engineer, a £30 million contract was signed between Polyspinners and V/O Techmashimport (the Soviet purchasing agency) to build a polyester fibre complex in Mogilev – 200 miles inside the western border of the USSR. A colossal plant covering some 300 acres the total project cost would rise to £100 million. It would have a workforce of more than 7,000 and turn out around 70 different products for everything from conveyor belts and tyre cord to suits and shirts. It was designed for an output of 50,000 tons per annum equivalent to the total output of the United Kingdom.

CHAPTER 1
LOM

My mind worked overtime trying to imagine what Russia would be like. We would be flying over the Iron Curtain. Would I be able to see it? All the news we saw was of Cold War and military parades; stern-faced men stood in freezing conditions watching huge missiles, tanks, and jack booted soldiers. They threatened us with nuclear bombs and generally didn't like us. I summed it up in my mind. It was grey – Iron Curtain grey, and it was cold, bloody cold! "Paint a rosy picture, why don't you?" I thought, pressing my nose against the Austrian Airlines Boeing 707 window.

Up above the clouds you could be flying anywhere in the world. Maybe somewhere there would be a gap that would reveal hidden territory and now the light was fading. As we descended, and after the captain had firstly made the announcement in German, he informed us of our imminent arrival at Moscow Sheremetyevo Airport on time, approximately 6.30 pm local time, and that the temperature was 0°C and snowing. "Great!" I turned to Arnie, "proper Russian weather." Arnie carried on coughing.

We had met at Heathrow Airport that morning. I shook hands with a sheepskin coat. What kept it rigid was difficult to define; male, five foot nothing in Cuban heels and I guessed about seven stone including the sheepskin. Arnie looked about seventy years old with a jaundiced complexion and a drooping pencil moustache. Added to that he had the worst hacking cough I have ever heard in my life. In fact he looked almost dead and he was travelling to the Soviet Union with me.

Over a coffee and a sticky bun I found out that Arnie worked for a company called Baker Perkins and he was going to install a Polymer transfer system. "The polymer chips are blown through" he did his best to explain. "Like a pea shooter?" I tried not to grin. Arnie put his head to one side giving me a look. "Yes… a bit like that."

Still I scanned the view, "thick cloud" as if anyone was listening. We were reminded to complete the embarkation forms, which had been passed round during the flight. Where was I going? - Mogilev. Why was I going? – Should I write Spy? I settled on Work. How long was I staying? - Three years. How much money? - Enough. Do you pick your nose? - Yes, regularly. "Are you okay?" Arnie looked concerned. "Sorry Arnie just daydreaming."

My first impression as I walked down the aircraft steps, was not the weather but the smell. It was strong and pungent, and as we stepped into the terminal building, the question was answered as scores of men lit up their strange cigarettes. Three-quarters squeezed cardboard, tipped with the foulest smelling tobacco. I was more of a social smoker but decided to try a Pall Mall that I had bought on the plane. "Sorry," I said to Arnie as he again started to wheeze on the thickening blue air. "No problem," he replied, "I used to smoke a pipe." That was obviously another question answered.

We eventually formed three queues moving towards sentry boxes, each housing a soldier. I was now up to the thick red line painted on the floor and a small woman dressed in a black uniform put her hand on my chest. "Passport," she muttered, along with something else I didn't understand. She tapped her finger on the embarkation pass I was holding. I nodded, "Yes." "Now," she said, as the man in front moved away. She grabbed my arm and pushed me towards the window. The soldier looked very stern, with a small round face topped with this enormous peaked grey hat. Around the hat was a red band, fronted with a gold coloured hammer and sickle on crimson star badge. He said something sharply. I shrugged my shoulders and slid the embarkation pass under the glass. "Passport," he barked. "Oh, sorry," I replied, and pulled out my passport from my sheepskin coat pocket. *"Otkooda?"* Again, I stared at him. "Where are you travelling from?" the woman whispered. "Oh, England," I said. Again, he spoke. "Where are you going?" she confirmed, "Mogilev." "Ah, Belarus," he responded. He spoke again. "How long you stay?" asked the woman. "Three years," I said. *"Tree Goda?"* asked the solider. *"Da,"* I showed off with the only Russian word I knew. "Tree God... Tree God!" Now I was on a roll. The soldier leant back in his chair, lifted my passport, looked at it for a moment, then raised his eyes and stared at me for what seemed to be a lifetime, during which time I am sure I could feel myself shrinking. Eventually, his right arm started to lift as if clockwork, and as it reached ten to the hour, the rubber stamp held between his thumb and forefinger slammed down on the passport, which he closed and slid back under the glass. I took it quickly and turned to Arnie, saying "Good luck," as the woman waved me through. I was in!

It must have taken best part of an hour to negotiate the baggage collection and baggage check. Hundreds of people pushing and jostling – survival of the fittest. Again, I stood close to Arnie, who appeared to be suffering badly. Eventually, I caught sight of a poster being held up, "Mr Grantham. Mr Hamer," written on it. I waved at the man holding the poster. He pushed his way through as close as he could to the baggage check and shouted, "Wait there." We watched him tug on the sleeve of another black-uniformed woman who was deep inside some poor sod's suitcase, clothes scattered all over the desk and even some on the floor. The traveller stood helpless with his hands on his head, pleading with the woman. Again, our man tugged at the woman's sleeve. She rounded on him, giving him a mouthful of something not very nice, as he jumped back sharply. Another uniformed helper walked towards our rep and pushed him back. "Looks like we're here for a while," wheezed Arnie. My cases were full to bursting and I searched desperately in my pockets for the keys before remembering that they were in my wallet. Eventually, after continued pleading by our rep the woman pointed towards us and waved us towards the desk. However, the crowd was such that we couldn't get through. She started to scream at people, presumably to make way. They didn't. The uniformed helper then got stuck into the crowd, pushing people back, riot police style. We shuffled through to the front of the queue and I lifted our bags onto the desk. Our rep held out his hand, "Mr Grantham?" I pointed to Arnie, "and Mr Hamer." We shook hands. "Mr Touse," he said. The official interrupted the pleasantries. Head back and hand on hip, she pointed to the luggage. Mr Touse interpreted. "What's in this case?" "Clothes," I said. "Open." "Shit!" I said under my breath while fiddling with the key. Arnie opened one of his cases and she started to root through his jim-jams, holding up his Marks and Spencer's dressing gown for all to see. I flicked the catches and the lid flew up. She picked up a jumper and dropped it on the table, swung the case round, thrust both hands into the case, pushed, pressed and kneaded, like grandma making dough. *"Vsyo,"* and she waved her hands. Mr Touse whispered in my ear, "Have you any cigarettes or chewing gum?" Fortunately, I had a couple of packs of Wrigley's and some Pall Mall in my hand luggage, which I opened. He quickly pulled out two packs of each and laid them on the table. Her hand slid over the goodies like a magician doing a card trick, and they disappeared as she beckoned the next victim to the desk.

Alexander Touse was employed by Techmashimport, the Russian department responsible for all major industrial machinery imports, their Head Office being in Moscow. He was about my height, five foot ten, thin, like Arnie, with extremely thick glasses perched on the end of his nose. He explained, with regret, that he needed to stay at the airport to meet four German businessmen who were arriving that evening for a meeting at Head Office. He also explained that, unfortunately, most of the hotels in Moscow were full due to the fact that tomorrow there was a big Communist Party meeting in Moscow; the delegates, from all over the world, having booked up all the accommodation. "I'll take your word for it," I said. "You're going to the Hotel Ostankino, and the taxi has been paid." He opened his wallet and gave us both 20 rubles. "This should be enough to cover anything that you need tonight, and I will see you at the hotel at 10 am tomorrow. Okay?" "Okay," we replied, "See you tomorrow."

We followed the taxi driver through the main doors and out into the Moscow night. Wet snow was blowing in a strong wind, then freezing as it hit the ground. The pavement was more like a skating rink. Arnie climbed into the back seat as I slipped into the front passenger seat. I called it a seat only because I sat on it, and maybe it was when Stalin was a boy, just like I called it a taxi, because that's what was written on top. It definitely was a rickety old rust-bucket Volga shed. He switched on the windscreen wipers. They didn't work. My side didn't have a wiper blade; his side did, simply to smear the advancing sleet. The driver countered this, supposedly, by positioning his chest up against the steering wheel with his nose pressed against the windscreen. To compound matters, he obviously had a very heavy right foot, and once this taxi was rolling, well, hang on for dear life, and I did. Now I know what it's like going down a bob-sleigh run with an idiot steering. Arnie just coughed in the back, without a word.

In the haze, I saw the lights change from green to red, and stamped my foot on the imaginary brake. The car started to slide and I thanked God there was nothing else on the road. The driver fought to keep the car straight and we ground to a halt half way across the junction. There followed a loud bang and the car jerked forward as another vehicle piled into our rear end. Arnie screamed in pain and, as I turned round, he slumped across the back seat, moaning, wheezing and generally fighting for breath. "Arnie, are you Okay?" The driver by this time was out of the cab and having a fistfight with the driver of the other taxi. I knelt on the front seat and tried to help Arnie to sit up. "I'm Okay," he panted, "I've hurt my back."

Shortly afterwards, we pulled off the main road and into a dark square surrounded by high-rise flats. To my right was a small dingy-looking building that was our hotel. The driver had moved to the back of the taxi and was gesticulating towards the boot, which he then kicked. It didn't open. I told Arnie to go into the hotel and sort out the rooms. It would be warmer inside, and he was definitely looking worse for wear. I would stay with the cab and get the cases. The back of the taxi was stoved in and the prospect of retrieving our luggage didn't seem that good. The driver, now becoming more agitated, was shouting at everyone within earshot, which was probably a radius of about a mile. Getting no assistance he eventually came over, planted both hands on my shoulders and obviously wanted me to stand here and guard the taxi. I assured him, *"Da, Da,"* before he disappeared into the gloom.

I must have stood there for over half an hour and the snow and wind were having an effect; my teeth chattering and my body shaking. I was freezing, bloody freezing. Then out of the blizzard came this dark figure carrying an enormous crowbar on his shoulder. *"Lom!"* he said, thrusting it towards me. *"Lom,"* I replied. He grimaced as he spit on his hands, and within five minutes ripped the boot lid completely off its hinges. He threw what was left on the ground and jumped up and down on it, cursing as he did so. Much as I would have loved to have watched this Russian war dance, I snapped my body back into action and snatched the cases from the hole in the back. The driver then jammed the remains of the boot lid back into the void, muttered something in my direction, probably wishing me a pleasant stay (NOT) before driving off. I, in turn, shuffled the cases into the hotel foyer. "Oh, God, warmth," I uttered.

First impressions of our Moscow hotel? A single over sprung glass door that I had to force my way through led directly into the reception area. The once parquet floor looked completely worn out, probably enhanced by the appearance of not being polished for several years. Against the far wall opposite the door was a small wooden reception desk painted a welcoming turd brown. The desk was unmanned. The over-riding sensation again was the smell. A mix of Russian tobacco just like the airport and a strange smell of decay or rot, I couldn't put my finger on it. Actually I didn't want to put my finger on it whatever it was. I found Arnie sat bolt upright in a tatty chair. He never moved as I approached, staring lifeless straight ahead. "Okay, Arnie, have you got the room?" "Room?" he replied, "I've got the key. Number 13." "Should be a treat," I laughed, without a flicker from Arnie. "Go up," I said, "and I'll get the bags."

One floor up and down the corridor, a single light bulb lit up the dingiest threadbare carpet. "Number 13," I said to myself. On the left, "nice door." It looked like cardboard with a strip of imitation red…well ex-red leather, held on with drawing pins. Arnie sat on the nearest single bed, head in hands. Two bare bulbs, now this was lavish. One bare bulb in the centre of the room and one bedside lamp on what appeared to be a wooden box between the beds. A chair-like thing and two planks of wood with a curtain across doubled up as a wardrobe. The room was completed with a large picture of Lenin pointing somewhere, to a hoard of people, "Probably west," I thought to myself. I somehow couldn't take my eyes off the picture and could not understand why until I got closer. It was hanging away from the wall at a crazy angle and looked dangerous. "No hidden cameras behind this baby" I informed Arnie without response.

Arnie said he was hungry so we decided to go and have a look for the restaurant. Just down the corridor we passed a door which was open. The room appeared to be occupied by a gang of waifs and strays, eating. "It must be the staff room," I said to Arnie. "Just a minute," he said, turned and disappeared into the room. His face peered around the door. "This is it," he said. He walked to the counter. The granny, dressed in a white smock said something in Russian. "Food?" asked Arnie gruffly. She uncovered two stainless steel trays, hotdog sausages in one, and what appeared to be watery mashed potato in the other. I pointed at both. Two sausages followed by a ladle full of slop were applied to each plate. *"Hleb?"* she asked. "Anything," I replied. She cut two slices of brown bread and dropped them in the goo. "Coffee?" I asked, and she poured ready-mixed from a large stainless pot. She pointed to a tray containing cutlery. I picked up a large spoon and waved it in front of her before dropping it on the plate. Arnie paid the woman. We sat down and ate, and what can I say other than it filled a hole. Arnie went to bed, while I walked down to the front door for a fag. I looked around the bleak, dimly lit square. I was right - Grey, Iron Curtain grey, and cold, bloody cold. "What had I done?"

CHAPTER 2
TANYA, THE TEA LADY

Miss Jolly said it and I believed it. With both hands firmly grasping the desk and fixing my eyes with hers she said calmly but firmly " if you don't pass your eleven plus exams Alan, I'll make you eat your school cap." You have no idea what effect those few words had on me. Every day before donning my cap and setting off for school or returning home I would stare at the hat and try to imagine having to take a bite. On several occasions I even tried it out only to pull the cap away from my mouth turning it in my hands before having another practice chomp, eventually placing it on my head. Only at this point would my brain allow me to pull a marble from my pocket and set off the half-mile or so.

Marbles were plentiful and the inevitable 'plunk' sound as one dropped through a grid only forced the hand back into the trouser pocket this time revealing the 'iron dowdy' later to be known as a ball bearing. These were completely different; these had to be won, usually in the playground and under serious rules of competition. Those who make the rules usually win and the older you are the better your chances are of making the rules.

I stopped on the steep hill down Harpers lane and stood looking as the sun sparkled on the dowdy. What a magnificent specimen it was and the weight of it. I bounced it carefully up and down in my hand. "Grids" I thought to myself, "too many grids." I slipped it quickly back into my pocket before kneeling down to pop a tar bubble that squirted a tiny jet of water into the air. That's when I looked up into the sky to check for planes or eagles. "Ah well" I would have to settle for clouds and started to draw the outline of a large puffy cloud with the end of my finger before attaching an imaginary rope to one end and pulling it so that it bumped into a neighbouring cloud, "klump!" I shouted. A quick visit to the toilet behind the bus terminus at the top of Halliwell Road. As smelly as it was I was always keen to see if the 'Kilroy wuz ere' artists had any new offerings. My reading wasn't good but Kilroy was special. His Humpty Dumpty head and big nose and eyes sticking up over the wall always made me laugh. Was it just me or was it all kids that spent most of their time either looking down at tar bubbles that encompassed the outer edges of cobble stones or looking up into space hoping to see something to run home and tell mum and dad about. That obviously did not include toilet graffiti.

"Mr Hamer...Mr Hamer! Are you ready?" Mr Touse touched my shoulder as I returned from another time and place. "Sorry I must have...." "How far do we have to travel?" asked Arnie. "Well, it's about..." Mr Touse scratched his hat, "in kilometres..., well it's a long way." "About 400 miles to Minsk" I said, "Then about 150 miles to Mogilev." "Well done, Mr Hamer." Mr Touse looked impressed. I omitted to say that I had just spent 2 weeks at London head office being prepared for everything Russia.

We walked out of the hotel and into a crisp, freezing, but sunny, Moscow morning. The area was mainly residential flats, quite stark in appearance and very quiet, eerie in a way, and grey. We walked on, turned a corner and into a large square with a huge monument of a rocket being launched. "The world's highest stressed concrete statue," Mr Touse explained with a hint of pride. "It's grey!" I pointed out, without response.

We dropped down into the underground - the Moscow Metro. The escalators were incredible; they appeared to go on forever, disappearing into the bowels of the earth. When we arrived on the platform, everything seemed very ornate and clean I thought; very clean, not a piece of paper or cigarette end anywhere. As the train scuttled along, I studied the metro map above the window. "Where are we going?" I asked. "Red Square," was the answer. Just two words and my pulse increased. Arriving at the platform I could see large marble busts against the walls and the floor, also marble, shimmered like a psychedelic ice rink. Up we went, a long way up, eventually emerging onto Red Square. My eyes seemed to take a while to focus. There was a covering of snow, well trodden now and quite treacherous. To my left, I could see St Basil's Cathedral; the coloured domes resplendent in the sunshine. "Across there," said Mr Touse, "is the Kremlin, and in the middle," he pointed, "You see the queue?" "Yes," I replied. "That's Lenin's Mausoleum. We have just missed the Changing of the Guard." "Can we get closer?" Arnie asked, and we followed Mr Touse across the square towards a black, marble building surrounded by people. At this point on the square the Kremlin wall behind the monument seemed to have grown significantly and the entire square looked to have taken on a completely new face. The scale of the sandy-red walls had a breathtaking effect. "Come on," said Mr Touse, "we'd better get those hats before you freeze." Little did he know that I was already frozen but from the inside, out. We moved up Red Square, away from St Basil's, and back over to the right. "Hotel Metropol," said the sign. "Come on, we'll get a drink." Mr Touse spoke to a smartly dressed man controlling all movements in and out of a large, ornately carved wooden door. The man ushered us through into a beautiful, warm restaurant. Now, this was a hotel. "Coffee cognac?" asked the waiter. I gave him the thumbs-up. Mr Touse gave us a short history of the Metropol, the oldest hotel in Moscow, and of other Moscow features, The GUM, or Univermag, just to our left, and the Bolshoi Theatre just across the road.

Following the reviver, we spent about half-an-hour in the GUM, searching for fur hats. Mr Touse said the best place to shop in Moscow was in the older quarters, the narrow streets behind the Bolshoi. The first shop we came to, according to our escort, was the best fur shop in Russia. The shop had a corner position and stood out from the other smaller ones. It had enormous modern windows to both sides displaying mink and sable coats of all shapes, colours and sizes. "My mum would have a field day in here," I said. They pulled out a selection of fur hats and Arnie settled for a regulation brown hat, which the entire population of Moscow appeared to be wearing. Not me, no chance. Not when there were silver grey specimens on offer. "That will do," I announced, strutting up and down looking in the mirrors. Mr Touse paid for both hats and out we went, fearless into the Siberian chill. What a dipstick I must have looked. Chocolate-brown sheepskin coat with the biggest, silveriest '*shapka*' in the whole of the Soviet Union. I was a walking Belisha beacon. "Look at me," the hat screamed. I matched the scenery... grey!

Later in the day we arrived at the railway station. Like most stations I had ever seen it had high ceilings but unlike the Metro the ornate stone walls looked filthy. We hung onto a metal pillar in what seemed to be a rip tide of people, while Mr Touse fought a war to collect our tickets. This was survival of the fittest, and any show of weakness on his behalf would probably have resigned us to staying in the capital indefinitely. His nerve held, and he came back clutching the tickets. By the time he returned, my bladder was ready to explode. Why I waited, I don't know. I should have followed my nose. This was my first real lesson for surviving in Russia. DO NOT USE PUBLIC TOILETS – EVER! To describe what lay within the toilet would be sickening. Suffice to say, consider fouling yourself and cleaning up the mess later.

We walked along the platform peering through the windows where possible, and some of the carriages appeared very cramped. Each carriage had a supervisor or guard dressed in black uniform with gold epaulettes, but unlike the airport security, no cap. Each carriage was numbered, and Mr Touse was talking to a diminutive lady at carriage No 8. She held out her hand and beckoned us on the train. "First compartment," said Mr Touse, and we shuffled in. Apart from the carriages being painted a mucky green colour on the outside, our compartment was not dissimilar to our corridor carriages back home. We stashed the luggage, apart from our hand luggage, in a second compartment and settled down. Not long after, we were off out into the Moscow night.

The lights at first twinkled but soon disappeared. The guard stood at the door - *"Chai?"* she asked. "Tea," translated Mr Touse. *"Chai,"* I replied. I stepped out into the corridor. Half way down, a man closely resembling an ape resplendent in vest and pyjama-bottoms leant on the window rail, puffing away on his cardboard ciggie. I still couldn't get used to the smell so pulled out one of my own and lit up. Mr Touse erected our table under the window just as our tea arrived. 'Russian tea' consisted of an ornate metal holder complete with delicate glass and filled to the brim with scalding hot tea - no milk, just a slice of lemon and two sticks of Caxap (pronounced Sahar). "Sugar," said Mr Touse. "It looks like Caxap to me." "Does it taste like Caxap?" asked Arnie with a flicker of a smile. "No, actually it tastes like sugar," I confirmed, licking the end. The tea was superb and actually the best thing so far, excluding Red Square that is. The train chugged on.

Later on, I walked to the toilet. Sat opposite was the guard, stoking up the boiler by feeding the fire with lumps of wood stacked behind a curtain. "Toilet?" I asked, and she pointed to the door behind me. I opened it and went in. Thank God I only wanted a pee. There was a bit of porcelain with two pieces of wood attached, but basically it was a hole in the floor with grab rails on the wall to hold onto. There was a hot-water boiler above a small sink and a lump of rough brown soap. Not having my towel, I shook my hands and walked out. "Thanks," I said. "Tanya," said the guard, with a smile. "Alan," I replied. She pointed to a folding seat. I pulled it down and parked my bum. We chatted for ages, not knowing what the other was saying and over another hot cup of tea we passed through a large town. *"Gorod Geroy Smolensk"* she said, pointing through the window. I nodded in agreement. All good things, as they say, and I stood yawning. *"Spokoyny Noche,"* she said. "Goodnight," I replied, and wandered back to our compartment.

Arnie and Mr Touse had changed into their jamas. I did likewise and jumped into the top bunk bed, Mr Touse the bunk below mine and Arnie bagged the lower bed opposite. The main light was switched off and replaced by a dim red light, which illuminated the snow-covered countryside. Suddenly it looked beautiful. "Mr Hamer, do you know the Ram of Derbyshire?" asked Mr Touse. "Not personally," I quipped, "but I hear some of the sheep are cute." Arnie chuckled, but no reaction from Mr Touse, who broke into song:

"There was a Ram of Derbyshire who had a nasty trick
Of jumping over fences and landing on his ****
Hey ding-a-ling, girl, whoever you may be
It was the finest ram, sir, that ever was fed on hay."

And on he went. Arnie was choking and I was laughing uncontrollably. It wasn't just the verse; it was more that it was being sung by a Russian with the weirdest squeaky voice. I tried biting the pillow. Thud, thud, thud, went the compartment wall. Somebody was not quite so impressed with the vocals. Mr Touse stopped immediately. Now he whispered, "Do you know any dirty ditties, Mr Hamer?" "Daniel in the lion's den," I replied, "but that's for another day. Goodnight," I said. We all agreed. I looked out over the shimmering vista and felt content.

Half-light broke in through a crack in the curtain window and there was a knock on the door. "Wakey, wakey," I shouted. Two groans in response. I climbed down and opened the door. Tanya was still door knocking further down the corridor. *"Chai?"* she asked. *"Da,"* I replied, opening the curtains. I looked out over a small village covered in a light dusting of snow. We soon washed and dressed as the train slowly trundled into Minsk. I kissed Tanya, the tea lady, on both cheeks and pressed a packet of Wrigley's into her hand. *"Do svidanya,"* she said, and we were off.

We moved to the front of the station and Mr Touse walked off to talk to a taxi driver, followed by plenty of head shaking and pointing. "Okay" he said, "we've got a taxi." "Where to?" I asked. "Mogilev," he confirmed, matter-of-fact-like. "In a taxi?" "Yes," he said, "It's the easiest way." "Can he drive?" I asked, tongue in cheek. "Of course," he said, not understanding the joke. "Don't worry, Mr Touse, things are getting better all the time," I said in summation. I think Arnie was past caring.

Once out of the city, certain things became apparent very quickly. The road to Mogilev had obviously been constructed in one straight line, as the crow flies, and the land appeared completely flat, apart from very gentle humps and hollows. It was a narrow, single carriageway road, with the occasional large pothole, which, if not avoided, shook the taxi violently. The overriding feature of the journey was one of beautiful desolation, fields, forests of silver birch and pines, rivers and lakes. Apart from the occasional lorry, we could have been travelling on the moon - nothing - no one. The drive was quiet; we very rarely spoke. I think we were all hanging on for dear life as the driver wrung out every leg of every horse under the bonnet, before slipping the car into neutral to coast the maximum distance. This routine continued for the entire journey.

After passing a number of old wooden houses, we came to a roundabout. On a concrete sculpture was written, MOGILEV but in Russian. *"Mogilev,"* confirmed Mr Touse. "Thank the Lord," said Arnie. "What does the name mean?" I asked. "Literally speaking it means Grave of the Lion King," replied Mr. Touse. "Oh great," I thought, "I'm a Leo." We ran through town before coming to a steep hill down to a bridge over a very wide river, the *"Dnieper"*. On about half a mile before turning right, *Ulitza Gagarina*, another mile, a left fork, *Prospect Shmidta*, and we pulled up. On our left there were three blocks of flats surrounded by a wooden picket fence. Mr Touse disappeared into one of the entrances, and soon reappeared with a tall man, and even taller woman. Grant and Dorothy ushered us down the path and into the next to last entrance. Grant pointed to another door to the left of ours. "The Spinners Arms," he said, "our pub." Through the doors we dropped our luggage and I followed Grant into a large dining area. "Gerry!" he shouted. "What?" replied Gerry, who emerged in his whites. "Any chance of some lunch for the new arrivals?" "No problemo," said Gerry in his finest cockney accent. A cigarette hung precariously from the corner of his thin lips. "Any preferences?" "Soup," said Arnie. "Anything," I said. "Ten minutes," Gerry confirmed. Grant pointed to another room, "library and table tennis."

We stopped on the second floor where Grant opened Arnie's flat and quickly showed him round. We carried on to the top, fifth floor. My flat was on the right, flat 25. Inside the door was a corridor leading to the bathroom, with a separate toilet. On the right was a kitchen with cooker and fridge. On each side of the corridor, there were separate flats. Grant opened both rooms. "Take your pick," he said. The flat on the left was bigger, with a balcony. I dropped my bags inside. "That's fine," I said. Grant suggested I had lunch and then call round at the office for an introductory chat. I nodded and thanked him.

I looked round my new home, my Russian bachelor pad. Inside a frosted glass door was a rectangular room around 25ft long by 15ft wide with a brown parquet floor. Immediately on the left was a single bed covered with a white linen duvet with an unusual diamond shaped cut out in the centre. Facing the bed on the right was a large antique looking wardrobe. Also on the right was a blue fabric double couch with dark stained wooden arms. Lastly in the bottom left hand corner was a small dining table. The balcony was fitted with a single plastic washing line and a thermometer attached to the side wall. The windows and glass doors were covered with white lace curtains. I leant on the large radiator under the window and surveyed my pristine new kingdom. "Not bad," I thought, "Not bad at all."

CHAPTER 3
POPEYE

Arnie and myself were invited to meet the lads and girls in the bar. I had tried to sleep, but couldn't. Probably the excitement had beaten off the jet lag, whatever! The shower had put new life back. Oh, yes, the shower. You have to be quick on your feet. You get the temperature just right, climb into the bath, wet your hair, somebody flushes a toilet in Minsk and the water turns to molten lava. Adjust a hot water tap in Smolensk, and not only does your water divert via the Siberian line, it also taps into the Gobi deserts, freezing, brown and full of sand. Anyway, an hour after starting, I felt refreshed. On with the glad rags – jeans and a snazzy sweater, then down to the Spinners.

This was novel, the first pub I'd been in without having my age questioned. It appeared there was a rota for bar duty, amicably agreed between the beer-swilling fraternity, of which I was to be an active member. My name was added to the rota; now I was one of the lads. Pete was behind the bar, another Bolton lad. Older and married, yes, but from home. "Pint?" he asked. "Big choice," I replied. Watney's Red Barrel was the only draught beer, lager was Tuborg, in cans and Mackeson was available in cans. There was also a range of spirits and mixers. Bar chits replaced money, so you could get completely pissed for nothing, or at least it seemed like nothing. When you don't see the money you don't miss it the same, so I tried a pint.

Basically, a hole in the ground, but well thought out, the bar itself had several tables and chairs. There was a dart board and a game of table skittles, plus a Shove Ha'penny board and to make it a real bar there were a couple of belts of horse brasses hung behind the bar. Then there was a tiny anti-room "The Sin Bin" Pete informed me with a very mischievous grin "for disco nights at weekends." With wagging finger he emphasised the point, "the bar is strictly for Polyspinners' contract workers and their wives only." After another mouthful of ale I duly conceded; "okay."

At around 10.30 pm, we moved from the bar to one of the guys' flats. About forty strong, we squeezed into his room and quickly decimated a prepared buffet before getting down to the main event. As we sat around the room, the introductions began. I stood up first, giving my name along with a brief résumé on my background. This was repeated around the room. Next time around, we had to sing a song or recite a verse. Fortunately, I was left till last in the round, panicking as the task came nearer. It wasn't that I couldn't sing, it was that I couldn't think of something appropriate. The Scots made the most of 'The Northern Lights of Aberdeen,' 'The Wee Cock Sparrow Sitting on a Barrow,' or 'The Bonnie, Bonnie Banks o' Loch Lomond.' They started it off and everybody joined in. Some of the girls were good singers. Mind you, others were bloody awful, but the girls had to get a rousing applause. The other guys, however, tended to bomb. Somehow, a West Country yokel doesn't do it singing an Elvis Presley song. The dirty verses I knew were anything but mixed company, especially when you're trying to get acquainted, so I went for it, 'She's a Lassie from Lancashire'. I started, and bingo, they all sang the song for me.

As always, any drinking party eventually deteriorates, especially after the couples bid their leave. It was now I understood that I would be living abroad with some hardened, worldly contract workers. Singing was superseded by drinking games, arm wrestling and an amazing barefoot, can-crushing contest; one which I was to regret the day after. Quite a simple game really. Stand an empty beer can upright on the parquet floor and try to flatten it completely with the fewest stamps of your bare foot. The next lesson was how to open a bottle of wine without a corkscrew. Simply remove the foil, grip the neck with one hand and slap the base of the bottle with the other. The 'hard-men' could achieve this in two to three slaps. The cork desperate to fly out of the neck leaving the white wine looking more like ginger beer. After breaking every bone in my right hand I finished up holding a tea towel against the base and hitting the bottle against the wall.

The main event was a nude wrestling match between the camp champion, a Scot, and an English challenger. With his dick firmly pushed up his arse and his balls doubling as ear muffs, England lost.

As I staggered home, there came a realisation of just where I was and who I was. These people were different, and yet they were British. I had met some real people tonight, including Tommy, a six foot four inch man-mountain from Sunderland. Denzel was the only Welshman on site and the part time schoolteacher with a class of around 20 British kids. Then there was the real 'Popeye', otherwise known as Jock from Aberdeen. This guy was a dead ringer, including the chisel jaw, pipe, lumber jack shirt and forearms like ham shanks, including, 'Anchor,' tattoo. I'm not sure about the spinach but treat this guy without the necessary dignity and he would probably eat you!

CHAPTER 4
GROWING PAINS

So what do you know at twenty-one? Well after considering the question for at least two seconds I suppose not a lot really - probably the basis of what's right and wrong, taken in the main from your parents, with a dollop of grandma thrown in. My recollections of my grandfather were vague, as he had died before my sixth birthday. I do, however, remember a kind man, always smiling, and always giving. I must have been blessed that way, a family who smiled with their eyes and whose generosity was boundless. Yes, me and my sister, Carolyn, were lucky children and happy, always fighting, as kids do, but content all the same.

I always considered myself to be the luckiest person on earth, fancy being born in Bolton, the biggest and best town in the world and in Lancashire, the Red Rose County, which, by the way, won the War of the Roses, and with undoubtedly the best football team in the country, the Mighty Bolton Wanderers. I raise both hands aloft in salute accompanied by a stifled roar even now as then. Thus is my passion for those magnificent men who have been privileged to don the shirt.

Being born on the 26th July 1948, I was christened Frederick Alan Hamer, after my father, and, just like him, was called Alan, the Frederick coming from my grandfather, Fred.

My mother was called Joan and my grandma was Ethel. My parents had a greengrocer's and fishmonger's shop at the top of Halliwell Road; by far the best end of Halliwell, although not posh, far from it, just proper folk! The majority of my formative years were spent at my gran's cottage across the road from our shop. Here I learned about the outside bog, dolly tubs and dolly blue, sugar butties, drinking tea out of a saucer, Toc H lamps and silver threepenny bits. Oh, yes, and cuddles, lots of loving cuddles - always worth falling off your bike for.

So, at twenty-one I was a loved boy, still living with my parents at the Albion Inn facing Bolton Bus Station in the centre of town. I had worked for Dobson & Barlow since leaving Smithills Grammar School, unceremoniously climbing through the classroom window one day never to return and academically a failure. 'Dobbies', as they were affectionately known, was a large textile machinery manufacturer based at Bradley Fold on the border between Bolton and Bury. An apprenticeship had been arranged by my Uncle Walter, who was one of Dobson's original 'Outfitters,' having installed machinery around the world, and in particular the 'Scutcher', whatever that was. Anyway, by now I had advanced to machinery sales in the jobbing department dealing with spare parts, 9 till 5 with plenty of time for seeing the lads, girls and drinking. What more could anybody want? What's more, I had plans to work in America.

In the summer of 1969, I had given the company three months' notice and was waiting for a US work permit. An ex-prisoner of war friend of my father, called Bos, had a very successful General Motors' car dealership in Crawley, Louisiana, and had agreed to find me a position, possibly cleaning cars to start, as well as providing me with digs and sufficient money to live. All I had to do was make my way down there, hopefully seeing some of the states along the way.

Mondays are never the best, especially after the weekend's excesses, but the brain has an escape clause when you're working notice. Jim, the Commercial Manager, worked at his desk just across the office and very rarely involved himself in my business, so it was unexpected when he put the phone down and said, "Alan, can you spare me a couple of minutes?" "Certainly Jimmy," I replied nervously. "Pull up a chair and sit down. Alan, I know you have arranged to go to America, but would you consider putting it off for a couple of years and going out to Russia for us?" "Sorry, what?" It must have been that gormless expression on my face, so he continued. "We need a materials engineer to work on the Russian project and I think you would be ideal." It was like being kicked in the goolies. I had forgotten how to breathe. "How long?" "2½ to 3 years," he replied. "Look, have a chat with your parents tonight and give me a decision tomorrow." He stood up; as if realising he needed a pee. "Don't worry; we'll sort out your contract." "Yes," I said, "I'll go." "Talk to your parents and let me know tomorrow," he repeated. "Okay?" "Yes, yes... don't worry... thanks, thanks." I walked back to my desk – "Yes! Yes! Yes!" I repeated quietly to myself, banging the desk with my fist.

I now had six weeks to get organised for departure, which included two trips to Manchester. The first was a detailed trip to Millets to get, among other things, the Admiralty weight winter warmers. Basically thick woolly vests, long Johns and socks that I was reliably informed would see me safely through a trip to the North Pole or up Mount Everest. Holding a sample vest I thought it wise to check with the manager, "will you be sending a Sherpa to carry the luggage?" A pained half smile was the best reaction I suppose I could have expected so I quickly pressed on with the inventory.

The second was a farewell trip to the Manchester Beer Keller that included cold weather initiation. This comprised a full and forced strip on the coach home, dropping me off around 2 am on a very cold and raining early October morning. When I say, "Dropped off," I mean thrown off outside Bolton Technical College at the top of Manchester Road and about one mile on the opposite side of town from home. If anyone saw me that night tiptoeing about hunched ape-like with two hands firmly grasping my nuts, I apologise. Eventually, I did get home to find my clothes wet through on the steps of the pub.

Monday 6th October 1969 at spot on 8am the company car arrived to take me to Manchester Airport. Not surprisingly, we were completely organised, the bags ready by the door, and my mum was running through the check-list. "Passport, tickets?" "Money?" Dad chipped in. That was his department. He had stuffed around £200 in crisp new tenners in my back pocket the night before. They were all there except for Carolyn who was studying at Warwick University. "Bye, Willie," I said, giving her a hug. Willie was our cleaner and had been with the family, well, forever. She pulled me into her enormous bosom, "Go on, sod off and annoy somebody else," she said. "Oh, Willie!" said my gran, "How can you say such a thing?" I gave gran a cuddle as the waterworks started; the tears flowed freely from her eyes that seemed to appeal to me and ask why I was leaving. "Don't worry, gran, I will phone and send you letters." "You'd better." I turned to my dad, whose face lit up with his trusted smile. His hand thrust towards me; I took it and squeezed. No words were exchanged – none were needed. We loved each other. So far, so good. As my eyes connected with my mum's, they sparkled as they filled with moisture. My chest appeared to leapfrog into the back of my mouth and I must have lunged into her outstretched arms. She stood proud, holding my hands, this woman who brought up her children to know love, respect and honesty. She could wrestle crocodiles whilst charming the Queen Mother. I had no fear of going, just a boyish thrill. The car moved off slowly and I waved until they were out of sight, but they would never be out of mind.

"Mr Hamer! Mr Hamer! *Avtobus! Bistro!*" The Russian dezurnaya (attendant come cleaner) was shaking me. "This is becoming a habit" I thought, "I can't be late on my first morning." The guys had told me to be on the bus by 7.30am. I looked at the clock; it was already 7.20. I grabbed at the Long Johns and woolly vest, socks, jumpers x2, parka, boots, woolly hat, and legged it.

On the road, at the end of the flats, stood two single-decker buses. Pete leant out of the front bus. "Come on, Alan, you're last," he shouted. I jumped on. *"Poechaly,"* said Pete to the driver, and the bus set off. "What did he say?" I asked. Oh, "Let's go," I was informed, "Pete is *'Poechaly'* man, this week". In all the mad panic I had forgotten to check the weather. Now, as I looked out of the bus, I was looking at a Christmas card. There had been heavy overnight snow, with drifts around 3-4 feet deep. In the early dawn light and clear blue sky, the scene was beautiful. We turned off Shmidt Street and onto Gagarin. Carry on down to the main road, turn right and past the end of the airport, right again, along a dual carriageway and then up a hill. Quite a challenge in these weather conditions; the bus sliding around and the driver constantly applying opposite lock. As we got to the top of the hill, somebody spotted a guy trying to stand up. He was obviously drunk, and everyone on the bus cheered as he stood up completely covered in snow. I craned my neck watching as the bus passed by. He fell over backwards. I shouted, "He's fallen again." Somebody shouted back, "he's dead." "Can we not do anything?" I asked. It would seem that this was a regular occurrence and many were not found until early spring during the thaw. The word was, "Never, ever lose it outside during winter, or else."

I had been told that the site was about the size of Hyde Park in London. If I had ever been, this would have been informative, but I hadn't. It will be the largest synthetic fibre plant in the world, but how big's that? Well, once over the top of the hill, I was to know. Still being built, and only a shell at this time, the Filament Yarn building was incredible. Half a mile long by one third of a mile wide. We passed along the length of the building, then past the Staple Fibre building and turned right. Right again and we passed the Pilot Plant and pulled up. "This is as close as a bus can get," said Pete, pointing to a barrier and several armed guards holding machine guns.

I jumped off the bus and sank up to my knees in fresh snow. "Where is the other bus?" I asked one of the guys. "The CJB bus goes round the other side of the Pilot Plant over to the Polymer building and DMT." He pointed to a tall building with a large, shiny metal chimney. "Over there," he said. Our bus pulled away. Like big kids, snowballs were already flying; the guards pulling away a safe distance, obviously not sharing our joy at such conditions. I had seen pictures of Prisoner of War camps during World War II, and this was just the same. Two wooden coning towers were connected by two high wire fences, topped with coils of barbed wire. Both the coning towers and double barriers were manned by machine gun toting army guards. At that moment, a convoy, of what appeared to be three large wooden cattle trucks, pulled up at the first barrier. "Bomb them," one of the guys shouted, and as if a platoon of commandos, we were soon hurling our grenade-like snowballs at the trucks. "Convicts," someone pointed at several pairs of eyes peering through the barred, square, cut-out holes in the side of the trucks. Quickly, the area around each opening was peppered with white blobs. "Shot," I said as I got a direct hit through the bars. "Come on, kids," shouted Poechaly Pete, "Work." We followed.

As we set off on our route march, I was informed that the convicts, a gang of shaven-headed madmen, were actually building the plant that we would be moving into, and that they were now in the Filament Yarn building - the next major structure to be completed. There were reports of Russian engineers supervising the erection being terrified after people had been killed or seriously injured by falling or having things dropped on them.

Inside the Staple Fibre building was like nothing on earth. Not cold but freezing, and dark as night, apart from the occasional arc light that lit up a basic concrete void. It was an enormous freezing tomb. We picked our way up a double flight of rough concrete steps and onto a corridor ... well - half a corridor - the left-hand wall still hadn't been finished; through a door on the right and into an office. The room was about 10 yards long by 8 wide. It had large windows at the far end, with a view over to Pilot Plant opposite, and to the right the barriers where we had bombed the convicts. Down the centre of the room was a large trestle table covered with a mass of technical drawings. At the far end was a wood-burning stove, which the guys had knocked together, and was now being lit to provide some basic warmth. A chimney was suspended by loops of string attached to the ceiling, and out via a hole in the window packed with wadding and masking tape. Four desks and chairs, plus a mountain of boxes filled with tools and spare parts completed the room.

"Don't get settled," said Norman, "You're next door with the boss." He turned right and stuck his head round the door opening. There wasn't a door on this office. "Your new man's here," he said, and allowed me in. "Alan," said Malcolm, "Come in." He walked from his desk in front of the window, hand outstretched, "Good trip?" "Eventful," I said. "Alan, meet John." I again shook hands. "John," he continued, "is our Chief Engineer and my number two." John's desk was at right angles to Malcolm's. "This is your desk." He pointed to a third desk on the left, just inside the doorway. Once again, there was a centre trestle table covered in drawings, and both side walls had metal racks covered in machine parts. "No stove?" I asked. "No," replied Malcolm, "We're hard in here." He pointed to a thermometer on the wall. "Minus 5," he said.

I had worked with Malcolm since moving to Machinery Sales, although he had a separate office off the main office in Bolton. He was our Technical Director and had been working in Russia as a Site Manager for about six months or more.

When you're twenty-one, everybody looks old, but I would estimate Malcolm to be in his forties. For his age Malcolm was a good looking guy with a well tanned complexion, dark jelled back hair and enormous bushy eyebrows. John, however, must have been close to retirement, certainly late fifties, with an oval face, rosy cheeks and thinning flyaway silver hair. As we were completing our introductions, I heard a familiar voice. "Mr Hamer!" "Mr Touse!" I said, without looking. "Alexander, take Alan onto the shop floor and introduce him to Mr Tchaikovsky. They are pushing to complete the pump room and need to check all the spinnerets before erection. I'll see you around lunchtime," said Malcolm. I called to see Pete, next door, to collect the packing schedule and then followed Mr Touse down onto the floor. As we arrived, about six men armed with crowbars and axes were stacking a mountain of sticky, oily bundles on the floor. A tall, middle-aged man with a long black overcoat stood watching. "Mr Tchaikovsky?" "Mr Hamer," he replied. "Alan", I extended my hand and we shook. He said something, Mr Touse translated. "He thinks you are too young." "Probably," I said, and smiled. He smiled back, threw his arm around my shoulder and gave me a hug. "Mr Touse, please ask Mr Tchaikovsky why the case has been opened before I arrived." He did. "You were late," was the reply. "Please explain to him that I cannot check contents unless I see a case untouched." He again excused himself by saying that they needed spinnerets to complete an installation in the pump room. I handed him the packing schedule. "Please ask him to sign for the contents and then I will check them." There followed a heated discussion in Russian, which was not translated. I said, again, "Please sign it." He held me in a long stare, pulled out a pen and signed. *Spasibo,* I said. *Pozalusta,* was the reply. "Now I'll get stuck in," I assured him. The ensuing handshake was solid and prolonged and I felt he realised that he wasn't dealing with a pushover but someone who would stand his corner.

Tchaikovsky ordered about four of the workers to remove the remains of the packing case, as the other two lads helped me with checking the contents. The corner that we were in was very dark and mind-numbingly cold. After the lads had told me their names, Sergey pointed at me and said, "Bobby Charlton?" "Rubbish," I replied. "Freddie Hill, far better player." "Manchester United," he went on. "Rubbish," I said. "Bolton Wanderers, best team in the world." Two hours later we had sorted the stock and I had two Russian pals, Sergey and Yuri, and two new Bolton fans who worshipped the real football God, Freddie Hill.

I returned to the office to write up my report. Trying to write wearing polar mitts is difficult. I took them off. Peter B dropped a load of packing schedules on my desk and explained what he needed and when. A trip to main stores was on the cards.

"Grub up," someone shouted from next door, and I was through before he had closed his mouth. I wasn't particularly hungry but my body shuddered with cold. I walked past the food - Lancashire Hot Pot and Red Cabbage which Gerry had cooked back at the flats and sent up in an enormous steel tray. I knelt down in the front of the stove, as if in prayer. "Bloody hell! Is anybody else freezing?" "No," was the reply, "It's quite warm in here."

The main topic of conversation over lunch was about the DMT plant, nicknamed the 'Dynamite Factory', due to the explosive nature of the chemicals produced, compounded by an explosion which had happened overnight about a week before I arrived. A centrifuge had been blown through the roof, resulting in a couple of Russian workers being seriously injured and a complete shut-down in the Pilot Plant production line.

Norman said something. "Eh?" I replied, not hearing him. He walked over to where I was sat, and at around six foot two tall hovered over me, his face portraying some menace. With an open hand, he slapped me across the cheek. "Pardon," you mean, horses eat hey," he instructed. "Christ," I said, shocked at the blow. He hit me again, but harder. "And don't blaspheme." He grabbed my ear as I checked my teeth. The rest of the guys were laughing. "Growing pains, Alan?" Something like that, I thought to myself.

Bert walked in. I knew it was Bert, because it said, "Bert," on the safety helmet he had just removed. "Where's the Dymo tape?" I asked, "I would like to put Alan on my helmet." It was next door.

Bert stood about five foot nothing tall but was solid, around forty years old and from Wigan. An Electrical Engineer with a gifted vocabulary, Bert had not only grasped the Russian language, he had added to it, and how! Leaning towards the Anglo-Saxon four-letter word weave, was novel in itself, but to break open Russian words and phrases and stuff in the 'f...ing' word was clever and very funny. *"Horosho,"* means, "Good." *"Horofuckingsho,"* is somehow, "Very good." Anyway, Bert was in the office and, as a result, the mood had lightened. The profanities rolled off his tongue like water off a duck's arse. I caught a glance from Norman and took the opportunity to nod towards Bert, my eyes suggesting the necessary slap. Norman laughed, "Are you kidding? He's a lost cause!" "What's that?" asked Bert. "Oh, I just got my head stoved in for saying, 'Christ.'" "What? What did you fucking say?" He came towards me with his fist clenched. Everyone started to laugh. "Oh, yes, very funny," I said. We shook hands. "So," said Bert, "are you on day-release from school?" "No," I said quickly, "I've been sent over to keep you old buggers entertained."

After lunch, I donned my woolly hat and set off to the Main Stores to arrange a transport schedule to Staple Fibre. About a mile apart, I had to walk past the DMT Plant and on past the Polymer building, which, at five storeys high, blocked out the sun. A high-pressure exhaust pipe blasted out a cloud of steam. At around 10° below zero, the steam was instantly transformed into a cloud of tiny ice needles which descended and swirled around in the breeze. I bowed my head and closed my eyes to slits as the needles penetrated the skin. As I tried to speed up in the knee-deep virgin snow, I lost my footing and landed on my backside. "First Christmas bump," I thought, "but probably not my last."

Leaving Polymer behind the site opened up. I got my first look at the main stores, a huge building about a third of a mile long. Outside the stores was a mountain of packing cases now covered in snow and vaguely resembling a familiar view from home looking up towards Winter Hill and Rivington Pike. A huge rolling crane completed the picture. It was a daunting thought that I was responsible for over 50 per cent of this machinery, worth around £35m. Well, it was mine right up to the time of erection. Oh, yes, and half of it was outside covered with snow, and this was only October. I hoped the packers had done their job right.

Inside the stores, half way along the far wall was an office. I knocked on the door and went in. Derek was inside; a Londoner working for CJB (Constructors John Brown). He was based permanently in the stores and arranged all materials movements around the plant. I sat down with him and discussed the can and cannot do's. I was introduced to 'Big Cyril' who had trekked over from the polymer building and who said he was from "Dawrsit" or somewhere exotic sounding. "Cawld as a penguins chuff out there!" he exclaimed. "Sorry?" Derek checked, obviously not paying attention. "Cawld as a nun's c...!" "A bit cold", Derek chipped in I presumed trying to defend my ears from Cyril's eloquent vocabulary. On the walk back, I decided how I was going to explain the can't do's, in fear of getting another battering.

Arriving back, I was confronted with a Russian girl, her blonde hair and angelic face hooded in a tight, woollen headscarf. She was dressed in the obligatory black *fufaika* - a padded coat, and black pyjama type baggy leggings. She was plastering the unfinished wall at the far end of the corridor.

Under all the clothing was a beautiful girl. Distracted I sat down at my desk. I heard her coming down the corridor and turned to get another glimpse. As she came into view, the beauty decided to hawk up a blockage in the windpipe or beyond, and with professional aplomb, pouted and spat out the biggest, greenest lump of phlegm that smacked against the wall and stuck. I turned away quickly. "Dear God," I thought, "What a lovely girl!"

Never again the admiralty weight vest and Long Johns; the itching was driving me insane. It was no contest; I would sooner freeze to death.

"Poechaly," shouted Pete, and Boris obliged. It was the end of a long, cold and sometimes painful first day. The rest of the week was just as cold, but this wide-eyed boy was determined to make the most of this amazing opportunity to learn. I was going to grab hold with both hands and hang on for dear life. I hoped the growing would get less painful.

CHAPTER 5
KIPPERS & CHAMPAGNE AT MINUS 37°C

Before you could say, "Bugger me, it's cold," it was Christmas Eve. On the work front, things had settled into a good routine probably because I had become more streetwise. Tchaikovsky was completely content, providing he got the wood for his summer house and garage. We were told that the packing cases were made from top spec Canadian Cedar, the variety that makes the best log cabins and, now, in this winterised tongue and groove condition, it was perfect for building. As Staple Fibre number one, Tchaikovsky was the man, and happy men are much easier to deal with.

Still without mains heating, average inside temperatures were minus 10-15°C, outside minus 20-25°C. It's amazing how you get used to it, providing you are properly dressed that is. Proper hiking boots, long, woolly socks, pyjama bottoms under a pair of jeans, two to three woolly jumpers, dependent on thickness, and a long parka style winter coat with a fur-lined hood, woolly balaclava and yellow safety helmet, plus special snow mitts finished off the look. This, of course, wasn't sufficient to keep you alive; movement was required, regular movement.

Mr Touse was a frequent visitor and always good for a belly laugh. My name had now been extended to, "Mr Hamer, them's um there." He skitted my Lancashire accent.

It was said that his 'little black book' that accompanied him everywhere was full to bulging with every dirty ditty known to man and many other things as well. Alexander Touse was 'the proverbial scribbler.' He was, however, still struggling with the concise version of Eskimo Nell. Whatever Pistol Pete and Mad Magrew were doing in the frozen wastes was causing a great deal of consternation, well, for Tousey anyway. After first removing the thick elastic band, he flicked through the pages before giving me a couple of verses of, "She was standing on the Bridge at Midnight." Still he was funny more for his squeaky voice and his general being than the actual verses. He was definitely not your average Russian male - slim and frail looking with milk bottle bottom specs, but he was a natural comedian. Even with his exceptional knowledge of English, Mr Touse was strangely out of place.

No, your average Russian male seemed to fall into two main categories, the Engineers like Tchaikovsky or his under managers, who were mainly hard-looking men, obviously intelligent but strong. Then you got the labourers, the *'Montage.'* We were told that they were simple country folk shipped in to do special erection projects. Whoever and whatever, these people were a breed apart. Not just hard, you could skate on these guys and girls. I had seen a man bury an axe into his own leg. The gash, about 6 inches long, was right down to the shin bone. He wrapped a strip of dirty shirt around the wound, pulled his sock up, pants' leg down and carried on working.

I saw a team of men; *'Brigade'* opening a huge case about 10 feet high and 20 feet long. Crowbar experts, they would ease up the corners; four men on top of the case, they would then work on one side, prising it out about a foot. Sitting down in a line, they would rock the side out with their feet and a chant of, *"Ras. Ras. Ras."* They then turned and walked the side down, arms out like a surfer. One worker left on top would drop down the crowbars and axes. He then jumped down onto the side of the case, now flat on the shop floor. I yelped as he landed directly on an eight-inch nail, the huge nail now protruding about 2 inches through the laces of his boot. He never made a sound, but carefully grabbed his right leg behind the knee with both hands and pulled the foot up and off the bloodied nail. He then jumped off the case, stamped his foot a couple of times, picked up his crowbar and rejoined the rest of the *'Brigade'* to carry on unpacking the case. As a child, I was brought up in a fruit and vegetable shop and had more than once stood on small nails, so knew the instant pain from such a wound, apart from the time off school recovering. I swear that I felt the pain more than he had. My gran always said, "No sense, no feeling." Maybe she was right.

I think it's important to know something of the recent history of the region. I was reliably told that one in three people were killed in Belarus in World War II. Mogilev itself was flattened as the Germans moved north towards Moscow. Only one building, the theatre, was left standing. Close to our flats, there was a large war memorial, a mound of earth covering a mass grave containing 5,000 bodies. It was said that if you stood by the grave long enough you would see the earth move. I have to say that I did! And I didn't! My thoughts however did leave me severely chilled. Communism meant that everybody would, or should, work. Don't work, don't live, literally. It was as if there was no place for pain, physical or mental, more a matter of getting on with it, keeping your end up at all costs.

The most extraordinary episode had happened a couple of days before. A regulation trip onto the shop floor for a chat with Bert took me up onto No 2 cutter platform. Bert was easy to find; you just followed a trail of sound, finding him inside a large electrical cabinet, beavering away. Five minutes' discussion and I set off back along the platform. At the end, near the steps, flames lapped up the left-hand side of the platform and about 20 feet into the air. I looked over the side of the platform but couldn't see what was causing the blaze, so

I quickly dashed down the steps and onto terra firma. About 10 yards away was a huge lump, I likened to the Hunchback of Notre Dame, sat on a small wooden box. The lump was busy welding a metal plate onto one of the feet supporting the platform. At the same time, a team of girls were working, polishing the rough concrete floor using buckets of water and big rotary grinding machines. The welder's lead snaked across the floor, through a large puddle of water and to a generator. The thick cable had split and a live electric wire sat in a pool of water produces fire.

My first reaction was to shout at the welder, without response, not a flinch! My next thought was for Bert. I shouted up repeatedly. By this time the flames had increased and the platform above, along with machinery and control panels alike, now turning black. "Bert!" I shouted again. I saw his head appear over the handrail. "What the f...ing hell?" "Get off," I shouted. As I did, the flames stopped. I turned round to see Sasha, a Plant Foreman stood alongside the generator. He had thrown the switch. I turned back to the hunchback, who was still tapping the welding rod, now to no avail. The man-mountain then uncurled. It was a woman, about five foot five and twenty stones, with a huge round face and oriental eyes. Sasha started to bark at her. It didn't sound pleasant. She, however, never uttered a word but moved steadily towards him. When she arrived, without warning she drew back a clenched fist and in one movement smashed it across his jaw. Sasha fell, as if shot, and did not move. The woman threw the switch back on, walked past the flames, sat down on the box and carried on welding.

After kicking the cable away from the puddle, both Bert and myself checked Sasha who by now was sat rubbing his chin before going back to the office for a cuppa and to tell the tale. I suppose the moral of the story is, "Don't mess around with a Russian woman when she's welding." I never saw the woman again and considered that Sasha may have relocated her to teach the convicts the art of welding.

Back at the flats, things were bouncing along. Working in the Polymer Building, and not one to be in the bar socialising, I hadn't seen much of Arnie. I did, however, bump into him on a trip to the market. The Russians laid on three minibuses and drivers that ran a shuttle service to and from town at twenty-minute intervals from 9am until 10pm. We had a good chat, mainly about work. The amazing thing was, however, that he looked 20 years younger. The cough had gone, the cheeks were rosy, and there was a definite sparkle in his eyes. I hadn't thought too much about it at the time, but one evening walking downstairs to the bar, I passed two attractive young ladies who smiled and said, "Hello." I heard them knock on Arnie's door and as I turned, disappeared into his flat. "Lucky, jammie old bugger!" I muttered to myself, "No wonder he's perked up." They may have been teaching him the language or Belarussian arts and crafts, but I doubted it. Whatever they were teaching him was doing him good. I hoped he had checked for spy cameras and wasn't entertaining the local KGB.

It had been recommended to me shortly after arriving, to check the flat for bugs. "Too late," I had told them after going over the flat with a fine tooth comb. We knew that they were there and among us, possibly working as dezurnayas and or interpreters. They, "The KGB," had taken over a complete office block just off Lenin Square in the town centre, around the time that Polyspinners' Engineers had started to arrive. Mogilev was an average sized town with a population of approximately 200,000 people and growing rapidly - obviously, with the development of the world's biggest synthetic fibre plant. There were no major military bases other than a small army camp, reportedly near a picnic spot that had been visited called Polikovichy. There was rumoured to be a major Air Base not too far away to the south, which made sense as we regularly heard supersonic bangs. We were also warned not to photograph any bridges. Obviously, a town built on the banks of Russia's second longest river, "The Dnieper," had a number of bridges, which I supposed if we blasted at the most strategic spots would disrupt both road and rail links, well, rail links anyway. At this time of year, with the river well frozen, people not only walk across the ice, they also drive wagons across. "No," I thought, "It is more likely that they wanted to monitor and add expertise in dealing with a large influx of Capitalist Pigs into an interior provincial town that had not clapped eyes on such people before.

Trips to town usually meant Saturday lunches at the Dnieper Hotel, Mogilev's only hotel. The Dnieper was on the main street and, actually, the terminus for our minibus service. Arrive for about 12.30pm after a good lie-in, into the foyer, turn right, up the stairs and into the restaurant. *"Pozalusta. Pozalusta,"* was the greeting, with a sit-where-you-like policy. We were welcomed like family into the restaurant, and always received special, if not charming, treatment from the staff, which begged the question, "Why?" Well, we were rich. You just had to compare what a top Russian engineer would earn, say Tchaikovsky, around 120-140 rubles a month. We, however, were paid living expenses and spending money of seventy-seven rubles a week, or three hundred and eight rubles a month. What's more, for us bachelors there was nothing to spend the money on, apart from food and booze, and that was very cheap. Well, for us anyway.

You couldn't beat a huge bowl of soup, *Borshe* or *Schee*, both with *Smetana*, or sour cream, as we know it. This was followed by mushrooms, oven-baked in herbs and sour cream, finishing off with a nice goulash, washed down with a bottle of Pliska - an Armenian five star brandy; a couple of beers, and back on the minibus in time for the football, live on World Service.

Speaking about the price of booze, a bottle of vodka cost approximately three rubles. On our minibus journey home, as we turned into Gagarin Street, about 500 yards on the right was a small food store. Outside the store stood a man facing the traffic and resembling a hitch-hiker. However, instead of sticking out his thumb, he placed his hand flat on his chest, his thumb tucked inside his coat and his forefinger and middle finger displayed and tapping frantically against his black coat. I had seen this display on a number of occasions, sometimes only the forefinger displayed. On my most recent trip, my curiosity had got the better of me and I asked about this repeating phenomenon. "It's easy," explained Vova, a site interpreter. "First thing to understand, is the different drinking culture in the Soviet Union." First and foremost, apart from restaurants, which were few, there were no pubs or bars as we know them, as places to socialise. Vodka, spirits, wine and beer were in the main sold in food stores for taking home. Taking booze home on a very limited budget, had to come a distant second to securing the food needed to live. This was even more important during long, hard winters. However, it was no secret that a large number of Russian men suffered an alcohol problem, which needed to be fuelled. Finally in Russia, once a bottle has been opened it is, "dead," the entire contents are drunk. Russians do not have screw tops because a top is never replaced, not on booze anyway. So, our man wanted a bottle of vodka but could only afford one ruble. The two fingers protruding on his chest meant that he needed two rubles. Another man arrives, also wanting a drink, and offers the man another ruble. The man retracts the middle finger leaving his forefinger extended until the final offer arrives, at which point the bottle of vodka is purchased, opened and split between the three men. This would probably happen in the darkness at the rear of the shop. There are places, particularly in bushes, where glasses are hung specially for the purpose. The glass would be filled and drunk down in one, *"Do dna,"* (bottoms up). Three glasses equals one bottle. Serious drinking, no frills. Vova, once again, gave us a quick lesson in survival and that Russian style hard drinking and Russian winters (*zeema*) do not mix.

Back at the flat, apart from a good size rug in the middle of the room, it was basically as I had found it. I had, however, bought myself a good stereo unit from one the guys who had brought a quality Bang & Olufsen unit back from his holiday back in the UK. A Gerrard 3000 deck with amplifier and two Sinclair speakers blasted out the music, certainly loud enough to get the neighbours knocking on the walls.

The main change had come in eating arrangements. At first, all meals had been taken in the canteen. I still went down for a hot English breakfast before work, when occasionally up in time. I was interested in cooking when I was at school and had wanted to be a chef. Now given the opportunity I decided to cook my own evening meals and was already a regular shopper at the local food store situated just a stone's throw from the flats. It was a medium sized stand- alone building with blindingly bright strip lighting. The shop sold most everything including fresh fish and meat. It has to be said however that most of the time this 'fresh' food looked anything but. Most evenings, arriving back from work, I would call in to pick up milk, bread etc. The fancy goods were bought from Gerry's chilled cellar beneath the flats.

Once a month, a Hungarianways articulated lorry would arrive at the plant to drop cases containing spare parts. As the buses took the guys back to the flats, I would travel with the Hungarian truckers, directing them back to the flats. We opened the gates and let the wagon pull right up to the cellar entrance. A human chain would then handball the goods inside, where Gerry would check against his delivery note. This process could take up to two hours to complete, leaving us with an Aladdin's cave full of goodies. The wagon then moved down to the Spinners Arms, where the draught beer for the bar was unloaded and replaced by the empty kegs.

I call them fancy goods, where in fact I mean goods from home – toothpaste, soup, baked beans, sponge puddings, Dundee cake, Lurpak butter, and my favourite Cadburys Fruit and Nut. Then we come to the drinks section. Gordon's Gin, Ballentine's Whisky, Martini, Tonic Water and Tuborg Lager in twenty-four-can packs were top of the hit list, along with a range of fags in 200s. State Express 777s were my choice.

Oh, yes, back to cooking tea. I had quickly become famous for my curry and chips.

I was now a member of "The 21 Club," a bachelor's club that started with twenty one members. As more wives had joined their husbands the twenty-one had reduced to around fifteen active members who shared out the duties, some on booze, some food and some entertainment. I was on food and once a week provided curry and chips for fifteen. Len, from Derby, who was founder member, was entertainment and arranged songs plus a comedy sketch. Following the show Len's Russian girlfriend would join us. Now the conversation would usually change to *Irena's* erotic lecture. Quite amazed I was to find out that she could explode up to 10 times in one evening session. Long after the subject had moved on I found myself staring at a point on the ceiling that was supposedly marked. I could only presume like a battle scar? These were things I definitely didn't understand.

Anyway, Christmas Eve meant a Christmas show in the canteen. A stage was set up and most of all of the tables removed to provide a dance floor. We, "The 21 Club," had been rehearsing for a couple of weeks and were performing *'There is nothing like a dame'*, from South Pacific. Dressed in my sailor's outfit: jeans, white T-shirt and white sailor's cap; specially made by the Mogilev W.I. the girls didn't stand a chance – not tonight. Anyway, we gave it a bash and brought the house down. After the concert, Gerry brought out the food, a hot buffet – 'the works'. During the recess, the disco was set up and off we went, twisting, twirling and all kilts flying. I was anything but a dancer, in fact I came from the old school of science which said, "Stand on the outside, catch the eye and pick them off as they get thirsty." That's fine when you're in charge - not out here. Out here the girls are in charge. You're like ducks at a duck shoot. They grab your hand, give you the cheeky wink and you're away onto the dance floor. Polite conversation was usually brushed aside with a good squeeze of your bum, followed by a rhythmical churning of the hips, plus the obligatory open-eyed stare. And these girls are here with their husbands?

A shy boy, sweat started to trickle down my neck and back. "Don't worry," said Tracey, "you'll be safe with me. Anne's on a mission to get you," Tracey continued to tease. "Oh, God!" I replied, "Not Anne." She was the notorious ball-breaker, and it was said that the 'Sin Bin' had been shortened from its original title of 'Anne's Sin Bin'. I had danced with her before, but to disco tunes, quickies! She was notorious as Queen of the Smooch. At this point I should get things straight, Anne was actually a lovely woman, married to Gary and they had two young children. Gary was about thirty years old and a diminutive figure; about five foot two and about eight stone wet through, with a full face black beard. The thing that made him stand out, well to me anyway, was his smile; he was always smiling. Maybe Anne had something to do with that. She was a couple of years younger and a couple of sizes bigger. Not big-big, no, just shapely. That was, however, until you came to the chest area. Dear God, what a pair of lungs! You could lose the Fifth Infantry Desert Rats between those dunes. The low-cut, black velvet, tight-fitting, slinky dress rounded things off a treat. Several drinks and a couple of dances later, the pace slowed as Chairman of the Board gave way to Procol Harum, and Anne struck. "I think you've been avoiding me Alan," as she gently took my hand and pulled me into the middle of the crowded dance floor. As they *'skipped the light fandango'*, her body entwined mine like a fly in a Venus Fly Trap. Her mouth nuzzled my neck and she whispered in my ear, "Hello, sailor." God, was I going to embarrass myself on the dance floor? "Hamer, chips!" Len grabbed my ear, "C'mon Tony

Curtis," he laughed. "Supper and you're cooking." "Sorry," I said to Anne, and kissed her on the cheek, "gotta go." Chip supper and Five Card Brag it was; then off to bed.

9.30am on Christmas day morning and my alarm went off. I sat up and looked through the window. A brilliant blue sky and a light covering of snow. I stood up and walked to the glass balcony door and peered for an age at the thermometer. Minus 37°C. "What?" I couldn't believe it. I was stood in the buff, cosy and warm, and it was minus 37°C outside. Christmas morning and we, 'The bachelor boys', were invited for a kipper and champagne breakfast in Gerry's canteen. I spotted Dave coming out of the other block of flats and round for breakfast. He started to run, head down in pain. I ran to the kitchen and jumped on the stool, quickly opening the quarter-light, the only window in the flat that wasn't sealed for winter. I stuck my head out of the window to give him a good verbal volley. It was like heading a brick wall, and when I opened my mouth I couldn't speak, the icy cold taking my breath away. I quickly pulled my head back in. "Shit!" I screamed, "Shi-i-i-i-i-t! That's cold."

Kippers and champagne are special and all the lads had a present from under the Christmas tree, a chocolate variety pack in a stocking and a pair of woolly socks for everyone. We sang several Christmas carols before opening the pub for more drinks. I stayed upstairs and helped Gerry tidy up until my phone call home came through. Between the canteen and the library, a wooden phone booth had been installed, with a light and chair. My five minutes on the phone consisted of four lots of Merry Christmas and you won't believe the temperature out here!

After a couple of hours in the bar I went back to the flat, showered, changed into collar and tie and was on my way to Norman and Nina's flat for dinner. Norman had worked two years at another plant at Novopolotsk, about 200 miles to the north. During that time, he had met and married Nina, who was originally from Chernigov in the Ukraine. Nina looked more Scandinavian than Russian, sorry Nina, Ukrainian. She was about five foot eight tall, slim, with short blonde hair and very athletic-looking. Not unusual, as she had been a competitive gymnast. She would tease Norman by kissing me several times on each cheek and exaggerating the kissing sound. "That's enough," said Norman, "you'll wear him out." "Chance would be a fine thing," I countered. Three other couples joined us for Christmas dinner, a proper turkey roast. During the meal, we found out that Nina had reared the turkey herself, keeping it in a cellar under the flats. "Awe!" was the consensus "poor thing". Norman had shied away from the whole thing and refused to get involved in its demise. "Nina did it," said Norman, "Wrung its neck." We all laughed. I looked at Nina's hands, "No problemo," I thought to myself, "hands that could choke a donkey." Fearing for my own neck I kept stumm.

New Year was very much like Christmas, apart from the special Haggis lunch arranged in the canteen and a very special 'Auld Land Syne', which seemed to carry on until the majority had dropped out through injury. At Jock's request and not wanting to disappoint, we also had a mass rendition of 'The Northern Lights of Aberdeen' to roll in 1970.

A couple of days into the New Year, we arrived back at the flats as normal. We filed in through the gate and down the path. Starting at the third entrance and running down to fence at the far end, was a skating rink. We had our own skating rink. Grant was waiting for us, more to stop the lunatic fringe from destroying the rink before it'd had a chance to freeze properly. He explained that the Fire Brigade had been during the morning. They had banked the snow to form a perimeter and then flooded the area, leaving a couple of hours before we landed. "Keep off it until tomorrow," was Grant's final request.

Sure enough, arriving home the next day we found a number of wives and children already using the rink. Going inside, Gerry had set up a line of ice skates for the borrowing of. Like a school kid, I dashed upstairs and quickly back down, grabbed a pair of skates, sat on the entrance steps and put them on. On tying the laces, the realisation kicked in. I had never skated in my life and was even useless on roller skates. "It can't be that difficult," I thought as I watched the kids going round. "Okay, gently does it," as I stood upright and shuffled across the icy path. Just as the thought that this was easy entered my head, my feet flew forwards and I crashed down on my back, driving the air out of my body. Everybody had stopped in fits of laughter and a couple of the kids came over and grabbed my hands. "Just give me a minute," I said, full of embarrassment. I decided to crawl onto the rink on all fours before plucking up the courage to get upright. "It's easy," repeated the kids, "Left, right, left, right," as they tugged my arms. We picked up speed and slowly moved to the end of the rink. "What now?" I tried to turn. No chance. This time I brought down one of the kids desperately trying to support me. This was going to be a painful process, but great fun!

During the evening drinking session in the Spinners, I came up with a great idea how to make the learning less painful. "Drunken skating," I said to the lads. "You fall over a lot but you don't feel anything." They laughed. "No, I'm serious. We finish up here and get out onto the ice." Needless to say, not everyone was convinced. After midnight, two intrepid skaters pulled on their skates and headed out onto the rink. I was right, you keep falling on your arse but you don't give a monkey's, you just get back up. Within an hour, I was flying, turning corners, and finished gliding on one leg, arms out to the side and left leg straight out behind me.

I careered head first into the snow banked around the rink and sat there with blood streaming from a burst lip. "Never felt a thing," I shouted. "Shut your noise and get to bed," Gerry shouted from Entrance 3. We laughed as we tiptoed back inside. Come the weekend, we had it sussed. Stereo speakers out on the porch with music blasting out, the rink was full, with a crowd of Russian spectators watching outside the picket fence.

I had lived in Bolton for twenty-one years, so I knew about 'dark satanic mills'. I grew up with one (The Falcon) staring me in the face. But a short walk and you could be in a magical forest or short, but energy-sapping bike ride you could be up Winter Hill, Anglezark or the Blue Lagoon; beautiful wild countryside - enough to lift the heaviest soul. Now, in Mogilev and deep in a Russian winter, despite the daily sight of snow, which in itself has a cleansing effect; the daily routine of work followed by weekends centred around drinking sessions and can-crushing contests, can have a dulling effect. It was a pleasant surprise, therefore, to hear that there was a ski bus arranged for the Sunday morning 9am start. I got to bed especially early, around 3am on the Sunday morning, and set the alarm.

A quick bowl of Corn Flakes, a cup of tea, and with several layers of woollies, skis on shoulder and out to the bus. Such was the novelty that we filled two buses, with the skis being transported in one of the minibuses. About three-quarters of an hour later, we pulled off the road and to everyone's amazement we were looking down over a natural valley covered in pristine, untouched snow. I looked around and instantly understood that this was a race to be first down. The minibus doors were thrown open and the skis were thrown out on the ground. I pulled on my bob cap and gloves, grabbed my skis and sticks, clamped my feet in, tried to turn and got pushed over by one of the kids. "Bugger!" It seemed an age before I was back upright and couldn't believe that no one had set off. I hit the slope exactly at the same time as Pistol Pete and Wigan Bert. Pete fell over. I screamed with laughter as we picked up speed. I had seen the Winter Olympics on telly and tried to lean forward in a crouched position, legs bent, just like the real thing, coaching myself, "Keep going. Just keep going."

We were still on a gentle slope but negotiating a hump in the land. The slope now fell away steeply. No pushing now, this was muck or nettles country, especially when I saw the tractor tracks across the bottom of the hill. I looked over towards Bert. "Hadn't he seen the ditches?" Just at that moment, I fell, possibly self-generated with fear. I was now ploughing down the hill head first on my back with my skis acting like anchors, slowing me down. I stopped. I looked across to where Bert had been. Nothing. I scanned down to the foot of the hill and saw a bottom, pair of legs and skis pointing skywards. This was a picture out of a comic book. Bert somehow forced himself out of the face of the ditch, his eyes plugged with snow. "What the f...?!" "Bert, the kids," I shouted. I looked round to see bodies littering the slope. Others were carefully setting up a slalom course down the hill. "Typical," I thought. I trekked on and disappeared into a pine forest.

I kept going until I lost the sound of people, and stopped exhausted in a small clearing, unclipped my skis and lay down in the snow. I could hear my grandma's voice "and silence like a poultice comes to heal the wounds of sound." I felt the sun warming my face and the beauty holding me, caressing me, welcoming me. Russia, clean, fresh, sparkling Russia. All mine! Strange isn't it lay here cocooned in a bed of pure white snow to think that during the summer months I would probably be covered in ants or some other biting bugs looking to infiltrate the nearest orifice. Not now, not even a bird to disturb the tranquillity. Mind you thinking, as I was that I could have laid there forever, that certainly was not an option. As the snow inflicted its first tell tale nip I blew out my final breath of steam and decided to rejoin life, bidding this most magical forest farewell.

CHAPTER 6
LOST WEEKENDS

Minsk is the capital of White Russia and is always a connecting point to and from Moscow. Every second weekend the company arranged a trip to Minsk; setting off after work on Friday evening and returning to Mogilev on Sunday afternoon. On my first visit, before Christmas, I had tagged along with some elder statesmen and had spent most of the time wandering around the city looking for bargains in the city's bigger stores. Cameras, I was informed, were good buys, particularly the Zenith E which was said to be an exact copy of the Pentax. Barry was the camera expert and he assured me that the Russians had copied it so well that they had even duplicated the odd fault that the Pentax was prone to.

We stayed at the newly built Yubilanaya Hotel, set on a main dual carriageway very close to the city centre and overlooking the new Minsk Sports Arena. The hotel leapt out of the ground like a large white twisted blade. What can I say it was modern? What was fascinating over breakfast were the Russian soldiers doing ski trekking. There were hundreds of them in their grey uniforms, machine guns across their backs, trekking over a huge course around the park opposite the hotel before dog-legging behind the arena, eventually turning full circle and running back along the river embankment. There was finger pointing and quiet laughter every time someone fell over. One such fall caused a domino effect, ending with a pile of soldiers and a subsequent ski stick fight. That made my mind up, "why should they have all the fun?" I asked following a fit of laughter. First stop was the sports shop where I picked up a pair of trekking-skis, sticks and a pair of quality Botas figure skates. Now I was armed and ready for a Russian winter.

Like most things tried on snow and ice, getting to grips with six-foot planks of wood clamped to the front of your feet will be a painful experience and particularly embarrassing. Once on your face or arse, with your legs, feet and planks pointing in different directions, just getting back upright can be an arduous and time-consuming operation. Unless you possess a steely resolve, simply cut them into three pieces and stuff them firmly into a dustbin.

After checking for spy cameras back at the hotel, I joined some of our party in the restaurant. The food, although good, wasn't the same as the Dnieper, or just maybe it was the chef's night off. The bar, however, was different class. Modern, large and very plush, with a centre bar, the front of which was frosted glass lit with blue down lights. Dim wall lighting, thick carpet, quality leather chairs and background music completed the ambience. To the average Russian, the bar prices would at least have been off-putting; to us they were peanuts. Even the prices for the list of cocktails which we decided to go through were insignificant.

Part-way through the evening we were joined by a girl. Tanya was an attractive girl in her mid twenties who spoke good English. Most unusual, as nobody apart from the interpreters spoke even a word of English. She also slotted into the party unnoticed, she was just there and part of the conversation, which, after several large cocktails, was becoming louder and looser. Within no time at all we were talking about Tanya. At the end of the evening my one and only concern was navigating my way back to my room, which I suppose I must have achieved, waking up in the early hours with the first of many trips to find the toilet bowl with the resulting 'Technicolor cough.'

As always, next morning breakfasts are quiet affairs, everybody unsure of the previous night's events and actions other than the absolute fact that you were pissed. Generally, people would semi-doze away the time until the bus collected us for the return journey, which always took half the time of the outbound trip. This was not a state of mind; this was fact. Since the very first trips, it had become routine for the singles to be accompanied by a full case of twenty-four cans of beer or lager. The aim was to finish the case before arriving in Minsk. The main reason for the controversy of the distance between Mogilev and Minsk was the length time it took to get there. The 'Speedwell Tours Special,' took about an hour to cover half the distance and a further three hours to stutter out the remainder. My washer was so shot that I took to sitting on the steps of the bus with my back against the driver's cab. My only trip to the party at the back was to pick up another couple of cans and ditch the empties. Trips out were now affectionately known as 'Lost weekends'. It wasn't that you were lost, it was more of a fact that you were determined not to the found, sober anyway!

On the Friday following my first trip to Minsk, I arrived home from work as usual, took a shower and put some tea on, when my doorbell rang. I opened the door and found Tanya stood there with another younger looking girl standing behind her. Tanya, without pausing for breath, came out with the longest nonsensical explanation as to why they were there. The top and bottom of it was that she, Tanya, was staying the weekend with one of the other lads and she wanted me to look after her friend, Vera. She pushed Vera into the flat, sliding a large suitcase through the door, which she quickly closed behind her.

"Hello," said Vera. "Hello," I replied, "Do you speak English?" *Nyet,*" was the answer. And she didn't, not a worthwhile word. She wasn't adept in the kitchen either, so I made tea, well, chucked a few more chips in the pan. Neither was she any good with the housework, although I was later informed that she did a stunning party trick with a vacuum cleaner. Anyway, she seemed a pleasant enough girl with short dark hair a pretty face and nice smile. What did trouble me though were her eyes. Looking as I do, beyond the bright blue eye make-up and over-long eyelashes, I searched for some sparkle. There was none. Not even eye contact, as if they would give her away.

Following the disco in the canteen and several drinks, we returned to my flat. Vera now came to life; this was her domain. At twenty-one, I wasn't a virgin but my experiences were limited. To me a bed was still for sleeping in. Vera, however, was completely comfortable in taking control. No inhibitions here. To her, things that I hadn't even dreamt of were commonplace. No sleep that night or the following morning either. I managed to make a break for it at lunch when Tanya came round and took her back to the other flat, "maybe," I thought, "for an afternoon session."

I went to town and did some shopping, calling in the bar for a couple of steadiers on my return. The general consensus among the guys was that they, the girls, were either looking for English husbands, KGB spies, or both. Whatever Vera was, she was certainly accommodating and possibly the right thing at the right time. By the time Sunday came around and she said, "Goodbye," never to be seen again in Mogilev or in Minsk, I sat on the couch and looked out into space, while I surmised, "At least you couldn't see her eyes in the dark and she did have a talent." I sat on, fumbling with my crotch. At least this is a better sore than a punch in the gob, a hell of a lot better.

A week later, I was back in Minsk, not at the Yubilanaya Hotel but the Hotel Minsk. Right in the city centre, The Minsk was a beautiful old hotel. Only around five stories high and painted a standard cream and brown, the Minsk however looked and felt solid. Quality wood, pillars, columns, high ornate ceilings, chandeliers and shiny wooden floors blending into thick carpets. My room was on the first floor looking out across the main street.

I had arranged to meet Lena, a young student interpreter from the plant. She was acting as personal assistant to Ludmilla, the chief interpreter and whose duties kept her working mainly in the Polyspinners commercial office at the flats, with Dorothy and Grant. Following a job in Staple Fibre the previous week, I had chatted with Lena. It appeared that she lived in Minsk and travelled home each weekend. "We should meet up," I had said. "You can show me round Minsk." I was amazed when she agreed, and we arranged to meet that Saturday across from the Minsk at 10am.

I was up and ready and looked across the road at around 9.45. I peered through the snow falling heavily and there was Lena, togged up in all sky blue, woolly hat, coat and gloves, with black boots. I grabbed my fur hat and ran out of the main entrance. She waved. "Where are we going first?" I asked. "For a coffee," she shuddered. About 20 yards down the road was a small basement café. It was different; it was nice. It reminded me of a place called the Casablanca at the side of Whitakers in Bolton. Carolyn and myself were regular customers for cappuccino coffee and Kunzel cakes, when such things were a novelty and an absolute treat. "Two coffee Cognacs?" she asked the waiter. He nodded. "Is that okay?" "No cakes?" I teased her. "You want cake?" she asked, now puzzled. "No, I'm only joking." She smiled, taking off her gloves. Sitting at a small table we chatted over coffee, the conversation only being punctuated when the café door opened and someone came in. She would quickly turn to check who it was, appearing to physically shrink in her chair. "Are you being followed?" I said, jokingly. She blushed and insisted, "No, no." I touched her hand. "I'm only kidding, joking," I assured her. The door opened and again she turned. "My brother is in town." "Oh, will he beat me up?" "No, but he will tell my parents." "Come on," I said, "We'll keep our heads down." We walked back onto the street. Fortunately, the snow was much lighter. "Put your leg in bed," I said to Lena. "What?" Her sparkling hazel eyes looked bemused. "Give me your hand." I held mine out. She did, shyly. Both hands were buried in my coat pocket. "Now you've got your leg in bed," I said, "Nice and warm," I laughed. "You silly man," she replied. "No, just mad really." We saw museums, state buildings, and churches that weren't churches. They used to be churches, some still were, I think. Two hours later we arrived back at the Hotel Minsk, "Just in time for lunch."

It's quite amazing the effect a warm room has after being outside in the freezing cold for a couple of hours. "Why is it," I asked, "that as the blood starts to flow and cheeks start to warm," I pointed to my cheek which was burning, "your nose starts to run?" I pointed to a drip hanging ponderously on the end of my nose. "It's the ice in your nose ..." she struggled for the word. "Melting, thawing," I confirmed. "Yes, melting," she agreed. "So why is your nose not melting?" "I am Belarussian, I am used to cold winters." "Then why are your cheeks red?" I pointed to her cheek. "Because they are very hot," she replied. "Exactly. English cheeks, White Russian nose, it doesn't make sense." "Oh, you!" She spread her arms. "Wipe your nose." I laughed and wiped my nose.

When the *Borsch* came, I sat back and laughed. "My God, I could drown in that." The soup bowl was enormous and full to the top with beetroot soup, finished off with a snow-capped island of *Smetana* (sour cream). Some large chunks of black bread accompanied the soup. "Have we ordered anything else?" I asked Lena. "You said Stroganov, didn't you?" "And chips?" I asked. "Chips?" She asked, bemused. "I must have chips every day," I smiled.

We were distracted by a slurping sound that was getting louder and more frequent. To our right was a table against the wall. A dirty-looking figure was hunched over a bowl of soup, his nose almost touching the rim of the dish and his spoon acting like a rotary paddle, sloshing the soup into his fixed, open mouth. "What on earth?" I gestured towards the tramp. "It is difficult," whispered Lena, "Everybody must be treated the same." "No," I said, "I'm not saying it is wrong, I'm just saying it's unusual in our culture. He's probably KGB," I said. "Shh." She put her finger over her lips. I picked up my spoon. "Here goes." I dipped my head. "Good luck," she laughed.

After lunch, we were quickly back out into the city, this time, however, setting off in the opposite direction. Now the sun was shining and, although around minus 10°C, it felt quite tropical. Lena did her best to give me some history of Minsk but she was definitely struggling to make it sound interesting. Apparently like most Belarus towns Minsk was almost totally destroyed during the last war, hence there was very little to see that was old, old. By the time the sun started to drop, we were across the road from Minsk Dynamo Stadium and Lena said it was time she had to get home. We walked back to the main street and parted company at her bus stop, a short distance away from the hotel. We agreed that we would meet up again and that we would see each other in Mogilev at the plant.

Maybe the tramp was a KGB man; maybe we were simply spotted or maybe Lena's nervousness was well founded, but she too was never seen again. Someone said that she was supposedly working for Techmashimport in Moscow but it was strange. She was pretty and shy, and pleasant, with a cheeky smile and I hoped, wherever she was, that she was happy.

A fortnight later I was back in Minsk and once again back at the Yubilanaya. This wasn't your normal trip though – no, this was by special invitation. We had been officially invited to attend the USSR –v– USA Amateur Boxing Tournament being held in the Minsk Sports Arena. I'm keen on anything sporting, so put my name on the list that was posted on the official notice board opposite the canteen. As time went by, and the number of British specialists and their families built up, there became more demand for places on trips. Normally I would have ducked out and let someone else have a weekend away, but I was keen on this special trip and made sure I legged it off the bus on the day the notice was posted.

We had arranged to meet up in reception at 7pm and set off on the short walk across the dual carriageway and into the Sports Arena. An official led us through to our seats, which were cordoned off from the rest. The front row was made up of judges and US and Russian officials. The second row, of twenty seats, was for our party, and a further four rows were for the US officials' family and friends.

No problem in identifying who was who. The Russians wore red vests with CCCP across their chests. The Americans wore blue vests emblazoned with USA, and in the main the US guys were black. Fortunately, I had a friendly American sat behind me. Tom gave me a brief resume on each boxer, Golden Gloves Champion, age and from which state. They were all Golden Gloves Champions or former champions and they almost all got battered, and I mean battered. Thumped, hammered, blitzed, pummelled, had the SH-one-T knocked out of them. One of the yanks, the heavyweight, a young man called Michael Spinx, made it through the entire three rounds. The Russian he was fighting, Yuri Nokurblokov, or something, appeared much older, shorter and wider, closely resembling a brick outhouse. Every time he hit Spinx the entire audience winced. The lad was being murdered. Somehow, he managed to stay on his feet, probably because he was able to run faster than Yuri. "Quick feet," Tom confirmed. "Not bloody quick enough," I muttered in response. All the boxers got a medal and a good round of applause. Some of the Yanks also got bloody big ice bags that they pressed onto painful looking wounds.

Unbeknown to us, the American officials had arranged a banquet at the hotel and it even included our party. Tom and his wife Ida had saved me a seat on their table and I decided to join them. I'm glad I did, as they proved to be wonderful hosts and genuinely nice people. It's amazing how people are stereotyped. My image of Americans was loud, brash and insincere. Well, the party was loud; twenty drunken Brits made sure of that. Never more so than when I decided to have a shadow boxing match with Michael the Battered. Have you ever seen a black man with a black eye? Both eyes had turned an iridescent purpley-blue. The discolouration also covered one cheek, which was swollen like a football. Anyway, he was fit enough to be slapped around for a second time. We slugged it out at close-quarters as he casually leant on my head with his left hand while I flailed away frantically. We finished up with both hands aloft, so I considered it an honourable draw.

Two hours later, I was in no doubt that these were some of the nicest, most natural and genuine people I had ever met; Tom and Ida in particular. Ida had definitely taken a shine and I had to promise several times to visit them at their home in the mid-west, Cincinnati, Ohio, to be precise. She linked her arm through mine and looked at me as if I was a long lost son.

Long after the boxers had been sent to bed, we sat chatting about Russia, the US and the UK. One thing we were all in agreement about was that it was good to meet people from different backgrounds and cultures and that doing more of it, either through sport or business contracts, could only prove to be beneficial and break down those established walls that we build up in our minds. At a time when all our minds had gone numb, adequately soaked in one bourbon concoction or another, we said, "Goodnight," and "Goodbye."

CHAPTER 7
FLATMATE

Living on your own is fine. I am naturally a loner and don't have a problem going back to my flat at the end of a working day and cooking for myself. The fact was that the extraordinary conditions that we were exposed to made us a close-knit community with a full social calendar, providing, that is, you wish to be included. We all have a choice. Grant, our office manager and interpreter, had called early week to inform me, due to the influx of several new starters, it was very likely that come Thursday I would have a flatmate.

Sure enough, on the Thursday evening my doorbell went and there was Grant with, "Ray," he said, holding out his hand. "Alan," I replied giving his hand a good hearty shake. "Get on," said Grant, disappearing down the stairs. I've always been one for first impressions being important and these were top-notch. You couldn't get past his grin, an enormous open mouthed smile with tombstones for teeth. Ray, at about 4 inches shorter than me, was in his mid-thirties, an oval face full to the brim with character topped out with reddish brown receding hair. He chuckled like a school chum. From Cheshire, an instrument engineer and married with a little girl. "Do you like curry and chips, Ray?" "I could eat a flock bed," he replied. "Flock bed, curry and chips it is."

Ray did a spot of unpacking and had a shower while I cooked tea. He didn't stop talking the whole time, giving me chapter and verse on the trip out, his life story from the age of six, the precise temperature of the shower water at all times and the state of his piles. I just kept agreeing. "This is gonna be fun; different but fun," I thought. We ate in my place. "Are you going to introduce me to the girls?" he asked. I sat upright in the chair and fixed his eyes. "What girls? They're all married. Anyway, you're married." "What? The Russian girls?" he looked puzzled. I was. "Anyway, my wife understands. I'm allowed to talk to them," he winked. "I would like to learn the language," he went on. "I'm sure you would," I confirmed. "Don't worry, Ray, there are plenty of young, attractive Russian teachers out there. I'll show you round town on Saturday and we can grab a bite of lunch at the Dnieper. Anyway, finish your tea and I'll introduce you to some of the gang in the bar."

The next morning, Ray gave me a shout. "Alan, breakfast's ready." I walked into the kitchen, still half asleep. "Poached egg on toast okay?" he asked. "Bloody fantastic," I said. We agreed to go to the local store after work and stock up on food, especially as he assured me that he enjoyed cooking. This, I thought, was going to be a match made in heaven.

Saturday morning we jumped off the 10am minibus to town, getting off outside the Dnieper Hotel. 200 yards up the main street, we went into the GUM, Russia's equivalent to Marks and Spencers or Woolworths. This was the same store as the one on Red Square in Moscow but about one-tenth of the size. It was, however, still by far the biggest store in Mogilev. First impressions when you venture inside, lots of shelf space and little to nothing on the shelves. Truthfully, the Russians could buy almost anything goods-wise. The only thing was that not all things were available at any given time, therefore you would find a large queue waiting to buy toilet paper or cups and saucers, because once sold out it could be weeks before they are back in stock. The other thing to understand was, a cup was a cup, not one of fifty different colours and designs. A pair of jeans was the same colour and design as those being sold in Minsk or Moscow or Vladivostok, and a *fufaika*; black and padded with down was the only thing I knew to be less fashionable than a donkey jacket. However if your sole aim was to survive a Russian winter this was definitely the thing to buy. People were practical because they needed to be. Anyway, Ray didn't fancy a *fufaika*, but instead, bought himself a fur hat. It was one of the cheaper ones with leather-type flaps and knebby front bit. I told him it looked great, "Yes, beltin," I said, "Suits you. It makes your face look thinner. Makes you look younger." All he could say was, "Bugger off." He kept posing in front of a large mirror, twisting and turning for that profile shot.

By now, quite a crowd had formed. This was a regular occurrence. Parts of the crowd were interested in whatever an Englishman was buying. For example, if Ray had been buying a wooden doll, there would have been a stampede for wooden dolls. The others in the audience were younger girls who were looking at me and giggling. Without appearing big-headed, I was somewhat of a novelty. After all, this was the interior and not on the tourist route. Most young people had never seen a foreigner before, wearing colourful clothes, especially in winter and with long hair. I had my hair cut twice a year whether I needed it or not, and by now the curls formed a long fringe over my sheepskin coat. It was a regular occurrence for people to stop in the street and stare, open-mouthed, as if an alien had landed. Oh, yes, and there was, of course, my boyish good looks! A couple of girls braved it and were stood talking to me. Telling them that I was English and didn't speak much Russian, *"Tolko chut, chut,"* didn't make a lot of difference; they carried on chatting. One of the girls was stroking my arm, well, stroking my sheepskin jacket. Ray was back in a shot. "Have we cracked it?" he urged. "Well, I don't know about you, Ray, but I certainly have." I introduced Ray to the girls as we left the shop and headed past the football stadium and on towards Lenin Square. The girls, in return, did their best to point out some of the places of interest, although I finished up guessing as to what they were saying. As we started to head back towards the Dnieper, the girls pointed towards the other end of town and said, "Goodbye," and we parted company.

As we walked back, Ray seemed amazed at the spotless nature of the streets. It must start with a child's upbringing at home and be followed up through school. Whatever it is, it works, and there is obviously a pride in their local area, their town, their state, their country. There is no litter, none at all, not even a cigarette end. The roads are lined with large concrete moulded urns. Everything that needs to be discarded goes into the receptacles, which usually smoulder with the number of cigarette ends discarded. "That must be the world's worst job," I said to Ray, "emptying the litter bins." There was no graffiti, no damage to phone boxes and possibly, most unusual, no kids throwing tantrums or gangs of teenagers causing bother. It would appear that in Russia grown-ups rule, and that seemed good.

We had a nice meal at the Dnieper, and decided to walk down towards the theatre. Ray took an interest in a shop displaying Bohemian Crystal and the local linen which was a speciality of the area. "You're like a bloody woman," I cursed as Ray picked his way through the shop's entire range. "It'll make a nice present for the wife," he replied. The shop was empty when we walked in, now, ten minutes later the shop was full of people pushing and shoving to get to the counter as if they were giving the stuff away. "I'll wait outside," I said, trying to force a way to the door. By the time I got there Ray was behind me, laughing. "Bloody Hell! Do we always have that effect? It's mad." We'd just started walking when we were caught up by three girls who linked arms and walked down towards the bridge. We stood for a while, looking down over the river, still completely frozen over with a good covering of snow. On the nearside bank was a church with a single mushroomed dome. I think the girls were saying that it was still a working church.

Anyway, the minibus was coming down the hill, and while Ray flagged it down I said, "*do svidanya*," to our escorts, who turned back towards town.

Saturday evening was spent like many before, down in the Spinners Arms, which always included the Saturday night dirty disco, when many a bachelor's frustration could be heightened even more by the 'Teaser Brigade' of young wives. The main thing was that everybody unwound and had a laugh. What followed the bar could vary, but there would come a time during the evening, or early hours, a critical point of alcohol degradation when decisions are made unwittingly. It's literally going with the flow, and that keeps going till dawn, somewhere. Now I had Ray, a person of reason, good judgement, good advice and more experience. "No more, Alan… Bed!" "Ray, you're right," taking a couple of steps back, "You're bloody right, off to bed it is, pan o' chips, and bed." That's another benefit of having a flatmate, they can cook the chips, when I would have burned the flat down.

What was a problem, however, was that Ray couldn't sing to save his life. You put some music on the stereo and Ray starts to sing along. "F.F.S. Ray, shut up, please!" He keeps singing, louder, impervious to the pain now being suffered by the entire block. "Alan? Alan?" "What?" I shouted back. "We need to be mixing with the locals and learning the language," Ray went on. "No problem," I said, "I'll sort us a night out next week. Just don't sing. Please don't sing." "Okay, it's a deal." "'Night Ray." "'Night Alan." "'Night Ray." "'Night Alan." "Piss off Ray." "'Night Alan."

On the Staple Fibre shop floor at the far end, beyond the bailing presses, worked a couple of Russian girls. They had been steadily polishing the concrete floor for a number of months. On first look, the girls closely resembled Michelin Men. On several occasions however I had caught a glimpse of something sweet lurking beneath several layers of clothing and four assorted head scarves. Anyway, I went for it, and somehow arranged to meet the two girls at the cinema at the end of Gagarin Street, 7.30pm that night. I dashed off to tell Ray. At first he didn't believe me and I had to swear on my Auntie Linnie's Lemon Meringue Pie before he took me seriously. "Don't forget, ready for 6.45pm, showered and shaved." I left him in the laboratory and went back onto the floor to take another peek at the girls. "Are you sure?" I thought. "Oh, what the hell, it might be fun."

We decided to be discreet and take the public bus to town. Big mistake! Buses are cheap - a ticket costing five kopeks, anywhere, and they get full…and I mean full; like sardines in a can. The secret is that unless you are travelling to the end of the run; in this case the railway station, DO NOT SIT DOWN! Anyway, we got on first, so Ray sat down on the front seat behind the driver's cabin. I, obviously, sat next to him. The bus then filled up to reasonably full, say thirty-two seated and thirty standing. The first stop was after the junction of Shmidt and Gagarin, where there were several blocks of new flats. There must have been another thirty people waiting to get on the bus. They wouldn't fit. The driver was getting angry and started shouting some choice language towards the rear of the bus, probably unable to close the doors. I was now cheek-to-cheek with Ray. An old lady draped over me with her bag and umbrella squashed into my ear. I would had stood up and let her sit down if I could've moved but there was no chance. Just breathing was a miracle. I looked through the window and realised that we were quickly approaching the end of Gagarin Street; our stop. "Shit. Ray, we need to move," I said. My voice must have sounded panicked. "Pull on the rail," said Ray. I managed to get my left hand on the rail and pulled at the same time, excusing myself in Russian and pushing the old lady. The daft old bugger pushed back violently and started to pummel my head with her brolly. "Push," said Ray, and again I heaved. There was a crack as the metal rail came away in our hands and swung down limply.

The driver slammed on the brakes and we let go. Everybody lurched forward and then rebounded back. First of all his hands appeared, clawing his way through the mob, then his face, white like a ghost, his mouth snarling. "We just need to get off the bloody bus," I said to him in English. Surely, he wouldn't hit an Englishman. He didn't, but he did enjoy physically throwing us off his bus, holding onto the collar of my coat and throwing me down the front steps, accompanied by a "Russian Ode to an English Git!" I, of course, once on terra firma, doffed my hat and bid him God Speed. I can't remember the exact wording, but better read another day. Ray, of course, was launched into my arms, desperately trying to keep his balance on the now treacherous slush. After composing ourselves, we started to laugh. I put my arm around Ray's neck and we set off towards the cinema.

I looked inside and outside at the front and at the back. We waited until 8pm and would you bloody Adam and Eve it, the girls stood us up. Ray had to pull me away at the end; I couldn't get my brain round it and was still chunnering to myself as we stood, yes stood, on the bus back towards the airport.

I must have yelped out loud as Ray turned round. "What's up?" he asked. "Someone just nipped my arse, hard," I replied. At the same time, several girls started giggling. I turned to see who was behind me. Just then my bum was nipped again. "What's going on?" I asked the passengers, in English. Two girls who were sat at the side held up their hands as if to say, "It wasn't us."

As we left the bus at the terminus, we were joined by five girls and one lad, slim and about six-foot tall. One of the girls introduced herself. "Hello," she said, "My name is Olya. I speak a little English." "My God," I said, startled, "Someone speaks English." We invited them up to the flat for coffee and they all came. While Ray was making a brew and sorting out one or two butties, I showed the gang my flat and stereo, some of them looking through my record collection. The girls were Sveta, Olya (who spoke English), someone and somebody else. Oh, yes, and Saba, a big guy with a cheesy grin.

I soon established whom the phantom nipper was when Sveta owned up, screwing up her nose as she pinched her fingers together. During that time, Saba slipped quietly away. "Don't worry," Olya assured us, "he is okay." I didn't worry. Anyway, shortly afterwards there was a knock on the flat door. Ray answered, and it was Saba, who shouted something in Russian. The girls responded and started to tog up for the elements. Olya insisted that we meet again at a concert and dance at the School of Foreign Languages on Lenin Square in the centre of town. "Friday at 7pm. We will meet you on the corner." She put her hand on my shoulder, "You will meet my friend, Laura," she said quietly. "She is very beautiful. You will like her." Her eyes were locked with mine, searching, pleading. I promised, hand on heart.

CHAPTER 8
ANGEL

I slid stealthily through the line of parked cars so as not to touch burning metal with my bare legs. I slipped the key easily into the Riley 4/72 lock, pressed the button with my thumb and unleashed a torrent of boiling air, like opening an oven door. Placing my left palm on the baking leather seat I winced as I quickly pressed the 'on' button on the car radio and turned up the volume. I looked back towards St. Annes open-air swimming pool where I had just left around a dozen or so of my friends splashing about in the water. Dressed only in flip-flops and trunks I had to wait until the seat responded to the slight sea breeze and then a keyboard began to play. I must have collapsed into the car, wafted into another world…

She skipped the light fandango
Turned cartwheels cross the floor
I was feeling kinda seasick
But the crowd called out for more
The room was humming harder
As the ceiling blew away
When we called out for another drink
The waiter brought the tray
And so it was that later
As the miller told his tale
That her face at first just ghostly
Turned a whiter shade of pale……………

My body was burning while I was frozen unable to take in what my ears were feeding to my brain. The sounds, the words stunned me. Even when the song had finished I couldn't move staring at the cars walnut fascia, pleading with a radio to play the song again. "Please, please, please play the bloody song again!!!!"

There are defining moments in everyone's life, there must be, at least there should be. There was a small crowd stood at the bottom of a short flight of steps. My eyes were drawn up the steps and to a doorway where there was a girl looking out. As I got closer, my eyes locked on the girl and stopped. What had brought me to this place, here, now? I was stood there, frozen in time; stomach trembling, hands shaking and heart pounding. Why? I was looking at an angel. Moreover, I was looking at the girl I was going to marry! I knew it. I was absolutely certain, and she still hadn't seen me, she didn't know I existed, but somehow, strangely, mystifyingly I knew her. She stood there, upright, strong and proud, looking out impatiently. Who was she and whom was she waiting for? Who was she looking out for? She was stunningly beautiful, her dark brown hair tied up in a large bun at the back of her head, her eyes dark and sparkling, full of confidence, full of life, even mischievous. They flickered my way momentarily, and kept going, not seeing me. "Alan!" Olya was beckoning me, waving frantically.

Ray was already inside when I got to the door. "Larissa, my friend," Olya pointed to the angel stood in the doorway. Her eyes quickly scanned mine as she turned impatiently and walked up a flight of stairs. Ray and several girls were waiting on a landing at the top. "You go." Olya shepherded us through and pointed down a row of empty seats at the back of the hall, now full of people. I walked about half way down, looked back and sat down. "Move up a couple of places," said Ray. "Another one." "Sorry Ray, I don't feel right." My head was in bits. Ray was next to me, then Olya and then Larissa, or

Laura, whatever her name was. I do remember keep glancing down the line. She didn't respond. There was a lot of chatter from in front, and a lot of people, well girls, turning round to look, a bit like Spot the Monkeys. Shortly after the company party arrived, coming in at the front of the hall and sitting on the front rows, I took off my sheepskin coat and sat back down as the concert started.

Lord only knows what the concert was about! I think there was a choir and a soloist or two, and people spoke in English and Russian, while I was in a completely different world. I can't even describe how I felt other than ill. Part way through the proceedings, about four of the girls snuck out of the hall. I must have looked panicked when I leant towards Olya. *"Pericur,"* she whispered, "They have gone for a fag" I confirmed to Ray. "What a gang," Ray whispered back. "Have you seen this lot?" he nodded. There was a continuous ripple effect as people turned to look, nudged the person next to them, chit-chatted, giggled. The only person who hadn't shown any interest in our presence was the girl who had blown me away.

The concert finished to a standing ovation and our official party left. Everybody helped to move and stack the chairs around the edge of the hall and someone cranked up the disco. The music wasn't bad actually and certainly not you're average *Muslim Magomayev* or *Rachmaninov* geezers that was usually pumped through the radios.

We formed a circle of about eight, including both Ray and myself, and I found myself dancing, facing Larissa. I wanted her to show some interest but was petrified inside, repeating to myself, "she doesn't like you, she doesn't fancy you." I was brought back to reality as Saba appeared from nowhere, grabbed Larissa's arm and dragged her off the dance floor and through the door at the back of the hall. Three or four of the other girls stopped dancing and quickly ran after them. My immediate reaction was puzzlement as to just what had gone on. My next reaction was anger and I walked quickly out through the doors and onto the landing. Larissa wasn't there but I could hear shouting below. I set off down the stairs but was met by the girls on their way back up, who formed a wall in front of me. *"Nyet, Nyet,* Alan, *Nyet!"* Olya shouted from the landing. She ran down and grabbed my arm, and along with the other girls pulled me persuasively back into the hall and back onto the dance floor. Ray was still dancing, his smile now bigger than ever. I moved towards Olya. "What has happened?" I asked. "Okay, okay, everything no problem," she said, "Dance with girls," she gestured with her hand. "Oh, just bloody dance," I said to myself. I looked round a group of attractive fun-loving girls, enjoying the moment. "Why not? Just dance."

I lay in bed, tucking the quilt up under my chin, thinking about her and trying to reason what had gone on. "Maybe," I thought, "he had done me a huge favour," Saba that was. At the time I thought I was going to implode, self-destruct. I hadn't even spoken to her. Stupid, gormless sod! Olya had assured me that they would come to the flat the following evening. Ray seemed happy enough, like a sand boy, he couldn't stop talking about the evening over a pint back in the Spinners. One or two of the lads who had been to the concert were intrigued when Ray announced that we had been there. They said that they were aware of something going on at the back of the hall, but unaware of what it was. "A gang of girls," announced Ray proudly. "They are coming round tomorrow."

"What if Saba comes with them?" I mused. "What if she doesn't want to come? What if? What if? Go to sleep!" I couldn't sleep, not a bloody chance. I lay there with a picture in my mind. She was standing at the top of the steps looking out. It was the most beautiful picture I had ever seen. It was perfection, it was a masterpiece.

CHAPTER 9
LIGHTS, CAMERA, ACTION

I must have fallen asleep during the early hours of Saturday morning because I remember waking up to a chorus of, 'Oh, what a beautiful morning,' from Ray the song-killer. "I'm having a shower," I said to Ray, who was in the kitchen eating. "Don't bother, there's no hot water and the cold water's brown." "Good," I said sarcastically, "I'll try a brown rinse." I poured some water from the kettle into a cup and brushed my teeth. "You were chirpy last night," I enquired. "It was good. And what was wrong with you? You were like a kid who'd lost his conker." "I'm all right and I've still got my conker, thank you." "What are we doing tonight if the girls come round?" asked Ray. "What do you fancy, Crep Susans and Mogilev Goulash?" There was a long pause before we said, together, "Curry and chips." "Just in case," I summed up.

I slid my way round to the shop through a sea of slush. It was the first week in March and the thaw was really setting in. It was going to take a long time to melt this thickness of ice that had gradually built up over a long, numbingly cold and yet mainly sunny, clear, dry and healthy winter. It's good to look back from time to time but now I was excited at what the future was going to bring. I was excited at the prospect of the evening ahead. I even spent an hour doing housework. I'm sure Ray thought I'd lost the plot.

"Lights, camera, action," I shouted from the kitchen. "What time are they due?" asked Ray. "Not a clue. They didn't say," I confirmed, or didn't. "Olya said they would come round." "Come and have a Martini, Alan, it will settle you down." "Martini?" I asked, sticking my head round Ray's flat door. "James Bond drinks Martinis," he gave me the tomb stone grin. "If they're good enough for 007, I'll have two. Actually, pour me a bottle. None of that fruit though." Ray poured me a glass. "Cheers." "Wallop!" I said, and the drinks were despatched.

At 8pm Ray and I started on the food. At 9pm we had given up. "They won't come round now, will they?" I asked Ray for the fiftieth time. "Probably not," he replied with an air of somebody who'd fielded the question fifty times. "It's your fault," I said, chucking him a can of beer. "How do you work that out, Alan?" "Well, you're the ugly get," I pointed out. "Oh, yes, and you're Mr Personality, aren't you? You didn't even speak to her. She obviously can't wait to see you again. She must have been charmed with your deadly wit," Ray summed up. "Nob off," I countered. "There you go, that confirms it. You have such a way with words." The doorbell rang. I put my finger over my lips and started to whisper. "Get the door, will you?" I pointed. "I'll be next door." I tiptoed quickly across the hall and into my room. "There's somebody at the door, Ray!" I shouted. "I'll get it!" Ray shouted back. "Good lad, Ray," I thought. "Not just an ugly get." Ray answered the door and I strained to hear some muffled conversation followed by a knock on my flat door, which swung open. I turned from the window; she was standing in the hall looking at me. She looked just as she had the evening before, wearing a dark grey skirt and jacket, a white blouse, buttoned to the neck, with a ruffled collar. The only difference was that instead of shoes she was now wearing a pair of knee-length black boots. I walked towards her, stretching out my hand. "Alan," I said, looking directly into her eyes. She held my gaze. "Laura." We shook hands gently. "Alan!" Olya threw out her arms and we kissed on both cheeks. "I been explain Ray why we can't come." She was off on one of her marathon explanations. "We have friends, go to Mogilev. We have to run away and catch bus and we come here. Laura," she points towards Larissa, "we come to see you."

"Look, don't stand out here, come into my room." I ushered them in. "Have a seat. Would you like a drink, something to eat?" "Drink, please," requested Olya. *"Perekoor Mozno?"* asked Larissa. "Can we smoke?" Olya confirmed. "Of course you can." I offered my cigarettes. "Do you smoke?" asked Olya, surprised. "Now and then. Usually when I have a drink." I offered my lighter. *"Pepelnitsa?"* asked Larissa. *"Pepelnitsa?"* And I walked to the kitchen and grabbed the glass ashtray from the drying rack.

We had coffee and Martini and whisky and sherry and coffee and cognac and chocolates and toast with butter and jam, and we talked. Well, Olya, Ray and myself did, Larissa not speaking a word of English. She did speak good German. She seemed to settle, at first sitting bolt upright on the couch, she looked more and more comfortable as the evening went on. Very possibly the booze. It was still an unusual evening, too many questions asked, searching for information, the language difficulties obviously a barrier, and Olya, God bless her, must have gone home hoarse. On several occasions, I felt Larissa checking me over, our eyes meeting. We actually had a dance together, well, more of a shuffle. The girls had been keen on my music collection and had been playing records all evening. Both Larissa and Olya were dancing near the window. I was fine sat watching Laura move but Ray convinced me that we should join the girls. "Up, you lazy sod." I jumped up with a smile. Everybody smiled, then laughed. We kept going in a way, but I did take the opportunity to get a good look into her eyes. Dark green eyes that gave very little away. I thought that she would tolerate me, at least for the time being.

After they had left to catch the last bus that left the airport at 11.20pm I sat with Ray, trying to explain the effect Larissa had on me. Ray was obviously aware that I fancied the girl, and being an intuitive person, understood that my feelings went beyond the normal boy/girl fancy, kiss, cuddle etcetera. What Ray didn't know, was the extent of my feelings. He couldn't - even I didn't have a clue what was going on. It was like disorientation; like constantly feeling off balance. Someone hits you on the head with a lump hammer and just as your head starts to clear they hit you again, and so it goes on. It's totally different to anything I had experienced before. Now there is no comfort zone, no confidence, and no control. "That's it, Ray, I'm out of control." "Well, just control yourself into the kitchen and do us a pot of tea." The great British answer to all problems through the years, a cup of tea. "Anyway, thanks Ray." "What for?" he enquired. "For being here, for tonight. For just being a mate." "Fuck off," Ray ended the bullshit. "Two bags?" "Three," confirmed Ray, "You can't beat a nice strong cuppa."

I managed to get some sleep that night, I was knackered, and there were good thoughts going through my head. I had actually kissed her goodnight. It was her hand, but she hadn't pulled it away. As hand kisses go, this was passionate, the real McCoy, and I got the long, lingering look in. Mind you, that would probably put her off for life, the old puppy eyes. I hoped she liked dogs, well, puppies anyway. I was doing it again, I was going nuts. Tomorrow would be a nice, relaxing Sunday. We had planned a trip to the bazaar; the market that was open every Sunday morning. Possibly a couple of beers in the Spinners, a nice meal and an early night, and Olya and Larissa had promised to call on the Monday evening. Sweet dreams.

The day went roughly to plan, apart from the unexpected stop on the main bridge over the Dnieper. A crowd of people had gathered on the bridge to witness the break-up of the thick pack ice which had covered the river for the last three months. A week of rain had caused the river to flood; the ice now breaking into huge blocks that were smashing and churning in the heavy swell, a bit like my stomach. One thing was for sure; today was not a good day to go swimming in the river. From what we had been told the river was dangerous any time and in the Mogilev area an average of three people a week were drowned. With those thoughts, it was a good time to carry on to the market.

Sure enough, around 7.30pm on the Monday evening, the girls arrived. This time we decided to use Ray's flat and spent the first hour chatting. "Do you like Laura's hair, Alan?" "Yes, I think she has beautiful hair." She once again had it tied up in a big bun. "Would you like to see her hair down?" Olya asked. "Yes, of course," I replied. They whispered together for a moment and then stood up. "We Okay in your room?" "Please go in," I gestured. They went in and closed the door.

It seemed like an hour went by but it was probably more like ten minutes when the door opened and Olya's face appeared. "Alan, come in please." Alan went in. Larissa stood in the middle of the room, smiling. Olya said something in Russian and Larissa turned slowly, showing her hair; dark brown and shining, even shimmering. It dropped over her shoulders, covered her back and finished resting on her shapely bottom. She turned back and once again I realised I was looking at an angel. *"Noo kak?"* she asked, hunching her shoulders and holding out the palms of her hands. "I'm speechless," I replied. "You're beautiful, an angel." *"Angel?"* she repeated the same word in Russian, *"Da angel,"* I assured her. She walked towards me and kissed me fully, warmly on the mouth. She might as well have kneed me in the nuts. It had precisely the same effect. I pulled her head onto my shoulder and ran my shaking hands down the waterfall of her hairline and held her hard against me. We stood there forever, kissing, touching, holding, warm. I breathed her in and I didn't ever want to let go, not ever.

The doorbell rang, followed by a loud knock. I ignored it. There followed a knock on my glass flat door. It was Olya and she was speaking Russian. Larissa pulled away with a strange look on her face. Olya's head appeared round the door. "Larissa, we must go." "Why?" I asked. "Alan, it's okay, we must go now," she insisted. "It's the big fella," Ray gestured towards the door. "Who, Saba?" I asked, already moving towards the door. "Where is he?" I opened the door onto the landing; there was no one there. Olya followed me looking frightened. "Alan, please. Okay, come in. We must go now. We will come back tomorrow." "Why is he here? Where is he? What does he want?" I was completely pissed off, but at the same time was concerned at the situation and the effect this guy had on the girls. There was something they were not telling us. I held back. Now was not the time to test things, the relationship was in its infancy, still very delicate and the simple fact was I loved this girl. I needed to hang fire, at least today. I asked to walk the girls to the bus stop, they declined and I didn't push it.

Larissa and Olya did come the following evening and the evening after that. They came every night, and things were great. It was just like happy families. The long Russian winter had relented and things were warming up nicely. Ray had turned out to be a genius around the flat, not only with his cooking but also as an instrument engineer. He had solved the shower problem by rigging an overflow valve, soldering a pressure gauge and tap in place of the blanked off bleed screw. Anyway, he was a rock and a great friend, but his work in Staple Fibre was quickly coming to an end. Commissioning on the first two of nine lines was underway and the pump room and laboratory where Ray's instruments were housed were now operating to specification. No sooner had he arrived and now he was leaving. "So what the hell am I supposed to do?" I asked him. "What do you mean?" He looked mystified. "Well, to start with there's the cooking and shopping." "And?" he insisted. "And there's the girls. What are we going to do with Olya?" "Look after her until I get back." "And when might that be?" "Later this year or early next year," he confirmed, "When the filament pump room is coming on stream." "Oh, great. I'll tell Olya to hang on."

Ray left for the UK the following Monday, and as usual Larissa and Olya came round to the flat early evening. We would usually listen to music, chat about the weather, maybe even watch TV. The programmes were something else, if not news then old Communist films or documentaries. However, now and again, there would be football or ice hockey, and that was well worth a watch. Olya was very understanding and would set off for the bus five minutes before Larissa to allow us a goodnight kiss and cuddle. She, Olya, was a lovely girl, and speaking some English, made conversation much easier. However, I was, by now, having feelings that were going beyond the need for conversation. They were all together more basic, and although I would wait a lifetime if needed, the feelings were definitely burning stronger. "Maybe," I thought, "I could waylay Larissa on her way home from college."

She was studying chemical engineering and was hoping to work at the Kombinat, which we were helping build. I could see part of the college from my flat window, but unfortunately, our other block of flats obstructed the path from the college over some development land, past our flats to the bus stop at the airport. I decided to wait at the end of the flats one afternoon, having arrived back as usual from work. I only had to wait around ten minutes when I saw Larissa walking towards me with some friends. She looked surprised to see me but said goodbye to her friends, although looking nervous. I decided not to speak just in case they hadn't realised that I was English. I waffled nervously with some broken Russian, gestured towards the flat, and we set off holding hands. I really felt like skipping down the path, but resisted.

"Now I've got you all to myself," I said, hanging onto the clothes stand. She looked at me, not understanding. *"Nichego,"* (nothing/it doesn't matter), I said, kissing her gently. She smiled a knowing smile. I asked if she was hungry, and decided to eat. "Gordon Blue," I said in my best Halliwell accent. "Chips and egg with Redex," I said, flipping the bottle of ketchup. She gazed at me if I was mad. *"Chto?"* (What?) I fired the stereo up and gave her lessons in chip butty eating, making sure to catch the excess tomato ketchup in the corners of her mouth with my tongue. We pushed the plates to one side and kissed for real, and for a long time. This created heat, which in turn created sweat that ran between my shoulder blades and down my back. We only broke for Larissa to go to the toilet.

I took the opportunity to change the music, choose the mood. Glen Campbell, he'll do. Probably a bit naff, Glen, but 'Galveston' and 'Rhinestone Cowboy', has to be a pleasant change from 'Yellow Submarine' and 'I am the Walrus'. I was beginning to feel like a bleedin' walrus. Mind you, I had been living a little like the walrus in the verse from Eskimo Nell, which goes:

> *"So back to the land of the frozen waste,*
> *Where the nights are six months' long,*
> *Where the polar bear wanks off in his lair,*
> *And the walrus plays with his prong."*

"Yes, I thought, "That's me." Just then Larissa interrupted my daydream. In the cupboard in the hall, stood a pair of Russian wellington boots, nothing else, just a pair of wellies. Whoever had been in the flat prior to my arrival had obviously bought a pair and then decided not to take them home. I had tried on the wellies, which fortunately were the right size, forty-two. They were very high, coming right up to the knee, so had been turned down about an inch at the top. "To stop the rain going down your legs," my grandma used to say. They would be ideal for fishing. The trips, I had been assured, would restart in the next couple of weeks. Larissa had taken off her boots and replaced them with the wellingtons and had now struck a pose in the doorway, a very seductive pose, tapping her right foot rhythmically with the music, and a look on her face asking, "Now, what are these?" I was dumbfounded and just about managed a wolf whistle. I just wished I had a camera to hand. What a picture! Oh, yes, and the doorbell rang. It was Olya. Larissa answered, and there was some muffled but seemingly heated conversation that appeared to centre on why she had not been home. Anyway, Olya came through. "Do you like boots?" she giggled. "No, we were going fishing," I explained. "Now? You're going fishing now?" She seemed amazed. "Don't worry, Olya, we won't go fishing now. You're here now," I assured her, with just a tinge of sarcasm in my voice. It turned out to be another lovely evening and as I tucked up in bed I couldn't help thinking just how that walrus felt, and my dad always said it made you go blind. It doesn't say that the walruses had white sticks. Leave it alone and go to sleep!

They say absence makes the heart grow fonder. Well, I was sure that there was no way that I could love anybody more, in fact I was increasingly getting worried that the two weeks holiday that I was embarking on could affect our brief relationship. Although I was sure that Larissa cared for me, I wasn't confident enough to be sure of her reaction to a break. There was also a nagging doubt in my mind about the situation with Saba, who obviously had an effect on our relationship and the group of Russian friends as a whole.

Another problem had arisen just the previous week and had come completely out of the blue. It started as just another day of work. I was on the shop floor with Tchaikovsky, and

Sid - our engineer overseeing the erection of bailing presses, when Malcolm and Mr Touse arrived. Malcolm discreetly took me to one side. "Alan, a delegation from the police has arrived and are wanting a chat with some of the bachelors. I don't think it's a problem but they would like to speak to you." "Yes, okay," I confirmed. "Mr Touse will go with you. They are waiting now." I walked back upstairs with Malcolm and Tousey, and while Malcolm ducked back into our office, I carried on past the main office to a small storeroom next door. Mr Touse knocked on the door and we went in. There were two men in their mid to late thirties and a woman who looked older. All three were dressed in plain clothes and no way on God's earth were they police. The three sat side by side. Another chair was set up in the corner, where Mr Touse sat down, and a fifth chair was set up on the nearside wall, facing the three. One of the men started talking. Mr Touse did his best to translate but looked nervous, very nervous, and started to stammer. "They are concerned that local girls have been reported visiting the flats on a regular basis." "Mr Touse," I replied calmly, "would you please tell these policemen, and women, that I am twenty-one years old, and if I wish to see anybody... anybody, then that is my right and my decision and should not be the concern of anybody else. Would you please explain exactly what I have said." Mr Touse now looked terrified, the blood visibly draining from his already pale face. He started to translate. The same man interjected, lifting his hand disdainfully to stop Mr Touse in midstream. He then continued to dictate to Tousey, who shrunk under the tirade. This time I stopped proceedings. I jumped to my feet. "Did he say prostitute?" I shouted at Mr Touse, who also jumped up; cutting off my advance towards the bastard. "Please sit down Mr Hamer," he urged. "Did he say prostitute?" I glared at the man who was still sitting. "They know nothing about me or about the young lady that I am seeing. They know nothing about my feelings and they talk about prostitutes. Not with me they don't!" I pushed Mr Touse, opened the door and stormed out and back to my desk. "That wasn't long," said Malcolm. "Sorry boss, but I snapped in there." I tried to explain but found it difficult to communicate. "Don't worry, Alan." Malcolm put his hand on my shoulder. "A couple of weeks at home will work wonders."

Larissa and Olya came round on the Saturday evening prior to me travelling home the following day. I hadn't said anything about the visit from the "so-called police" and whom we (the lads) were in full agreement, would have been the "KGB warning off squad." I didn't want to worry them. Instead, I tried to find out what Larissa wanted as a present from England. She was obviously very surprised and even embarrassed at the suggestion. We agreed that it would be a surprise. They did ask to borrow my record collection while I was away. "Take you're pick, please," and we filled a large shopping bag with the LPs and singles. Laura was in no doubt as to the exact day and date I was returning to Mogilev and promised, crossing heart and hoping to die, to call. Olya, as usual, allowed us a couple of minutes to say goodnight. We kissed and held each other close, soaking up the warmth, enough to last a fortnight.

CHAPTER 10
NIGHT, NIGHT, SWEETHEART

Polyspinners had come to an agreement with the Russian Kombinat, that they (The Kombinat) would pay for one flight home each year and Polyspinners would pay for the other. The company would pay for the first trip and it was accepted that we, as individuals, could pay our own flights in rubles and claim the money back in sterling. Great then to exchange Mickey Mouse money for £180 or so. For a twenty-one year old, in 1970, I was now quite well off.

The lads were still meeting at the Boar's Head on Churchgate. Black Velvets all round, followed by a couple of pints of scrumpy at Ye Olde Man and Scythe, a couple of Aussie specials at the (S)Wine Lodge before meeting up with the girls for cocktails at the Brass Cat. Just as if I'd never been away.

The lads want to know whether I get to see any football and what the pubs are like. The girls are eager to know about the weather, the shops and, "What do you do at night, Alan?" Linda One asked, all the girls' eyes piercing my head. "Sleep," I answered, tongue in cheek. "No, yer know," Janet backed her up. "Oh, you mean the blindness thing?" I grinned. "I bloody hope not, no, we mean, are you getting any?" "She means have you met anybody?" Janice tried the cultured approach. "Are you kidding? I hold audition nights during the week, with the winners coming back for the weekend." "Stop messing about," said Linda Two, "or we'll take you round the back and give you a good seeing to." "Oh, yes please." I threw my arms out, "Take me please." Just then, a great spade-like hand crashed down on my head. It was Big Nick, Thos, Lopper and Skimmer. "Hamer, toreet, pal?" We hugged Russian style. It was good to be back with the lads, and that included the girls.

Even more special was to give my sister a cuddle and spend some time with her shopping in Bolton, including a trip to our favourite café. I even went to a party at Chorley College with her, although God knows why. I think I was checking up on a lad she was dating called Bill. Now Bill seemed fine; it was some of the other buggers I worried about. Too many pairs of sandals and rosy cheeks for me. The longer the night went on the more the smell of "wacky backy" drifted around the hall and the wider the eyes became. It got like a scene out of "Village of The Damned."

Anyway, I made my excuses and sodded off back to the Albion, going the long way home via Belmont. Just to drive was a pleasure, no radio, just listening to the 3-litre Jaguar engine purring effortlessly. I had noticed the headlights in my rear view mirror, but what the hell, he wasn't passing me; this cat was flying. It was only dropping down from Belmont Road with the road lights, that I spotted the bloody police car, headlights flashing. Their car, now exhausted, just managed to pull in front. I stopped. The traffic bobby slowly climbed out of the car and walked to my door, checking the registration number on the way. I wound down the car window, which was soon fitted with a large, red, copper's face, his hands gripping the door. "Good evening, Wing Commander," he said calmly, "Are you having difficulty getting it off the ground?" I tried desperately not to laugh. "Sorry officer, I thought it was somebody having a go – yer know?" "Driving licence?" he requested. I took it out of my wallet and handed it to him.

He looked at the licence then looked at me. "Are you Alan's son, from the Albion?" "Yes," I replied. He handed back the licence and brought his face back to the open window. "In future, if you're going to drive at that speed, make sure you're not being followed by a police car, okay? Now, get yourself back to the Albion," he tapped the roof of the car a couple of times with his hand, before returning to his car.

It was two o'clock in the morning when I unlocked the side door at the Albion and walked into the kitchen. On the sideboard were lined three policemen's helmets. I opened the bar door. Dad was still serving behind the bar while mum was sat at the bar with a crowd of friends. "Where are all the lads?" I asked, pointing to the row of helmets. Dad pointed to the taproom. I craned my neck round the end of the bar and there was another group sat playing dominoes. "Al, come and give your mother a cuddle." She held out her arms, wrapping me up in them when I arrived. I had to run through the night's events, including the run-in with the traffic police. After I had finished, mum announced to all and sundry, "Alan's in love. He's got a Russian girlfriend and she's very pretty." "Mum," I said, exasperated, "I'm off to bed." "Night, night, sweetheart." She gave me a kiss and let her red faced son slope off.

Before returning to Russia, I had a special day out shopping with my mum and sister, who were keen for me to take something special back for Larissa. We finished up with a mini skirt, a pair of cotton summer pants and a psychedelic cat suit with flared bottoms and a zip-up top, plus lots of pairs of tights. I also hit the record shops to stock up on the best albums.

CHAPTER 11
ALL'S WELL THAT ENDS WELL

"Technical problems," our interpreter said "don't worry they're finding a replacement plane." After about an hour, we were ushered through the departure lounge and out onto a bus that trundled along for about ten minutes, stopping alongside a plane stood outside a large hanger. "What the hell is that?" one of our party pointed to this dark green thing with wings. "It's an old Soviet troop carrier," I said. It was a twin propeller plane with a low-slung cabin almost touching the ground. As we walked nearer, people started to go white in the face. "Say your prayers now," I shouted, "It's a bleedin' rust bucket." I love flying, and I like to wind people up, but this looked seriously dodgy, even more so when we got on board. The air was musty, no, sour, maybe. What was left of the leather seats appeared to be going mouldy. I managed to grab a shiny window seat on the left-hand side under the wing. On sitting down, there was nothing receptive in the backside region; no springs, no cushioning, nothing. It was just like sitting on a cold pavement or like a chilling recollection of my first Moscow taxi. A cold shudder ran through my body. There was a seatbelt. I fastened it tight.

The left-hand engine eventually fired up, shedding a cloud of black smoke, but for all the din, the propeller did seem to be spinning okay. We started to taxi. Every nick in the concrete sent the backbone into spasm and rattled the teeth. It was just like driving a glorified go-cart but with solid tyres. It was so uncomfortable I started to laugh, but no one else saw the funny side. There was no conversation at all, just fear. As I looked round, it was etched in people's faces. The plane ground to a halt and stayed there for an age. "Maybe they are warming up another plane," I comforted Hazel, sat in the aisle seat opposite.

There followed a loud metallic bang that shook the plane. I looked through the cabin window and a guy's face was close enough to slap. He raised a sledge hammer high above his head and swung it, and again the plane shook. "Have you seen this idiot out here?" People stood up and craned over to watch as he repeatedly slammed the sledgehammer into the plane. Eventually I had to let go. "He's a Russian instrument engineer," I said, "Just a small technical fault." Again, no one understood the humour. I wasn't sure I did. "Sit down, please. Sit down." The stewardess was bringing another tray of boiled sweets down the aisle. "Excuse me, what is Boris doing with the hammer?" I asked the young woman. "It is okay, no problem," she assured me. "Obviously not," I concluded sarcastically. I turned to Boris and winked. His expression didn't change but he did load the hammer onto his shoulder and walked back from the plane shouting to somebody before disappearing behind the fuselage. Immediately the revs were increase and the plane trundled on, not even stopping at the end of the runway. Maybe the pilot thought that if he stopped again we would all try to escape, so he just rammed it down the runway and up into the wide blue yonder.

The flight was great, not too high, and it was a nice clear day. I was sure we flew over Gorad Geeroy Smolensk, and on over tiny villages surrounded by vast open fields, now beautifully spring green, and large forests with the occasional glint of the setting sun reflecting on small lakes and rivers. The atmosphere on board had started to improve and I was aware of laughter coming from the back of the plane. Once again, the stewardess was making her way down the aisle, requesting people fasten their seatbelts and handing out sweets to make your ears pop. The pilot pulled the handle marked 'landing gear' (in Russian) and it felt as though the floor beneath my feet had fallen away. "Here we go," I thought to myself, and could see Minsk airport away to my left.

We hadn't figured out what the problem had been but were in absolutely no doubt as we touched down on the runway. It was then that the pilot hit the brake pedal. The plane lurched violently to the left and off the runway, the uneven ground thudded beneath my seat. Just to help things even more, a couple of the women started to scream. I'm sure one was the stewardess. I stuck my head down and hung on.

We were down and my head was still connected to my body. "Oh, thank you, God." The pilot said something in Russian; it brought applause from the passengers, all 20 of us. Personally, I could have wrung his bloody neck, the mad bastard had nearly killed us, but as my gran always says, "All's well that ends well."

RUSSIAN AIRCRAFT SERVICE MANUAL
1) SIEZING BRAKES
    a) Apply lubricant.
    b) If there is no lubricant, ask Boris to hit repeatedly with sledge hammer.

CHAPTER 12
INTO THE BOTTLE

To say that I was glad to be back in Mogilev after two weeks' holiday would probably seem stupid. Yes, I had loved being home and seeing everyone but I was excited to be back in my new home. I was looking forward to getting back to work and I was counting the seconds until I saw Larissa again. I was like a dog with two something's. No matter, landing back just in time to catch last orders at The Spinners was timing to perfection. A couple of pints of Red Barrel were slotted down without touching the sides, followed by a sound night's sleep.

Whether I was out of the habit of getting up at 7am, I don't know. I do know, however, that I had missed the works' bus and was forced to dash to the office, arranging for a taxi to take me in. Not the best first morning back. After the false start the day went fine, most of it spent catching up with the position on the shop floor and bringing the paperwork up to date, as well as plans for the weeks ahead, jotting everything down in my little red book. The ritual cheer followed John's turn as *'Poechaly'* man, and off the bus went.

The guys had told me that the Saturday morning fishing trips had started, the minibus leaving the flats at 5.30am. I called and added my name to the list before retreating to my flat. First job was a trip to the local shops to pick up basics like spuds, bread, milk, sugar, eggs, plus one or two personal specials, *pilmeny, kolbasa(*cured meat sausage) *and ogurtsy(*pickled cucumbers), plus vodka, wine and lemonade.

Something struck me as I came out of the supermarket. There was a line of motorcycles outside, from small 250cc bikes through 350cc Jawas to 500cc Dnieper combinations. It was obvious that these bikes had been kept indoors during the winter months and now, in the spring, brought onto the streets. While 99.9 per cent of people were unable to afford a car, motorcycles were both affordable and available. There was a crowd of men outside having a smoke and talking bikes, while the girls were doing the shopping; a bit like back home but bikes not cars. The guys were staring at me, two hands full of shopping. "Evening," I said, as I passed by. "Maybe I should get one," I thought to myself – then again...!

Back at the flat, I treated myself to pilmeny and chips. Pilmeny are small pastry pouches filled with a very tasty mincemeat type stuff. Just deep fry until crisp, very tasty and excellent with a plate of chips. Jump in the shower for a good scrub down, and I was ready. Maybe not. I decided to get dressed.

Shortly after 7.30, the doorbell rang. I ran to the door and opened it. Larissa stood in the doorway, stunningly beautiful, even cast in the light from a single 40-watt landing bulb. "Coming in?" I asked in English. She walked straight into my open arms, where we remained, back together. *"Gdye Olya?"* I asked. I think Larissa was telling me that she must have forgotten I was back so she had come alone. She eventually took off her coat and we moved into my flat. I put a new LP on the stereo. I held her hands, looked deep into her eyes and told her just how much I had missed her. Being that Larissa didn't speak a word, she hunched her shoulders in that, "I haven't got a clue what you're talking about," way, so I slowly, deliberately leant forward, holding her eyes and kissed her, at first gently but increasingly stronger and more passionate, eventually pulling away, still holding eye contact. "You know what I mean," I thought to myself. "She must know." "Anyway," I said, "Presents. *Podarok.*" *"Da?"* She sounded pleased but shocked. I had left my case stood at the foot of the bed. I grabbed the handle and swinging the case up onto the bed flicked open the lid. I had a carrier bag full of different pairs of tights. "Some for you." I grabbed a handful and held them out, "For you," I confirmed, "and some," I pointed to the remainder, "for Olya." *"Da, da, Olya,"* she confirmed. In another carrier, there was a nice silk blouse and a dark brown wraparound miniskirt. She held them up with a look of amazement. I think she asked should she try them on. *"Pozalusta."* (With pleasure), I nodded, and gave her the thumbs up. "I will look away." I placed one hand over my eyes. She put her hands on my shoulders and turned me round. "Don't worry, I won't peek," turning part way. She gently slapped my shoulder. "No, no, no, please." "Be quick I can't wait," I shouted. "Okay." I spun round, opened my mouth like Bob the Fish and collapsed backwards onto the bed. "Frog's knob!" Larissa stood swaying her hips provocatively. My eyes must have stood out like chapel hat pegs. The blouse was a low-cut, crossover type thing, sexy. The skirt, however, was positively rude, magnificently rude! Laura turned and I could see the curve of her wonderful bum. "Dear God, take me away." Larissa's face was a picture, she could barely contain herself at my reaction and changed from inquisitiveness to appealing, to warmth. *"Spasibo,"* (Thank you). She pulled my face between her breasts and kissed my forehead. "Next." I gently slapped her bottom. "And now for the main present." I held up the final carrier bag and handed it to her. She peeped inside and her mouth opened, looked at me and back to the bag, as she slipped out the multi-coloured cat suit. Laura said something in Russian. "It's a cat suit," I confirmed, and turned with my back towards her. "Go on, try it on," I said. She was already changing. *"Noo kak?"* and I turned my head. What a picture, it fitted her perfectly and she looked beautiful. She stood in pose and played with the zip, questioning me with her eyes, up, down. "Definitely down," I said. "Ah, ha," she teased me. *"Moya mama* e *sestra,"* I tried to explain who had helped buy the presents. Laura looked tearful and threw her arms around my neck and kissed me long and caringly, tenderly, wonderfully.

I was so much in love, Boris could have hit me with that sledgehammer and I wouldn't have felt a thing. At a time when Laura was trying to explain why she had to go, I was trying to explain why I wanted her to stay, how I felt about her and that I wanted, desperately wanted to make love to her. Nothing before had prepared me for this but the feelings I now had were hurting, physically and mentally hurting. What was getting in the way was the language; I simply couldn't explain and express my true feelings.

When I went to the bog, Larissa took the opportunity to change back and seemed adamant that she must go. I agreed to let her go on the promise she would call tomorrow. She promised. We repacked the presents into two carrier bags and set off to the bus stop. Stood in the shadows away from the others we held hands. Only when the bus arrived did we kiss, briefly, as friends would kiss, apart from the eye contact. I held her hand until the last second and waved as she stood at the back window, and didn't stop until the bus disappeared round the corner. I looked up into the starlit sky and thanked somebody up there for bringing me someone so wonderful, so beautiful. I knew that I was the luckiest man on the planet. I floated back to the flat, resisting the opportunity of a pint in the Spinners. I wanted to think, not drink. I was in love, but how do you describe your feelings? "Surely she knows, anyway just tell her and even better show her."

The trip back from work the next day was great. I stared out of the bus window at a fine Mogilev evening, children playing on swings and with footballs, while my head was already in a dream world. What would she wear? It wasn't warm enough to wear the mini skirt, anyway she would probably save it for a dance, a special occasion. The same would apply to the cat suit. She would cause a scare walking through Mogilev in that. Either of the outfits would cause an accident or two on the swings and would cut short a game of footie. "Al… Alan, are you getting off?" Peter gave me a friendly clip round the back of my head. I stood up in a daze, "Mr Alan, Mr Alan, eh?" The driver was holding his finger against the side of his head. "No, Boris, it's you that's bloody mad." I put my hand on his shoulder. "Mr Alan, lu-lu," I confirmed. Boris laughed and slapped the steering wheel, "And Boris, I don't care." I turned and skipped down the path and up the steps, all the way back to my flat.

Tea was quick, followed by a shower and change; blue silk shirt, best jeans, white leather belt with fancy silver buckle, black slip-on shoes, ivory and leather choker. A quick Elvis top lip impression in front of the mirror – I was ready.

I sat in silence on the bed with my back against the wall, listening nervously for the sound of footsteps on the stairs. I hoped she would come alone as she had she had the night before. Olya was a lovely girl and always a good laugh and, maybe more importantly, a good interpreter, but I thought that our relationship now needed to move beyond that. I knew we needed the intimacy that is impossible as a threesome. I checked my watch, it said 8.15pm. They nearly always arrived just after 7.30pm and the buses ran every fifteen minutes. Maybe she had been held up or was waiting for Olya. I walked through into Ray's old flat and peered through the window towards the airport. I couldn't see anyone.

It was a nice evening so I decided to walk across to the bus terminus. I found a position at the end of the first block of flats where I could see the bus stop and also the entrance to my block. The first bus came and then another, without any sign of Larissa. I walked back to the flat, made a coffee and sat upright on the couch. Maybe her parents had seen the presents; maybe they had asked questions and maybe they had stopped her going out. Perhaps she had a cold and wasn't fit to come out. Tomorrow I would get off the works' bus and wait for her on her way home from college. There must be a reason. She had promised that she would call tonight. There must be a simple explanation why she hadn't. I sat on, thinking, "Tomorrow. Bring on tomorrow. Everything will be okay."

I did exactly as planned and stood at the end of the flats until the last stragglers from college had long gone. "Just time," I thought, "to get changed before 7.30." I ran inside. Again, I took up my position on the bed and listened. Nothing. What if she had had an accident? I didn't know where she lived. I knew it was through the far end of town, but where? I realised I didn't even know her name or Olya's. How stupid is that! What if she's lying in hospital? How would I find out? What was I going to do? I needed a drink. I poured a glass of Ballentine's and drank it in one. The drink only fuelled my anxiety.

Olya had borrowed most of my records before I went home on leave. Larissa had been but she hadn't brought them back. She had called for her presents. "No, that's nonsense," I told myself, "she was not that sort of girl." I knew her better than that. No, she must be ill or injured, but my stupidity meant I could not contact her or Olya. "I can't be with her when she needs me." And what of Saba, what part had he played? Maybe he had threatened her or even hurt her, or maybe he was with the KGB. What if they had warned her off, or even her parents? I had another glass of whisky and paced round the flat. I played Simon and Garfunkel's new hit, "Bridge Over Trouble Water." The words made sense, they fed the need to drink; it would help me sleep – it didn't.

Days now became a routine. The work becoming more difficult, yet strangely acting as a release, focusing my mind. When you're part of a team the mind has to function positively. However, increasingly my mind was being invaded with negatives, self-persecution and drink.

Waiting outside the flats I now had a habit of turning away from people approaching, both Russian and British, so as not to acknowledge their presence. Before I was always pleased to smile and speak to people. It was not only a common courtesy but something that was so simple yet uplifting. Obviously such things had stopped mattering.

Now that glasses had lost their usefulness drinking was done from the bottle and by the bottle, my inner being was being washed away. I was retreating into a foetal position, assumed each evening as I curled up on the bed.

During the first 15-20 minutes of getting home, I would drink a litre bottle of spirits, any spirits, whisky, gin, brandy or vodka, it mattered nothing. The thing was that as I drank from the bottle, my entire inner being including my mind would dissolve into some foul vapour that was somehow regurgitated, back into the empty bottle. The bottle now full could be discarded in the bin. Borne out of guilt and a feeling of self-stupidity, there comes a self-loathing. Who else could I blame? Once desperation had now given way to fated acceptance that I had lost her. Tears that had soaked my pillow had given way to icy cold squalor. I was dirty, inside and out, and that was how I should be, a dirty, broken, drunkard who neither asked for nor wanted any understanding or pity.

Now, as weeks turned into months, there were fewer and fewer recollections. I suppose it's like being caught in a whirlpool being dragged deeper and deeper. But when you have long since given up, you simply don't care. There was no lack of money to fuel the habit, although by now the volume of drink needed to pass out was difficult to quantify. I was even imposing myself on decent folk running the bar, staying until I was thrown out. Sometimes collapsing on the stairs up to the flat, and one night waking up having burned a large hole in my jumper with a cigarette and my stomach badly blistered.

By this time I wasn't eating. I was using the canteen for meals but was finding it difficult to get food into my mouth my hands shook so badly. The food I did manage to eat was more often than not spewed up, either down the bog or if at work, any dark corner I could find.

People did show me concern. But how many times can you turn the other cheek? I had no difficulty now in telling people to mind their own business, and in a very simple English.

I even saw a Russian engineer cut in two. Staple Fibre commissioning was running at a pace and ICI engineers were doing trials on the Line 5 cutter platform. I was behind Line 4 bailing press with Sid, the fitter. He didn't speak a word of Russian but by grunting, pointing and throwing things at them, they the Russian fitters climbed all over the presses and put them together like clockwork, and what's more they loved him. Anyway, Tony, one of the ICI specialists, was working high up on the cutter platform with the Russian. Tony had popped off somewhere and left the guy working on the cutters when he dropped his spanner into the hopper. He then made a fatal error, deciding to climb down into the hopper to retrieve the spanner. The bailing hopper was like a huge V-shaped funnel, into which the cut tow yarn dropped, a bit like cotton wool. Inside the hopper was a magic eye, or beam of light, which would be broken when sufficient cut yarn built up inside the hopper. This automatically started a rotating paddle which fed the yarn into a tramper box. By climbing down, the fitter broke the beam and the paddle fed his legs into the tramper. At this point the man started to scream, obviously aware of what came next. The paddle spins for a matter of seconds before it locks, at which point a five-ton tramper arm attached to a hydraulic ram slams down and compresses the yarn inside the bailing press ready to be strapped for shipping.

Before Sid could reach the press and hit the emergency stop button, the tramper arm had taken him off at the waist. The front of the tramper box was made of a reinforced glass, just like a giant television screen. My eyes were transfixed to the screen, which by now was covered in a red mist. Tony must have been making his way back to the cutters but arrived too late. He climbed down inside and pulled the top half of the man out on his back. My sole contribution was to collapse onto my knees and sick up. I just used it as another reason to feel sorry for myself, hiding myself away in the office until it was time to go.

I seldom phoned home, finding it difficult to hide my condition and answer questions about Laura and what had gone on. My mum never stopped reassuring and telling me how much I was loved. She was never a fool and knew something was wrong. "I'll drop you a line," I promised, before finishing. I never did. Mums have an impact, don't they, and I found it difficult to get back to the flat before breaking down, collapsing on my bed in a flood of tears. I could see her face and her eyes full of understanding, and her smile that melted ice. I wanted her to cuddle me like she had as a child when I was hurt or upset. She would sit and hold me on her knee until the hurt had gone away. Not now. I grabbed a bottle of brandy and took a long swig, the intake stopping my blubbing.

Why is it, when you get into a spiral, you become so bloody selfish? You don't give a toss about anyone or anything. It's just, "Me, me, me," and "Why?" Oh, and of course, "Why me? Why should she leave me? Me!" You can beat your chest all you want but somewhere along this ride to hell, you have to ask the question, "Who would want to even acknowledge the existence of a dirty, self-centred, drunken bum like me?" It's like seeing an injured hedgehog in the road; you may swerve out of its way, but stop and move it... Why...so it can die slowly? I don't think so. You probably feel that by leaving it someone will come along and put it out of its misery, quick, decisive. End of story.

CHAPTER 13
GORKY PARK

It was a Friday in July. The heat was suffocating and I was having difficulty getting through the days sneaking away to be ill. My stomach had been giving me problems, at times doubling me up with pain. I had seen the Harley Street doctor on his last visit to site. He had prescribed a course of tablets for what he diagnosed as a peptic ulcer, possibly caused by drinking and an irregular diet. I suppose it's easier than saying, "You're a piss-head and your body is beginning to shut down."

I was trudging up the stairs behind Gordon. He had only arrived on site a couple of weeks before and was living in the flat across the landing from mine. I was struggling to hold the key steady enough to guide it into the lock. "Do you fancy some tea?" Gordon asked, leaning on his flat door. "Sorry?" I mumbled. "I've done some potato hash and there's tonnes of it." "I'm okay," I said shortly. "Two jumbo bottles of wine to wash it down?" Gordon turned, accepting my refusal. "Half an hour?" I stuttered. "Yeah," he acknowledged as he closed the door.

I stripped off the clothes that I had worn day and night for far too long, and turned on the shower, leaving it to settle and run off the brown sandy muck while I looked for something clean to wear. Only one turquoise silk shirt remained wearable and my best jeans, which I threw onto the bed. My hair was getting quite long, the last cut being on the April leave. Even then I had a trim on top but had left the back quite long. It needed three good washes before I got the requisite squeak. I certainly needed a good scrub elsewhere and paid particular attention to the wrinkled retainers and bellus endus. Maybe it would be easier using sandpaper. Eventually I towelled down and got dressed. Before leaving the flat I picked out my last litre bottle of Chivas Regal. "May as well go out in style," I thought.

Gordon's flat was very basic compared to mine. A bed, couch and small table and that was it, but the smell of food was great. He brought through the wine and two half-pint glasses. I took the bottle and filled the two glasses. *"Do dna!"* I said. "What's that?" Gordon looked puzzled. "Bottoms up," I confirmed, drinking the wine down in one. Gordon was in his late twenties, a big guy, standing around 6 foot tall and quite heavy. Anyway he seemed a decent guy.

We certainly didn't chat over our Tatty Ash, not even after the lubrication of two litres of wine and a litre of whisky. Any talk was strained and certainly not memorable, but maybe that was down to me. The food, on the other hand, seemed to be sitting well and so far my stomach had accepted it. The drink, however, was not having its usual numbing effect, in fact quite the opposite, and my head started to burn. "Do you fancy a pint in the Spinners?" Gordon asked, while clearing the table. I sat on the couch, holding my head in my hands. "No," I said quite calmly, "I'm going to town for a fight." I stood up and walked to the door. "Good luck." Gordon walked back to the kitchen.

I don't know how I got to town and I don't know how or why I got to Gorky Park, but I was standing outside the open-air dance hall and music was coming from within. I handed some money to the woman in the hole in the wall and took the ticket that allowed me through a manned gate. Inside, there was a group performing live on stage and there were hundreds of teenagers. Most of the girls were dancing, with a good number of lads milling around the outside of the dance floor.

A girl came towards me, grabbed my hand and pulled me onto the dance floor. I tried to dance but couldn't, my legs not in time with the rest of the body. The girl seemed to understand and moved in close, wrapping one arm round my waist, the other hand on my shoulder. She smelled wonderful; her short orangey, red hair shrouded a cute face with big brown teddy bear eyes. After a couple of songs another girl butted in, the redhead passing me on to a very attractive blonde girl who held me at arm's length, giving me a good coat of looking at before pulling me into the web of her arms, her face and lips nuzzling into my neck.

We slowly shuffled around for a song or two, until I spotted him. Saba was stood with a crowd of lads over to my right. He was staring at me with that unusual smirk on his face, the one that drove me mad. The feeling in my legs suddenly came back and I discarded the girl and marched straight for him, bumping people out of the way. I grabbed his throat with my right hand and kept marching him backwards towards the stage. *"Gdye Larissa.* Where is Larissa?" I repeatedly spat the question at him. The group had stopped playing by the time the couple reached the stage. By now, I was screaming at him, "Where is Larissa?" His face never changed, just a sickly grin, looking down at me. Realising that everything had gone quiet I let go of his throat and looked around. I was surrounded by 20 or so lads. *"Gdye Anglichanin?"* Somebody wanted to know where I was.

A figure barged his way through the crowd. Built like a rugby prop forward, he didn't stop coming. Then there was an amazing white flash as his fist connected with my chin. Now my legs really did turn to jelly, and I hit the floor, hard.

Now, you have to see things from their side. A drunken Englishman crashes your party wearing a silk shirt, Wrangler jeans, a chiffon neckerchief, with long hair down his back. He starts shouting his mouth off and trying to choke one of the lads, in fact the leader of the gang. "Kick his head in," would have been my decision and they rightfully obliged and I blacked out.

The next thing I remember was being dragged, a pain in my left arm, which was draped over someone's shoulder and a strong hand gripping mine. I managed to lift my head and saw a line of policemen moving quickly into the crowd of people trying to get out of the open gates. My head was pushed firmly down. "*Militzia, Militzia*," the guy who was dragging me whispered quietly but firmly, not stopping, and we crushed through the gate. Somebody grabbed my other arm and we increased speed, my feet incapable of catching up. People were still running past us and I began to feel pain in my hip and legs, but on we went. Eventually, the pace slowed and I managed to ground my feet and walk, in a fashion.

I had lost a shoe and my left foot and toes started to burn, blood was dripping off my chin. I pulled my arms away and felt at my face, checking my teeth. My bottom lip was burst and I spat out a mouthful of blood. My ear was sore and blood ran down my neck. My body now racked with pain, only sharpened my senses. I had to go back and find my shoe but as I tried to turn round, the boy who had dragged me out tugged at my arm and pulled me back. As young as he was, he was stronger than me. I pleaded with him, I needed to find Saba, and I needed to know where Larissa was. He appeared to understand but kept pulling me away, only stopping when we joined a crowd waiting at the bus stop on the hill overlooking the river. He mentioned Larissa's name and, although I didn't understand much of what he was saying, I did make out that she wasn't in Mogilev. She was in the Ukraine; something he repeated several times. Larissa was in the Ukraine.

The bus still hadn't arrived when I was abducted by two girls who grabbed my arms and frog-marched me off towards the bridge. They didn't speak, just gently but firmly escorted me away towards home. "I can't walk properly," I explained to the girls in English, pointing at my left foot, "No shoe." I stopped belligerently. One of the girls bent down and pulled off my other shoe throwing it over the bridge and into the river. "No problem," she said in Russian, and started to run off. I tried to chase her but couldn't run, grabbing the bridge wall to stop me from falling. Both girls were now laughing and beckoning me on. I kept hold of the bridge until the culprit walked towards me. She put her hands on my shoulders and kissed me gently on the cheek. She said something, and her friend handed her a handkerchief which she spat onto and started to wipe the blood off my neck and mouth. When she had finished, "*Poechaly*," I said, and again they linked my arms and off we went.

It was a long walk back to the flat, but we laughed, joked, nipped and slapped one another making light of the journey. I wasn't sure whether they were laughing with me or at me, or at my feeble attempts to speak Russian. Whatever, the girls were perfect company, so much so that I completely forgot about my aches and pains and the fact that I had walked all the way without shoes and socks. Even the girls had removed their high heels and stockings in favour of walking barefoot.

In the early hours of Saturday morning, we arrived at the flats and I asked the girls to come in for a coffee. They declined, pointing to my watch. They had to go home, which was well, "Over that way," pointing back the way we had come. They asked if I would go to the dance next week and I promised that I would, and, in turn, gave them a long hug and a kiss goodnight. I stood watching them go arm-in-arm until they disappeared.

I limped up the stairs again feeling the pain invading my body. I showered carefully, checking the cuts and bruises, before brushing my teeth and climbing under the single sheet on my bed.

I said a prayer for Belarus, thanking the girls who had seen me home safely, asking nothing in return. I prayed for the young boy who had helped me out of the dance and told me where Larissa was. I prayed for the guy who had chinned me and the lads who had kicked me, for treating me the way I deserved to be treated, the way I begged to be treated. As I choked on the tears I asked God to look after Larissa, wherever she was or whatever she was doing in the Ukraine. I couldn't help but be selfish and ask if he could find it in his heart to bring her back to me, and I fell into a long and restful sleep, knowing and promising I would be a better person.

CHAPTER 14
ARISE, SIR ALAN

Gorky Park, although painful, was good for me and served as a reminder that there was more to life than lying on a bed snivelling. Don't get me wrong, I wasn't about to give up drinking, but I was determined to give up giving up. I was certainly going to rejoin the human race and try and mix socially with workmates and townsfolk alike. Along the way, I did break a promise and that is something I try not to do. No, I didn't go back to the dance the following Friday. I didn't want to cause any more problems. It was, after all, their dance for their enjoyment. I wasn't about to make it therapy for a spoiled *Anglichanin* git with a drink problem.

It may have come as a repercussion from the park fracas but the following week, Malcolm asked John to give us five minutes alone and came and sat on the end of my desk. He explained that it was common knowledge that I had been suffering a personal loss. This in turn had had an effect on my drinking, my character and my work, which, from his standpoint was his greatest concern. As a result, he had asked admin to arrange two weeks' leave. I should assess my position and, hopefully, come back fully refreshed, ready for the increasing challenge ahead. Without telling him of the park incident, I did assure him that things had changed and that I was determined to sort the problem out. I also wanted to confirm that it was leave, and I was coming back. I thought it good of him to assure me that he now needed me more than ever. Anyway he would be on leave at the same time, so should I or my parents have any concerns, we could meet up back home. Oh, and there was one other matter. My sister, Carolyn was getting married and it coincided with the leave.

It's early Saturday morning, with the sun just rising in a clear blue sky and a low mist lazily hanging over the fields. Eight intrepid fishermen, one interpreter (in the form of Mr Touse) and a Russian driver are all flying along in a minibus about 30 miles south of Mogilev. It's early but by now we are all in good humour and Mr Touse is going through his rugby songs medley. You know the ones:

"Last night I contemplated masturbation,
It did me good, I knew it would,
Tonight I will repeat the operation,
It's my desire to pull mi wire."
To the tune from the opera 'The Marriage of Figaro.'

I'm sat on the back seat and turned round for my flask, in a bag behind me. I saw something through the back window that made my jaw drop. "What the bloody …? Grab a camera!" I shouted, pointing at a black flying object that had cut across the road behind the bus. It could only have been 500 feet up. It was big and black with a long pointed nose that hung down and it seemed to be flying very slowly. I could see that the undercarriage was down, so it very probably was landing. "Get a photo of that." I was pointing at the object flying just above the fields at the side of the minibus. "No, no, no!" Mr Touse started to panic. His ghostly white face no longer displayed any signs of humour. "You can't take photo!" he shouted. "Get a bloody photo somebody, it's a bomber!" I shouted back. Mr Touse said something to the driver and the bus started to swerve violently. "Whoa…we're only joking Mr Touse," I assured him. We continued to be thrown from side-to-side until the plane disappeared behind some trees. All the guys looked stunned at what they'd seen. "What was it?" someone asked. "It looked like a bloody big bomber to me, but did you see its nose, it was hanging down?" We talked about the object for ages and seemed to agree that we were not meant to see it and that it was probably a secret war plane. Tousey's response also fuelled our intrigue. No more MisterWise-crack ingHappyRussianChappy. Well not today anyway.

We arrived at a beautiful lake that we hadn't fished before. Basically round, the lake had several large bushes and overhanging trees around its edge. It also had a nice amount of weed in the margins. Before too long I had a nice bag of roach and perch, with the odd silver bream.

There were, in fact, two lakes; the second smaller lake further along a track and down a short but steep hill. I climbed an old silver birch tree at the top of the hill overlooking the lake. I must have stood there for well over an hour watching a beaver building a dam. I'd never seen a beaver before, and to watch one close-up in the wild was simply stunning. I lay against a large branch spellbound at the view. Now this really was voyeur's paradise.

Around lunchtime, we trekked back to the minibus and presented the driver with a reasonable sized pike that one of the lads had caught; steamed pike being a delicacy over here. I threw my arm round Tousey's shoulder and assured him that I had only been teasing him with the strange plane. He also apologised for losing it but explained that it could have got him into trouble had anybody found out. On the trip home I sat quietly scanning the sky and surroundings wondering. In the near future, I was to find out where the plane was going and why we never went fishing again at beaver lakes. It would be some time later than that before I was to find out what the strange black object was flying low over these Belarus fields. As it turned out Britain and France had one almost identical.

I certainly got my arse well and truly kicked when I arrived back in the UK. "You've been worrying us all to death, so get your head up and be thankful." My mum held my head up with her hands before prescribing a traditional mothers hug. As a boy only she had the power of healing and I was still her boy.

Carolyn and Bills wedding was back at St Pauls, Halliwell and our old vicar Mr. Bracewell had come back specially to conduct the service. Me and sis had some photos taken in the gardens and managed to have a quick heart-to-heart, followed by a long and moving cuddle, a brother and sister moment. It was a simple realisation that the family dynamics were changing, and quickly.

Carolyn and Bill shot off on their honeymoon and the following day I was picked up by Malcolm in the company car but not before one for the road in the Albion. Malcolm promised mum and dad that he would keep a close eye on me and whip me into shape. I think if I hadn't reminded everybody of the time, they would still have been sat there having another one for the ditch. Anyway, I was better now. And why shouldn't I be? Gran had done all my dirty washing, two suitcases full. Willie had fed me up on her famous Lancashire Hot Pots and I had been anointed with the healing balm that is family and friends. Yes, I was better. Not whole, but better.

We met Dorothy, our site administrator, at London Heathrow. She had spent her leave with family in Canada. She was an extremely English rose, quite posh actually and standing over 6 foot tall, quite imposing. I could only guess at her age, probably I thought, early to mid-thirties, with a quite a deep almost austere voice, but funny, very funny. "The Three Musketeers," she proclaimed when we met. I had an inkling that this would be a trip to remember.

We took a taxi from Sheremetyevo to the Hotel Rossia, the new 5-star hotel, positioned on the river at the south end of Red Square. We would be staying overnight and flying to Minsk after lunch the next day.

Dorothy chuckled, "Time for a drinky-poo, or three, and a bit of sightseeing." "Not sure about the sightseeing," said

Malcolm. "Hang on," I said, "you've just had me drying out for two weeks." "Then we definitely need to get you back into shape," Dorothy summed up. We arranged to meet up in our west wing reception. This hotel was the biggest in the world and with twenty-odd floors and over 3,000 bedrooms, was a logistical nightmare. "It's a good job that the lifts work," I thought. Mind you, when you get to your room it's worth it. My room was a suite with a breathtaking view over the river and I could see some of the mushroom domed chapels inside the Kremlin walls. After showering I checked the room for cameras, but still resisted the opportunity of some light relief, thinking that somebody could be watching. Even worse I visualised a group of middle-aged Commies pointing out a crooked little finger depicting my manhood. No, I decided to have a doze.

A lovely August evening, we walked across Red Square and on my advice decided to eat at the Metropol. Malcolm then suggested a cellar bar he knew under the National Hotel on the main road running north at the top end of Red Square. The place was so nice, the conversation so good, and the endless supply of booze so calming, we completely lost track of time. I lost count of the cappuccino and cognac chasers we had, but on my umpteenth trip to the bog, I realised my legs had lost the plot. Shortly afterwards, Dorothy jumped to her feet, "Come on!" she ordered, "we've got to see the changing of the guards." "When?" asked Malcolm. "Now, the 4am changing, we've still got five minutes," she said, pulling at Malcolm's hand.

We emerged onto the street, which was now eerily dead. Dorothy grabbed our hands and dragged us along like an impatient master dragging two reluctant puppies. We were running, or at least Dorothy was running, while Malcolm and myself were stumbling, falling, gasping for breath. We ran through the subway and onto Red Square, the clock above Lenin's mausoleum was already chiming. She carried on tugging us along across the cobbles; the sound of our footsteps echoing off the Kremlin walls was almost deafening. About 50 yards short of the guards, Dorothy stopped running. Both Malcolm and myself collapsed into heaps on the ground. "Bloody, bugger, dam!!!" she screamed, "we've sodding missed it." I started laughing, Malcolm joined in. Dorothy doubled over, her hands grabbing her knees and acting like pit props. She started laughing, hysterically. "Sod off," she spluttered mid-laugh, which made us laugh even more. Eventually, Dorothy gave up and sat down on the cobbles with us. "Cigarettes on Red Square," she announced, handing round the fags. We lit the cigarettes and blew the smoke skywards. I started to choke, causing the others to start laughing again, the laughter echoing around the square. Apart from the guards we were the only ones there. We stopped momentarily, hearing a loud metallic clunk, followed by the squeak of rusty hinges, as a black metal door swung open in the Kremlin wall.

Four dark figures emerged from the door and started to walk slowly towards us. We sat staring at the figures growing larger as they approached. Dorothy took a long drag on her ciggie, "Ah, well," she said, "they're coming to take us away, ha-ha, hee-hee." We also started to laugh again. The quartet stopped, talking and scratching their heads. I'm sure I heard one say, *"Anglichany,"* in a resigned voice. They turned and started walking back towards the gate. "Come on." Dorothy stood up. "Where are we going now?" "To follow the Yellow Brick Road." She pulled us up. We faced south towards St Basil's, linked arms and almost in unison, skipped off. *"We're off to see the wizard, the wonderful Wizard of Oz."*

We grew tired of skipping long before we reached St Basil's; maybe a touch of reality eating its way back into our tired heads. As we walked past St Basil's, Dorothy stopped, "Hey there's a flower" she pointed up the wall. "St Basil's Cathedral wallflower. I want it." "It's too high up," stated Malcolm soberly. "I want it and you're getting it for me," she said calmly. I looked up and, sure enough, high up the ornate stone wall there was an unusual dark flower growing out of a crack. I took off my shoes. "Okay, Malcolm, I'm going to have to stand on your shoulders." "No chance, you won't reach it." He started to walk away. "Malcolm?" Dorothy shouted, "Come back here. Look," she carried on, "you peg him up and he can stand on my shoulders. Okay?" "Certainly, Dot." He interlocked his fingers and bent his knees. I put my hand on Dorothy's shoulder and my left foot in Malcolm's hand. He boosted me up the wall and somehow I managed to plant my right foot on Dorothy's shoulder before looking up, my fingertips just reaching the flower, which I gingerly eased out of the wall, root and all. Coming down was much quicker, skinning my hands as I came. We finished in a three-way huddle, jumping up and down as if we had scored a goal in the Cup Final. After the celebration I dropped onto one knee and held out the flower, "Ma'am, your flower." Dorothy took the flower, "Arise Sir Alan. Back for a nightcap," she said, and off we went back to the hotel.

When we arrived at the Rossia, the main glass doors were locked. While we banged on the enormous doors Dorothy did her Harry Worth impersonation. Standing at the end of glass with one foot and one arm raised this 6ft 15ins lunatic appeared to be flying. I sat back down on the ground to behold this wondrous site. "Dot, you weren't out flying a couple of weeks ago were you?" She let her wings and undercarriage come to ground. "What are you talking about?" I waved my hand before standing up. "Don't worry Dorothy, it's just me having a flash-back." Shortly afterwards Dorothy's foot connected with my arse.

I was late meeting up with them for breakfast, one reason being my poor orienteering skills, finishing up in the wrong restaurant i.e. Level 4 south-west rather than Level 4 north-west. Oh, well, I got there in the end, wherever it was. One thing was for sure, and that was the mother of all hangovers that I had. I couldn't believe it when I saw the two bottles of champagne and a bottle of cognac. "You must be joking," I said, pointing at the booze. "Hair of the dog," explained Malcolm. "Anyway, we've drunk most of it." Needless to say, we polished off the lot, along with a full Russian breakfast. Not much different from an English breakfast, except you're eating it in Russia and you're drinking a shed load of booze with it.

CHAPTER 15
A GOOD IDEING

Back in Mogilev, the heat was really on, and not just the daily temperatures that regularly climbed above 30°C. At the Kombinat, the Filament Yarn building programme was way behind schedule, which was now causing ripples from the Plant directors, down. Word had it that the convicts that were building the outline structure, had set up traps that had severely injured and even caused fatalities among the supervising engineers. Chilling news then, that in order to get things up and running the Russian guards had built a temporary dividing wall so that work could commence in the spinning hall, which was a high-rise section facing the Staple Fibre building. Oh, yes, and as luck would have it I was first in.

John joined me and we met with several Russian directors and engineers outside the armed post and barricade. We were issued with special security passes and stick-on identity badges which I stuck on my safety helmet. The group was flanked by machine gun carrying soldiers, and I wondered whether this would happen on every visit that was made.

Basically, there were two small arc lamps high up at each corner of the building, which left around 50 per cent of the building in almost total darkness. The ground was compacted and clay-like, and at two opposite corners were huge, rough, wooden barricades. On close inspection, I could see eyes looking through, and there were strange banging and screaming noises. Some of the guards shouted and kicked the barrier; immediately the eyes disappeared and it fell quiet for a moment. The group moved back towards the door, up some rough concrete steps and onto a metal platform about 30 feet above the ground. We stood for a while, John drawing a rough sketch of an 'A' frame that needed hanging from the upper girders to enable the movement of heavy erection parts within the structure. Once an agreement had been reached, John went back and left me with two engineers and an interpreter to sort out a schedule for moving packing cases from the main stores.

The discussion turned into a heated battle, the engineer insisting that all machines should be moved at the same time. However, how many brain cells does it take to realise that you cannot fill a void with huge packing cases and allow labourers to complete a quality concrete floor? They assured me it would happen. "It's your bloody plant," I said, "get on with it." I turned away in exasperation and felt a bump, my safety helmet flying into the air. As my eyes re-focused I looked at the point of a steel spike, 2 inches from my forehead. The spike had been welded onto a girder and positioned perfectly to stick through someone's skull, and but for the peak on my helmet, that skull would've been mine. "That's it," I said, "I'll come back when the area has been made safe."

I did go back a couple of days later and managed a high balancing act; several times walking across girders that spanned the void 30 feet up. Peter wasn't so lucky when he stood on a booby trapped platform section and fell through, skinning one side of his body and breaking a couple of ribs. He had to be taken to the nearest hospital and was sore for weeks.

Back from work, I was out training with the football team. Training took place, as did matches, on a permanent football pitch set up on the airfield, just far enough away from the runway. We had been enrolled into a Mogilev works' league, which kicked off in September and ran through October and November until the big freeze, to recommence March, April and May the next year. I was a decent standard, having played for the school team but some of these guys were ex-professionals. I just managed to squeeze in at Right Back. "You may not be the best footballer but you're certainly a dirty bastard," the team manager summed up. The famous Roy 'Chopper' Hartle played at Right Back for Bolton, and he was known to have warned a tricky Chelsea Winger, "If you go past me again cock, you'll finish up with gravel rash." I just couldn't think how to say it in Russian. Obviously, the best thing about any training session is a shower followed by several pints in the bar.

Saturday mornings were spent fishing, a different venue every week and all mind-blowingly beautiful, quiet and relaxing. One week on the river Drut, which was out West on the Orsha road. Turn right at the tractor factory and keep going for about 20 miles, past the prison partially hidden by a pine forest. The river meanders gently on both sides of the road and disappears below a railway bridge over on the right. Wanting to explore, I set up a spinning rod and a reel bag full of various spoons and mepps spinners and set off upstream to the left of the road.

I had caught a couple of nice sized perch and missed a big pike when I met up with Barry who had just caught a small Jack Pike which he was taking back to the driver. Barry told me that Gary had caught a big fish that was definitely worth a look, so I made my way back towards the road. Gary was our fishing king and was Irish Pike record holder and secretary of the Irish Piking Association, or some such organisation. "How's that for a roach?" He held up a specimen, the likes of which I had never seen. "It's bloody huge," I confirmed, staring at this magnificent scale perfect silver pig with fins. Photos were taken of the beast and a couple of scales removed to verify the species before returning it to the water.

Several weeks later, we were sent a copy of the Angling Times, which included an article on the catch, entitled, "Is this a record-breaking roach?" However, on checking the photo and the scales, Gary's fish turned out to be an Ide, common to Scandinavia and the Soviet Union and closely resembling the roach. The news didn't overly bother Gary. "Back in Ireland," he assured everyone in the bar, "a fish that size would make good pike bait." One of the camp comics couldn't resist, "Gary, I told you that you were overdue a good Ideing". That did it, I thought, "night all!"

Summer Sundays usually included a minibus ride and picnic at various local beauty spots. I decided to go along, if only to keep out of the bar for a while. This week's trip was to a popular beauty spot and historical site called Saltanovka. It was the site of a battle during the Napoleonic Wars, when it was said that Napoleon's army was caught crossing the frozen river. During the battle the ice broke up drowning hundreds of French soldiers.

Anyway, while parents unpacked their picnic baskets and kids chased one another and skimmed stones across the lake, I followed a path along the side of the valley and into woods of Silver Birch. About half a mile on, I found a suitable man-sized rock and sat down overlooking a narrow lake. On the other side of the lake was a gentle slope, again lined with Silver Birch. This was a beautiful blue, sunny day, with just enough breeze to take off the edge, and the sun seemed to light up the silver trunks that reflected in the ripples on the water. Being a dreamer, it doesn't take a lot to set my mind free and this hypnotic scene was spin washing my head and enriching my body. It was as if the birches replicated two opposing armies, the stand off reflecting in the water. To think that something so beautiful today could have been so unimaginably brutal all those years ago. Maybe those torn bodies somehow live on in these trees now smiling at one another across a rippling lake.

My God, that's what I call visual stimulation. Better get back before I miss the bus, but before I do, one last lingering look, I may never see anything as beautiful again. On the bus back home I looked through the bus window and listened to people talking about the quality of the ham sandwiches, particularly those with the pickled onions. Was it me? Am I the fool? "Frankly," I surmised, "I couldn't care less."

Tuesday evening and I had a new flatmate, Parker, in his late twenties, six foot plus and with fair hair. He definitely wouldn't be lonely here. He didn't say where he was from, save to say that he said that he was so famous that they had named the borough after him, and that most people rode bikes. "Why?" I asked, and, "Was it Holland?" Anyway I certainly had never heard of a Parkerborough. "No, my first name!" now I had got him flustered. "Think diesels," he said, "They make Diesel engines there." "Oh, they make engines there and ride push-bikes. Great advert," I said. "Well, it's flat," he explained. "Yeah, flat and bloody boring. It's no wonder you're no good at football." I struggled to keep my face straight. Parker laughed but I wasn't sure he knew that I was pulling his leg. Maybe we need more time to get to know one another better. One thing was for sure we had more than enough Peter's, so he was definitely Parker.

He was a pot of tea man, so we drank tea and ate Dundee cake and chockie biscuits. He told me that he wasn't into football and wasn't a big drinker. "Just like me," I assured him. "I hate the bloody stuff," my fingers firmly crossed. He didn't cook either. "So it's Gerry's or starvation," I went on. Anyway, just like Ray before him, he assured me that he was a good waker-upper. What else do you need for starters? I didn't see a lot of Parker during the rest of the week as he was always off with the fairies by the time I got in from the bar. What the hell, he was big enough to look after himself.

Saturday was the last official fishing trip, and any future outings would be arranged during the week, weather allowing and subject to demand. Anyway, today was going to be beautiful weather-wise and although we were down to four, I was determined to make the most of the tranquillity. We left about 8 am heading out on the Gorky Road to the north-east. After about forty-five minutes, we turned off the main road and onto a rough track, we followed the dirt road through a wooded area followed by a clearing and through the centre of a small village of about a dozen wooden houses. A girl watched us pass and looked as if she had seen a bus load of Martians. I tried to wave but didn't think she had seen me. We bounced on, back into a forest and after a couple of minutes crossed a field and pulled up at a river, "The Pronya," the driver announced. The river was reasonably wide and quite fast flowing. I scanned the area, and to my right I could make out a small lake, the sun glinting on the water.

The other three guys wanted to fish the river for pike and I didn't, so I bid my farewell and set off up the field and past some large bushes that sheltered this end of the lake from a cool breeze. Another 10 yards and there was a nice grassy bank with an open swim between two patches of weeds; it certainly looked fishy. I quickly set up a float rig and plumbed the depth, which was around 4 feet, about three rod lengths out. "Perfect," I thought, and started off using break flake that I had steamed the night before. After about fifteen minutes I caught my first fish, a small but plump Crucian Carp, the first I had seen in Russia. This was soon followed by three more at roughly ten-minute intervals.

My concentration was broken by a familiar sound that was getting ever closer and louder. It stopped for a while in the general vicinity of the minibus, before again moving closer. Around the bush came two young girls wobbling slowly along the uneven path on a huge twin cylinder motorbike. The bike, almost stalling, passed behind me and I felt a hand brush the back of my head. I turned round to see the bike catch the slope and veer to the left as if being sucked into the water. I jumped up, as the rider fought for control, the bike trundling slowly into the lake that swamped the engine, producing a big gasp of hot steam. I just managed to grab the rack behind the saddle with my fingertips that was sufficient to stop the bike's progress.

Fortunately, both girls were wearing wellies. The pillion, who had exited the bike on the left and who looked like the girl from the village, stood in her baggy shorts with one boot under the surface. The pilot was wearing knee-length wellies similar to mine and was stood in the water, her turn downs looked like Plimsoll lines. Between us, we managed to heave the lump of a bike up the bank onto a flat piece of ground and onto its stand. At that moment the driver of the bike completely lost it and attacked the pillion, slapping her and pulling her hair. At first shocked at the reaction I decided to brave it and managed to pull the cats apart.

The pilot was an attractive girl with short black hair, but with a mean looking downy mouth and dark, piercing eyes. The pillion was blonde with a more rounded face, and unusual vacant eyes, if not a vacant expression. She sat down to empty her boot and I grabbed an old towel out of my fishing bag and gave it to her. "Alan," I told the girls. "Sveta," replied the dark haired girl. "Luba," mumbled the blonde. I told the girls I was 22 and asked how old they were. They whispered to each other and agreed that they were sixteen, the belated answer suggested otherwise. Neither of the girls much above five feet tall or over-developed, although Sveta was making some impression on the T-shirt and looked quite shapely in her tight black tracky bottoms. I asked was it papa's bike, to which I got a very sharp, *"Nyet."* I think it belonged to her *dedushka*, (grandpa). Whatever, it was certainly too big for these two girls and there were no 'L' plates.

I stood staring at the bike for ages before it dawned on me that it was British, the kick- start was located on the right hand side. Although the beast was painted from top to tail in a mucky dark green it reminded me of an old 500cc BSA my uncle owned. I remembered vividly that he had taken me on the pillion to see the Queen's visit to Bolton in the 1950's. Still, this bike looked even bigger and older. I decided it was a 650cc at the very least. One thing was for sure, it was a bike and not a boat and it was definitely wet!

I knelt down and found a tool compartment and luckily there was a box spanner that I used to removed the spark plugs, cleaning them the best I could. It was then that I spotted the 3 rifles engraved on the crankcase. "It is a BSA!" The girl nodded "*Da.*" I waited momentarily for any more information, but there was none. I tested the plugs, holding them against the manifold. Sveta decided that she would work the kick-starter first standing on my fingers that were wrapped around the kick-start rubber, trying in vain to force the pedal down. "Thanks for that," I half protested again without reaction. A couple of slow cranks either side was enough to show that there was still some life in the old beast, well in the spark plugs anyway.

I left the plug leads hanging down and tried to tell the girl to leave the bike for 10-15 minutes to let the sun dry it out. The girl flipped and started pointing at the plugs, I think ordering me to put them back. "So what?" I thought, "You want them back, I'll put them back." After replacing the box spanner and oily rag, I again pointed to my watch. "Ten minutes," I said. "Leave for ten minutes."

I pulled out a new packet of 20 State Express, which certainly caught their attention. Both girls were suddenly in my face. "Please, please," they begged. "You're not old enough." I tried to put them off. No chance. I took out two and gave them one each. *"Spitchky,"* (matches), Sveta ordered. I had a box of Swan Vesta's in the bag but it wasn't there. The blonde girl was giggling and she offered me a light from the box of Swan she had pulled from her pocket. I held out my hand and she removed most of the matches before returning the box. Once the dark foxy girl had pocketed her share she immediately went back to the bike.

After first standing upright on the kick-starter she adjusted the valve lifter with her left hand opening the valves fully.

Even then she had to hop on the pedal to reduce compression sufficiently for her body weight to turn the engine over. She then cranked the engine over repeatedly with a number of short jabs of her foot. The engine merely seemed to gurgle in response. I tried to open the throttle, to clean out the chamber. Sveta calmly pushed my hand away and looked daggers at me. I had obviously interrupted a well rehearsed routine. She turned on the fuel tap and slowly cranked the kick-starter while priming the carburettor, part closing the valves and finding compression. She jumped up, swung her left leg up and back, at the same time switching her weight back and down, greeted by a small puff of grey smoke from the exhaust. She then repeated the process twice, each time adjusting the valve lifter, before starting to crank the engine again. "Here," I said, feeling guilty just watching the girl, "I'll have a go." She took a long drag on the ciggie and eventually took a couple of steps away.

"Now see what a man can do," I thought, opening the throttle fully and turning the engine over. Tickle the carbs, find compression, press. The kick-start wouldn't budge even when I put my 11½ stone on it. I gave it a swing, nothing. I fiddled with the air intake screw, flooded the carburettor and gave it another kick. "That's it, it's still wet." She pushed me out of the way like a naughty little boy and went back to the same routine.

Not surprisingly, during the second cycle the bike decided to fight back. The girl was still determined to kick the bike into submission when the engine let out a loud crack and kicked back violently, throwing her skywards, the bike exhaling a cloud of white smoke from the air-intake. "Satisfied?" I said, in English. She grimaced and, with a look that could kill, took a kick at the bike uttering something not fit for a man's ears. She turned and held out her hand for another ciggie. "Sit down for a minute and I'll think about it." I walked to my spot on the grass and sat down.

Eventually she sat down at the side and Luba, who had been meticulously going through my fishing bag and had everything spread out on the grass, decided to sit behind me and play with my hair. She was like a child playing with a dolly except this child smoked and pinched stuff. I grabbed a flask of coffee, poured a cup and offered it to the girls, which they drank but commented that it needed more sugar. They refused a cheese and onion butty, but did take a block of Cadburys fruit and nut to enjoy later.

Both girls, by now, were getting very touchy feely. Luba, with the vacant eyes, wanting to know what every item in my bag was called, and what it did. Sveta, the extremely sinister firebrand, pointed to and touched every article of my clothing. After first removing my choker and trying it on, I explained that it didn't suit her and she needed to put it back round my neck before I broke hers; all, of course, in my best English. She asked about my jumper and checked the label before moving onto my Wrangler jeans. I knew she liked them by the way she stroked them but her eyes had always been fixed on my leather belt and large steel buckle. At least I certainly hoped it was the belt. She grabbed at the buckle and tried to unfasten it, losing her temper, she pulled at it. *"Nyet,"* I said, firmly, looking straight into her eyes. "How much is the belt?" she asked. I wasn't sure whether she wanted to know what it had cost or how much I wanted to sell it for, so I told her I didn't understand.

I tried to bait up and start fishing but Sveta had this annoying knack of distraction, again wanting a cigarette. I looked at her again and realised that she really was just a kid, a confident wily, intimidating, tough nut but still a frail-looking kid. Luba looked slightly older and could have been sixteen. She could tie the back of your hair into a good pigtail though and I felt the plait down my neck. I turned round and thanked her and she in turn responded with a lovely smile.

Sveta who must have felt that she was being ignored kicked my foot. "Why is your hair so long?" she asked. "Why not?"

I shook my head. She jumped forward and kissed me full on the lips, while throwing her right leg over mine she eventually sat down on my thighs. "Give me a cigarette," she demanded, her eyes piercing mine. I took out the packet and offered her one. Sveta said something to Luba who responded by putting both hands on my shoulders and forcing my head back. I tried to dislodge her hands but instead she grabbed both hands and quickly knelt on my arms pinning me down. Sveta in turn grabbed the packet of cigarettes. Making sure she had my full attention she took one out slowly and placed it between her lips. She then took a match from her pocket and looked round for somewhere to strike it. Eventually she settled for the zip on my jeans. Just to prove who was 'the boss' she calmly leant forward and blew the smoke in my face. She handed a fag to Luba and placed another on my chest before dropping the packet down the front of her T-shirt.

At a time when I was feeling extremely nervous as to what her intentions were she stood up and walked towards the bike. Luba jumped up and joined her and they again started to whisper. I let out an audible sigh before standing up and walking over, trying to appear calm and asked for the cigarettes back. Sveta, simply laughed as I made a fist and waved it at her. "Water off a duck's back," I thought, "She doesn't give a toss."

Luba said that they had to go home and Sveta again turned to the bike, which I figured should be reasonably rested. She didn't hold back this time, even when the bike showed some pluck by repeatedly kicking back. I offered to give the bike a push but by now the girl was manic; nothing was going to stop her. She again tickled the carburettor, closed the valves and meticulously stroked the kick-starter pedal finding compression at its most upright position as if she was priming a bomb.

The bright sunshine framed her, high over the bars. Apart from the cigarette delicately hanging from her pouted lips and her rubber boots flexed under tension she could have been an athlete set in her blocks waiting for the gun. "This time," she said, setting the throttle, she flew backwards like a gymnast, crashing the kick-start through. She flailed at the twist grip while riding the back-fire and instantly delivered a second kick somehow managing to throttle the monster into life. A huge cloud of blue exhaust smoke choked all three of us.

Both Luba and myself applauded, while Sveta took a celebratory drag and bowed the hero. She ran towards me, jumped wrapping her arms and legs around me before kissing me hard on the lips. She cursed and rounded quickly when the engine cut out.

This time after a couple of laboured cranks to prime the engine, one hefty kick was enough to fire the bike into life. She swung her leg over the saddle and with one pelvic thrust rocked it off its stand. Her tiptoes barely touched the ground, but she held the bike upright with a certain ease. Luba climbed on the back with her bag of pilfered treasure, putting her arms round Sveta, who eased the gear pedal into first and off they went. "Bloody hell," I thought, "now that was different. Fishing, fishing, please some bloody peaceful fishing." I sat down with my hands shaking and smoked the last cigarette.

I didn't say a word to the lads until after we had passed through the village. I saw the bike, but not the girls, outside one of the houses. Anyway, I had to let the lads know something once they had spotted the pigtail. They'd heard some noise but thought that it had come from the village and, anyway, they had been happy as Larry catching several pike, including one monster of a fish over 10lbs.

They found it hard to believe that I hadn't chanced my arm with the girls and did not believe me when I said that the girls had actually frightened me to death. They looked like delicate young girls but I was on their territory and at their mercy. The foxy dark-haired girl was certainly the dominant character and if she had wanted my belt and jeans or anything else, she would have taken some stopping whether I'd been willing or not. Just watching her trying to start the bike was proof of that, talk about giving it some wellie.

I remember, at the age of sixteen, returning home from a friend's house late one night and walking through the arches of the town hall square; there were three women stood smoking in the shadows under the side arch. As I walked past one of the women grabbed my hand and pulled me back while the other two grabbed my arms. They asked one another if they should rape me, as if I was a piece of meat. Fortunately, after much pleading, one of the girls spoke up for me and they let me go. I ran home quicker than I have ever run in my life. This day, although in many respects comical, had brought back those memories. Young and pretty girls, yet, in their domain so very powerful.

Chapter 16
SHEEP'S HEAD

It was quickly becoming apparent that this was a country of defined seasons, quite unlike back home where one season seems to be very much like the next. Over here you have no doubts. Summer, it's boiling, while in winter it's freezing. Spring, you get a little bit of rain and lots of *moshki*, a gnat-like insect that drives you nutty during May when the fruit blossom is on the trees. Now we are in autumn, and although you can still get nice days you can equally get colder, rainy days and soon expect the early snowfalls. The thing is, more often than not, it is a dry climate and very healthy providing that is you are dressed correctly. Anyway you certainly know when to break out the winter gear as the Russians to a man don their fur hats.

As notices for weekend trips were usually pinned up on Tuesdays during working hours, the wives were first on the scene, very often filling all available places before any of the lads got home. So the 21 Club decided to bite back. We arranged our own trip to the 'Bobruisk Treacle Mines'. We did qualify that: i) all children must be accompanied by at least one parent, ii) due to the sticky nature of the mines it was recommended that wellington boots and rough clothing should be worn, although overalls would be provided, iii) pilferage of treacle lumps would result in prosecution as free samples would be issued to everyone before returning home.

Anyway, on my way to work on that Tuesday, I had pinned up the poster. Sure enough, on arriving back at the flats we discovered five takers booking fifteen places out of the thirty-two places allowed. There was definitely some ribbing in the bar that week, and proved our point that either the ladies put their names down without even checking what the trip was or were dim enough to believe that treacle was actually mined. Afterwards, they said they didn't look, but I'm not sure.

Back at work, we were completing all nine lines in Staple Fibre. It does the heart good to see wagons rolling off site carrying bales of finished yarn. Basically staple fibre is melted polymer forced through spinnerets. Spinning machines then draw, crimp, heat set and package the tow yarn before cutting and baling. Staple fibre is used in cotton and wool type products like shirts, blouses and suits.

In Filament Yarn we now had an office that was close to being finished and gave us an area to duck into for a cuppa. This was going to be a must once the winter started to bite. It was also the week that the convicts had been moved out of Filament and into a services workshop out towards the main stores. This, in turn, allowed the removal of the temporary wooden walls that had divided off the plant, which could now be seen in its full and awesome glory, half a mile long and one-third of a mile wide. Even though still very poorly lit, standing at the spinning room door at the end of the main corridor projected a view that was breathtaking. I have never before seen a corridor approximately 10 yards wide that disappeared into the distance.

Malcolm looked at a group of us with his thumb cocked over his shoulder, pointing down the building. " This is going to be a big job..." he held the pause. "One" he lifted his finger; "we're behind schedule". " But the Russians..." somebody tried to counter but was cut short. "Two," his eyes narrowed. "We are not being pulled down this place kicking and screaming." He turned sideways and pointed. "We are going to push the Russians right to the far end...okay? Finally, this isn't just going to be the biggest filament yarn facility in the world...it's going to be the best." "Yes boss." I agreed feeling myself stand to attention.

Back in the Staple Fibre office, Malcolm wanted a chat about how things were progressing. We also discussed the possibilities of pulling back a couple of months lost time in Filament and agreed that as things stood, it was improbable. "That's why I've decided to get you some help and we've arranged for a guy called Ted to come over for a few months and help out. He arrives next week, so you'll need to take him under your wing and show him the ropes." I nodded as all good subservient workers should, not wishing to point to my lack of wings and still not knowing where the bloody ropes where stored.

We had word from the office that several new starters were due to arrive on the Tuesday evening, and decided that the 21 Club would host a special welcoming party, or, as some of the guys put it, "An initiation party." Simple food, get pissed, do a turn, can crushing, up chucking, the lot. And that's before we hit the bar.

We met at Len's flat, around 7pm. I took the usual kitchen sink curry and a mountain of chips, and Len greeted us with a Mogilev special Screwdriver punch in a stainless steel bucket nicked from the Spinners. By the time the party arrived, we were already extremely merry and in mid sing-along. The guys filed in one by one, as if going into the dock for sentencing and were followed in by Gordon who had arrived back from two weeks' leave. "Alan, your man's outside but he's had a bad trip," Gordon spoke quietly into my ear. "Who, Ted?" I asked, standing up. "Yes, Ted, he's on the stairs." I walked quickly out of the flat, and sat half way down the flight of stairs was a hunched figure. I walked down and put my left hand on his shoulder. "Ted, are you all right?" His face lifted slightly and I could see the tears flooding down his face and his nose running. "Have you got a hanky?" I asked him, feeling in my own pockets. He lifted his right arm and repeatedly wiped his shirtsleeve across his face. Ted's age was difficult to assess in this mood, but I estimated him to be in his late forties or even fifties, with wild dark curly hair disguising a receding hairline. He wore a blue and white lumberjack style shirt and a pair of old-fashioned baggy, grey/blue jeans. His eyes although blood red appeared lifeless. "Come inside," I said, pulling him onto his feet. "Come on, it's home-from-home in here, all guys in the same boat." We walked slowly up the stairs and into the flat.

He moved into the centre of the room and without warning his right arm shot out like an old signpost on a country road, his forefinger pointing towards the window. "There's a green-eyed yellow idol to the north of Kathmandu." His rasping, Bolton accent cut through the noisy room and everybody sat open-mouthed. I could only liken the scene to those turning pot heads that you find on a funfair and try to throw balls into. Thirty men sat silently while Ted recited Eskimo Nell from start to finish and word perfect. When he'd finished, everyone stood and applauded. "Get the lad a drink," someone shouted, and Ted was accepted into the Polyspinners' clan.

I managed to have a chat with him during the evening and established that he was married and lived in a busy suburb to the east of Bolton town centre. He also admitted that he had never flown before and had found the travelling very difficult. I didn't see him leave the party but he certainly didn't make it to the pub. "No matter," I thought, "he will be okay."

The next morning, I travelled with Ted on the works' bus and took him straight up to the Staple Fibre office where I introduced him to Malcolm, John and the lads next door. I then showed him how to complete a packing list report and asked him to go through a handful of missing parts reports and draw up an order for replacement parts. "Simple," was the word I used to sum up. I left him to get on with things while I set off for Filament Yarn to check a load of machine parts, only coming back just before lunch.

"How's it going Ted?" I asked. He grunted, not looking up. I looked at the replacement parts' list and nothing was on it. I picked up the missing parts' reports that I had left in order, and they were completely mixed up. Most disturbing though, was that Ted had continued looking at a report he was holding with both hands. I moved behind him and couldn't believe that he was holding the report upside down.

I decided to break for lunch, during which time Ted hardly spoke, even though I gave him a lot of opportunities to express himself. After lunch I took him with me to check a case of spares down on Staple Fibre shop floor. When we arrived, Ted picked up a nail extractor and started to open the case. "Ted. Ted!" He carried on removing nails. "Ted," I touched his arm, "we don't unpack the cases, we check the parts inside." He put down the nail extractor, turned his back and started to cry. "Now we're in trouble," I thought. I put my arm round his shoulder, realising that he wasn't a well man. "Come on, Ted, let's get back upstairs."

He walked quietly along with me to the engineers' office where, fortunately, a couple of the lads were checking technical drawings. I grabbed him a chair and poured him a cup of tea. "Pete," I said quietly, "keep your eye on him for a minute, will you?" I walked next door and, fortunately, Malcolm was at his desk discussing something with John. "Malcolm, we have a big problem." I told him the full story. Malcolm looked exasperated but listened till I had finished. "Okay, Let's go and have a chat with him and see if we can get through, if not I'll speak to Dorothy and arrange travel home for him next week."

Ted was stood in the corner, face against the wall and sobbing. "Ted." Malcolm's voice was sharp and he turned round sheepishly. "We'll get you home next week. Until then, you'll have to pull yourself together, okay?" He nodded and sat down.

The only time I had an opportunity to catch up with Ted was at breakfast in the canteen, and trying to get him to speak was almost impossible. Our nurse had called to see Ted in his flat and popped round to let me know how he was. "To put it in a nut-shell" she explained "Ted's had a breakdown, probably caused by taking him out of his environment and setting him down 3000 miles from home."

I had arranged a phone call to his wife for 1pm that Saturday, so I had to tell Ted and remind him each morning. When Saturday came and Ted hadn't appeared, I decided to go round to his flat. I knocked on the door for almost 10 minutes, shouting through the door that he needed to speak to his wife. Eventually, he opened the door in his pyjamas. I grabbed an overcoat hanging on the coat stand and made him put it on. He followed me down in his slippers and stood outside the phone booth while I got his wife on the phone. "Hello," I said, "My name is Alan and I'm working with Ted. He's fine but he needs to have a word with you, can you hold while I put him on?" I held the phone out for Ted. "Have a word with your wife, Ted." He took the phone and shouted down it, "Put sheep's head on luv, I'm home Monday!" then slammed the phone down. He walked straight past me and back to his flat. "Bloody hell, that says it all," I thought. "Talk about short and not so sweet." I didn't know whether to feel sorry for Ted, his wife or the sheep. I could just feel sorry for me, as I was going to be doing all the work and I was soon to learn what twenty-four-hour shifts were all about.

Difficult to take in and do, very simple to figure out. Work twenty-four hours, come home and sleep for twelve hours, then back to work for another twenty-four hours. Friggin' awful, but I understood it was necessary. The Russian directors didn't give a tupenny toss that it was their fault that the building was months behind. They wanted to get back on schedule, and we wanted to drive them even beyond that.

Over the months, we had built up good working relationships with our Russian counterparts, built out of trust, honesty and hard work, alongside genuine friendships. I had visited a couple of engineers' homes for dinner and drinks. The earlier language barriers were now not as significant, particularly at work where a large part of communication in both English and Russian or Belarussian was technical, machine parts, or bad language; that is unless you were around Norman, the 'speak good English tutor.' One thing, however, had completely thrown me. When you work with people on a regular basis without knowing their names, you just pick them up. For example, in Staple Fibre there was a group of technicians on one section: two Sashas, Petya, Sergey and Mihael. I thought Tchaikovsky; the team leader, shouted "Slushai!" and Sasha jumped to attention. "Right," I thought, "he's called Slushai, not Sasha. A day or so later, a similar thing happened with Petya. "Slushai!" and Petya responded. After a week or two, I realised that Slushai was a very popular Russian name and, obviously, started calling the lads 'Slushai'. I was obviously amazed then, when I found out that Slushai was in fact a command meaning 'listen' or 'pay attention'. By that time I had forgotten everybody's real names anyway.

I needed something to lighten my life and the load, and that came in a surprising package. It was the end of October and the weather, although not as cold as last year, had broken and we looked forward to another long, cold but fresh and healthy winter. The new office in Filament had been tiled out and glazed, and even had a central heating radiator. A long trestle table and a couple of desks and chairs completed the room. I was the first to set up camp. Now, with the twenty-four-hour shifts, it was literally a camp. Oh, yes, and the surprise package, we, or at least I had my very own cleaner, not called Slushai but Vika. Now Vika was eighteen years old and what I would generally describe as a 'big girl' about five foot ten, with an excellent pair of lungs and very friendly. Yes, she was nice and she was chatty and she smiled and laughed and giggled and flushed up, red in embarrassment, and she spoke quite good English. "Not bad," I thought, for your average every-day office cleaner. She only worked part-time, still attending some college or other or, as I said, "Four days at KGB headquarters, and definitely not cleaning." She giggled and went red. I looked forward to her working and found her company therapeutic. I still regarded myself as damaged goods, suffering from bouts of depression, particularly during the evening hours when my mind returned to the *what ifs* and *why hadn'ts*? I was still madly, sickeningly in love and maybe more than ever it hurt so bloody much.

Now, more and more, Vika made me smile, and moreover I believe she started to know that there was a connection. So when one day I asked her if she would come to the flat, she jumped at the chance as well as jumping at me giving me a huge squeeze.

I was still working irregular hours, so arrangements to see her were difficult but we did manage to get together two or three evenings each week and soon the rendezvous included sleeping together. At this point, I noticed a marked change in Vika. The fun-loving, shy laughter giving way to a more serious, calculated and somehow repetitive relationship. Don't get me wrong, I certainly wasn't grumbling. No, just like the worn out man who visited the doctor and whose diagnosis was that his capacity for wine, women and song was the root problem, I also was willing to give up singing. Still, the relationship, although having its obvious rewards, was increasingly lacking something. I knew all too well, that 'something' was love, but that selfish streak never goes away, does it? It becomes hard to understand when you are brought up with certain principles, that sleeping with someone when you know very well that there is no future, can be thought acceptable, but she was here and she was warm and she was certainly willing, and it was okay.

Anyway, Norman nabbed me during lunch one day at work. "Alan, we've found you a nice girl." Norman stood in front of me and spoke slowly and clearly to ensure my attention.

"Does she go?" I asked, with a cheesy grin, and tensed to dodge the blow. "No, she doesn't go," Norman said, seriously, "And if she did, she wouldn't be doing it with Nina around." "Right," I agreed. "Listen," Norman went on, "Saturday night seven o'clock, the cinema opposite the tank. Okay?" "No problem. What's her name?" "Svetlana, I think." Norman wasn't sure. "Ah, Sveta, we've met. Black hair, cruel eyes, chain smokes, curly teeth, spits a lot, walks with a bit of a run. I know her." Norman turned, with a look of exasperation. "Saturday at seven, okay?" "Okay. Just tell her not to forget my cigarettes." That was enough, I thought, "he's going to kill me." Anyway, wild horses wouldn't have kept me away. I was intrigued, having only been on one previous blind date, and she didn't turn up. Mind you, thinking about it, how would I have known if she had or hadn't, I'd never seen her before.

Saturday night I dressed as smart as I could – you know, best or cleanest jeans, spit on the shoes and all that. I even put on clean underwear – not that I was expecting to get that lucky. As is the way of things, this time of year everything is covered and I wore my sheepskin and fur hat. I jumped the minibus to town and then grabbed a taxi outside the Dnieper, a quick run up to Lenin Square, turn left and down the hill, and up the other side to a main roundabout with a huge green tank perched on a concrete plinth. On the base of the plinth was a large red flag inscribed with the words, *'Glory to our Soviet Red Army.'* There were hundreds of such adornments around Mogilev, on buildings, works, schools, shops, everywhere! The only thing that was more prevalent than a flag or banner in the Soviet Union was the Soviet Red Army. There were soldiers everywhere. Sometimes it looked as if 50% of the population was in the armed forces.

Anyway just to the right of the tank is the sports shop from where I had bought most of my fishing gear. They also sold camera equipment and other odds-and-sods. The shop stands in front of Pechersky Park, Mogilev's biggest park. There is a large forest, lakes, including a boating lake and even a ski jump, and no, I didn't have a go, I'm writing this book, aren't I? At this point I must get something off my chest. Having stood at the bottom of the ski jump I couldn't help but wonder; "how do you do that for the first time?" It's like somebody saying to me, "Alan you can ski can't you?" "Yes" I reply. "Good, just have a go off the ski jump." "Pardon?" "Just ski down the side and throw yourself off the end." "And then what?" "Try to lean well forward." "Right; fall out of the sky head first?" "Exactly!" "Okay." Now I realise it's quite easy. Still I wonder how many 'first timers' actually make it out of accident and emergency?

I've already passed the cinema, which is back down the hill in front of a massive new high-rise development. You can tell from the random rubbish about tanks and ski jumps that I was a good ten minutes early but Norman, Nina and Svetlana were already there, waiting. Nina gave me her usual kiss and cuddle and Norman shook hands before Nina introduced me to Svetlana. "Alan, Svetlana. Svetlana, Alan." I took her gloved hand and kissed her on each cheek. *"Zdravstvuy,"* (How do you do?) which is actually a shortened version of *Zdravstvuyte*. "Hello," I replied. She looked a nice girl, maybe eighteen years old and five foot five tall, pretty face, light make-up, shortish brown hair under her mauve knitted hat, and a knee-length mauve woollen coat with a fur collar. She smiled nervously and her shy brown eyes tried to hide her anxiety. "Come on, last one in gets the popcorn." I tried to lighten the mood. "Anyway, what are we watching?" I asked, gently holding Svetlana's hand. Norman and I hung back to buy the tickets, Norman questioning, "Well, what do you think?" "She seems lovely," I told him, watching Nina in deep conversation with Svetlana. "Probably checking her ring size," I thought to myself, and chuckled.

The film was about this guy and a tank. He lived in the country and these Germans came and killed a lot of the village people including this attractive woman who kept giving him the eye, before she was dead of course. He in turn did some nasty things back and he blew up a Panzer Division and gave up his life for the village, and nobody lived to live happily ever after. Then we looked at one another and laughed. Lord knows why we just laughed in a quiet sort of way, probably feeling embarrassed.

We came out of the cinema and walked along chatting in English, with Nina interpreting. She, Svetlana, was attending college, and liked *kolbasa* and fine art. We kissed goodbye, as we had greeted, and I left all three outside her apartment block, deciding to walk back down to town before grabbing a taxi home. I didn't see Svetlana again; the underarm deodorant must have turned her off. I would have to live with it.

CHAPTER 17
LENINGRAD

Early November brought a special weekend trip To Leningrad. I say "special" for a couple of reasons. First of all, we hadn't been to Leningrad before and it was said to be one of the most beautiful cities in the world, "The Venice of the North," I believe it is called. Secondly, we were setting off Friday so having an extra-long weekend break. About twenty-five of us set off from Mogilev by coach to Minsk airport. This included four bachelor boys, Mike, Dave, Ronnie and myself, or the three older farts, and D'Artagnan the young apprentice, as I was better known. Our hotel was the Oktyabrskaya, standing in a main square at one end of the main street in the city centre. At the other end of the main street was the Hotel Astoria, approximately one mile apart.

Now, I know this sounds disgraceful, but it's probably only a bunch of British guys that could visit one of the most beautiful and historical cities on earth, be pissed when they arrived, be even more pissed when they leave and, in between, see or know that they have seen absolutely sod all. In our defence, it was November and cold with sleet and snow. Not what you would call ideal conditions for visiting the 'Avrora' or the Winter Palace. Some of our more sober members came back with stories of the Hermitage. "After the Louvre in Paris probably the most famous art gallery in the world. A place that you could walk around for an entire week and only see a fraction of the exhibits." Now… to an uneducated drunken

Brit, that's like giving a bloke a nob so big that it doesn't fit. Anyway, we had a different agenda on this culture visit. We were going to attempt a new world drinking record.

On the Saturday morning we walked down the main street and visited some of the shops and cafes along the way – I just don't remember which ones and why. We had planned to make our way to the Astoria and achieved our goal by late afternoon. Both the Astoria and the Oktyabrskaya were among Russia's oldest hotels, the Astoria certainly being the most ornate. One could say it's "absolutely marbleous," but that would be too cheesy. There was certainly a nice bar with a bit of a desert island theme, palm trees, fishing nets, treasure chests.

Around seven o'clock, we moved into the main restaurant for dinner. Not just a grand piano here, they had a stage with a full orchestra and a couple of singers doing famous opera pieces. It was a very nice accompaniment to a caviar and champagne banquet. We lasted a couple of hours before the soprano got a little too much, deciding to retire to the nightclub.

It looked like a big cave, with smaller areas like grottos with dim (Toc H) lighting. But most important it had a bar with bar stools. I found myself a spot at one end of the bar and was soon on first name terms with the bar tender, "Yuri," he said. "Yeah, Yuri Dozyget," I confirmed. "Get the bleedin' drinks in." It's amazing how easily the Russian rolls of the velvet tongue when you're pissed. The other lads were hovering around the dance floor like bulls on heat, checking out the talent. My only concern was how to keep my head from hitting the bar top, propping it up with both hands.

"Hamer!" Somebody grabbed my hair and rattled my head like shaking a coconut. Mike pushed his mouth right up to my ear, "She wants you… come on she wants you," he repeated. My eyes tried to focus and I looked past Mike and saw a very attractive girl stood looking directly at me, beckoning me with the forefinger of her right hand. "Go on, she fancies you." Mike was getting giddy. I looked back at my long glass of Black Label and soda and was attempting to get my hand to it when it was suddenly kidnapped by another hand, warm and soft but strong. She pulled me off the bar stool, across the dance floor and into a dimly lit grotto where she turned, wrapping her left arm around my waist, her right hand slid straight down the front of my jeans and into my Y-fronts, her hand cupped, gently supporting my nuts. I looked directly into her eyes and had this sudden urge to cough. "That's it, she must be the local doctor." Her fingers continued to explore, her face hiding the imminent disappointment, although there was definitely some life down there. "Inga," she whispered, continuing to massage me back to life. "Alan," I whispered back, strangely short of breath. "I'm very pleased to meet you." She pushed me against a wall and we kissed, long and hard.

Whether we were getting more animated or the gasps and grunts louder, I was looking out and could see that we were creating an audience. I think the lads were selling tickets, and from my point the bomb was already ticking. I put a stop to the action, grabbing the top of both arms and holding her at arms' length. "Coats... we're going." I held her hand and pulled her back to the bar, grabbing my sheepskin from the back of the chair. She, in turn, led me over to a table where two girls sat drinking. They exchanged a couple of words in what sounded distinctly like gibberish, before she collected her sheepskin coat and we left the nightclub.

We walked through the hotel and into the main reception area with its brown and cream marble floors, walls and enormous sweeping staircase. From the ceiling, hung the biggest, most ornate chandeliers I had ever seen. We stood against the staircase wall holding hands and checking one another out. Inga, I thought, was in her early twenties, with shoulder-length, jet black hair and a straight-cut fringe just above her thick, black eyebrows and electric blue eyes. She was a very attractive girl, who so far had hardly spoken a word. After first telling her that I was from England, "Where are you from?" I asked in both English and broken Russian. "Finland," was the reply. She then proved her prowess with the language by saying, "Hello," and "Thank you." We both laughed at the attempt before starting to kiss again. She was again playing with my man bits but this time from outside my jeans, having undone her blouse and placed my hand inside. I might have been pissed but was ever increasingly aware that this was a very busy reception area and we were getting some very strange looks. I was in no doubt at all what Inga wanted, but not here, definitely not here. I watched a middle-aged couple talking to a uniformed porter and could see him staring directly at us. "Oktyabrskaya," I whispered in her ear, "We need a taxi," as I fastened up my coat.

We walked through the front doors and out into the bitter night air. We jumped into a taxi, and within ten minutes arrived at the hotel. We took the lift to the third floor where we were greeted with the shift dezurnaya sat at her large desk in the centre of the landing. She was a big, stern-looking woman, who hadn't even lifted her head to acknowledge our presence. "Room 306," I said nervously in Russian. Now she looked up. "Who is this?" She pointed to Inga. "My sister," I told her, trying to smile. She said something I didn't understand but was obviously some lecture on hotel rules, after which she dismissed us with a wave of the hand. I felt quickly in my pockets and pulled out a new packet of State Express and a pack of Wrigley's gum. I placed them gently on the desk in front of her, "Room 306, please." I put a lot of emphasis on the "please". "I don't smoke." She pushed the present back towards me. "Sterling?" I asked, pulling out my wallet. Now she lost her temper. "Go," she ordered Inga. We bid a hasty retreat, laughing as the lift doors closed. "What a bloody dragon," I said in English. Now Inga took control, pulling me out of the hotel, along the street and onto a dark side street, only stopping at a shuttered doorway. She took off her coat and mine, and ingeniously joined the two together, making a sheepskin tent. The tent was quickly lowered over our heads before getting straight to it, fumbling, freezing, shaking, shivering, puffing and panting, and fifteen minutes later we were back inside ordering coffee cognacs at the bar.

Time wasn't as precious now and she seemed to relax and enjoy the moment, both speaking our own languages and not understanding a word but it didn't seem to matter. Inga was leaving to go home at 8.30am and we would never meet again. After a long embrace I put her in a taxi and waved until she disappeared. I pulled out the cigarettes that had remained untouched and smoked my first ciggie for ages, feeling slightly dizzy but good.

I couldn't wait to get back up to the third floor. The great lump of a woman still sat there in a world of her own. "Room 306, please." I held my room card right under her nose. She fumbled in the drawer and pulled out the key. "Thank you and goodnight," I said sarcastically and walked, shoulders back, head high, along the corridor and into my room.

I don't know whether it was a late breakfast or early lunch, but either way was more about the consumption of alcohol than getting the day off to a healthy start. I did well, I thought, to field the questions about the night before. The other guys had either drawn a blank or got so drunk they didn't remember. I surmised having nothing to bother you up top makes for easier sleeping, especially on the way home from another lost weekend. I could vaguely make out people talking about Leningrad, some happy at what they had found and some disappointed. Everybody had been offered Icons and most appeared to have hung on to their sheepskin coats and jeans. I visualised some of the mementos, Avrora in a bottle, Winter Palace in a glass dome with snow, Leningrad Rock…ahhhh.

CHAPTER 18
S NOVIM GODOM

I always thought that winters would be better spent hibernating, that is, of course, back in the UK. Over here, it's far too good to miss. Don't get me wrong, you certainly wouldn't go out for an evening stroll in your jumper and slip-ons. I don't care who you are or how old you are, put a load of guys into fresh snow and I guarantee that they will clod a snowball or two. Why not make a snowman, grab a pair of skis, a sledge, ice skates? Here you can, any day and every day. Obviously, the sky is grey when it snows but most of the time it is clear blue and the air is dry and healthy; it's bloody wonderful, a veritable winter wonderland.

The fishing trips and picnics give way to ice skating and skiing trips. Also, the football gives way to indoor sports like table tennis and other indoor games, if you get my 'snow' drift. Actually, one wag said that such was the action in the two blocks of flats at weekends, that it was now being picked up as a special feature registering on the Richter scale. I hadn't a clue what he was on about, but hey, ho!

I had joined the newly formed table tennis team, which had been entered in the Mogilev League. Actually I wasn't a bad player, having played as a kid for St Paul's, Halliwell, then the YMCA, and more lately for Dobson & Barlow's in the Bolton League. It was great; you got out in the evenings visiting different venues and meeting people. Actually, the only thing you didn't get, and I missed, were the sausage rolls or cheese and onion butties after the match. Here you got a handshake and, "Piss off, you jammie English git!" They said it of course with the best painted on smile that they could muster.

Work goes on as normal and because we are in Russia, we are working the hammer and tongue system, brush up arse so you clean as you go. If it moves, oil it. If it doesn't, paint it, and run for your life when there's a welder about, because they are guaranteed to set fire to something. Actually, we had a specialist welder coming out from the UK to do the rough, on-site jobs that nobody else would touch. Mick comes out for one-week or two-week contracts and works a fourteen-hour day, getting back in the Spinners for about 11pm just when most people are calling it a day. He lands in the bar still in his work gear and looks more like a pit man, but covered in burns and blisters, with bloodshot eyes. He told me last visit what he earned, and get this, £1,000 a week, clear. Yes in 1970, he earned £1,000 per week in his hand and he's scabbing all the drinks off us.

We've also had several new lads arriving from Dobson's to work in Filament Yarn erecting the 110 drawtwisters, most of which were still in packing cases waiting for me to check off. Three of the guys, Steven, Deano and George, are bachelors in their mid to late twenties and are already initiated into the clan. Deano is a climber in his spare time and has already had a go at a local works' chimney, climbing unaided to the top. "Then what?" I asked yawning. "Then I pissed down the chimney before climbing back down." Sometimes you really shouldn't ask. George is actually married and seems quite sensible and steady, with a great smile. Steve, on the other hand, has quickly gained a reputation as a woman's man. Proof of the pudding is the reason we have met up tonight, holding a special party for Steve who has just returned from his final treatment to clear a dose of the galloping nob rot . It's obvious to everyone now that rubbers are important, even the Russian variety that come in various sizes and are packed in full-length boxes, necessitating rolling your own. Anyway, as Steve said, "Do not get the clap."

His first visit to the doctor entailed having a huge syringe full of this battery acid type stuff pushed up his Jap's Eye. They quickly drop the load inside and a nurse grabs your old man and squeezes holding the fluid in for about five minutes, by which time it would seem Steve is screaming. Eventually the nurse lets go and he fires the burning liquid into a piss pot. He emphasises, "That's the easy bit." He continues. "They get this metal contraption, the umbrella!" he explains, as some of the guys already firmly holding their plums decided that they have heard enough. This steel rod-type thing is again pushed up the Jap's Eye, and then a screw is turned, opening the umbrella, which is then pulled back down the passage. This process is repeated twice, each time the screw being given one extra turn. Since that time, Steve has been peeing, when possible, while immersed in a bath full of warm water.

Today he went for his second, and hopefully last, treatment, which was just a repeat of the first visit. The doctor had confirmed that he was now okay but today's treatment would make sure. Steve having first confirmed that he was quite sore seemed mystified why the doctor had ordered him off sex for a further week. All that, on the top of the fact that he was finding having a 'Jodrell Bank' very painful. We promised to get him pissed every night for the next week – that way he wouldn't give or get a toss either way.

It's amazing the reaction of men listening to another man telling them about the treatment for a man's complaint. I started off scratching my privates, followed by the cupping of the family jewels, and finished up trying to stop myself going for a pee. Well, when you've sunk about ten cans of lager, that's a pretty impossible job. I wondered how women went on! Maybe it entails some sort of rubber bung and a bloody sight bigger umbrella; maybe over here one of those round loo brushes. Anyway, now we've had a few drinks, stuff Steve! If he wants to go round firing off his cannon willy-nilly, that's his fault.

Soon enough Christmas 1970 is upon us. Lots of parties, plenty of shows and dances and, as the previous year, Gerry's special Loch Fyne kipper breakfast, followed by a phone call home, were the highlights. Vika was still calling regularly and our relationship was holding up as it should between friends. However there was still this huge gaping hole, this nausea that turns your stomach each day, every day, every time you allow your mind to run free. It's a little trip as you walk, a little tug on your arm as you run. It will not go away so get on with it.

I have a photo of Carolyn and me on her wedding day, Carolyn resplendent in her wedding dress, snow white, glowing, and me at her side looking so proud. Mum said that they (Carolyn and Bill) were planning a trip to Jersey in April, around the time I was due for leave, and whether I was able to take a week with them. Sounded good to me, especially as my money was being paid into a Jersey bank, ex-patriot stuff and all that. It would give me a chance to buy one or two bits and pieces tax free, followed by a week back in Bolton. "Tell them to book me a room," I concluded.

The Russians were gearing up for another riotous New Year's bash, the only time the shackles came off at work and men could go around greeting other men with a mass kiss-in and back-slapping party. There were, of course, certain individuals that it was important to avoid. Big Sasha fell into that category, a huge, lovable man who ran a gang of *'montagniky'* (erection workers) in Staple Fibre. He had this aura about him that, during the warmer months, would attract flies. Sure enough, he spotted me trying to sneak out of the Staple building. "Mr Alan!" he shouted, holding out his arms. "Sasha." I tried to sound surprised, his gang already in fits of laughter waiting for the head-on crash. Sasha grabbed me, lifting me off my feet and held me there suffocating, my face stuck firmly into his odour-ridden *fufaika*. *"S Novim*

Godom." (Happy New Year.) He kissed me on both cheeks, his hairy face skinning my cheeks as he did. *"S Novim Godom, Sasha."* I patted him on his back as a mark of submission. He put me back down. "Right, you bastards!" I walked round the entire gang, kissing them and slapping their backs as hard as I could. That was before I was whisked away into Sasha's tiny den.

He'd cleared some rubbish piled on a stool. "Sit down." I sat down. One of the lads arrived with a glass nicked from the water machine. Sasha carefully sat a large lemonade bottle on the table and I knew right away what my medicine was, "Finest, pure *Samogonka*," he confirmed, with a grin from ear to ear. He undid the pop bottle top as if the home-brewed vodka was nitro-glycerine, tilted the glass and poured the vodka, stopping when it formed a skin standing proud of the glass. The hooch looked like coconut juice and appeared to have the consistency of coconut juice, but I was bloody well certain that it wasn't going to taste anything like coconut juice. Sasha undid a small bag and took out a large chunk of black bread and a lump of *Salo*, or dried and salted pork fat. From his pocket he took out a large penknife and cut a chunk off each. *"Do dna,"* he ordered. *"Do dna,"* shouted the gang, hovering in the doorway. I bent my heard forward until my lips touched the glass, picked it up and sank the contents in one as ordered. "Fucking hell!" I jumped off the stool, my guts rejecting the burning tar I had thrown down my throat. Somebody had the sense to slap my back hard enough to keep my heart beating. *"Hleb, Hleb."* Sasha pushed the bread toward my mouth. I bit into it quickly, chewed and swallowed. *"Voda.* Water, please, water," I gasped, as the tears ran down my face. One lad ran off with the glass, leaving the others doubled up with laughter. Sasha tried to pass me a piece of pig's fat but I refused, in my finest Anglo-Saxon. The lad returned with a glass of brown ditch water that I sank in one. "Okay, bugger-lugs, your turn." I took the bottle and filled the glass to the brim. "Don't worry," I told Sasha, "it's like nectar," I showed him by kissing the ends of my fingers. "Come on." *"Do dna."* He picked up a chunk of bread in one hand and raised the glass with the other, while his gang clapped rhythmically. *"Ras, ras, ras, ras!"* they chanted as he sunk the potion in one. He stuck the bread under his nose, inhaling deeply before biting off a piece and chewing furiously. "Good," he said in a faint, raspy voice. He held up his hand and I followed suit, our hands colliding with a loud crack. *"S Novim Godom,"* we said simultaneously. *"Noo kak?"* Sasha asked, rubbing his stomach with his hand. "How was it?" I replied, and stuck up my thumb, "Great!" I wanted to tell him that a pal of mine had just been treated for the clap, with the very same concoction being shoved up his bell end, but gave up, finding the translation too difficult. I left him sharing the remainder of the brew with his team.

The New Year's dance saw the canteen filled to the rafters with one of Gerry's special banquet tables and disco to die for. What made it even more special was the time difference of two hours with the UK time, giving us two New Years in one; twelve midnight Russian time and 2 am being twelve midnight UK time. Both events finished with the big circle, 'Auld Lang Syne' and Frank Sinatra blasting out 'New York, New York', with everybody high-kicking lumps off one another. Trying to get round and kiss about fifty ladies can be both difficult and rewarding, while making you a bit of a specialist in techniques. Anyway, it was seen as a bachelor's duty. If you could get through it without messing your pants, you had done well.

I braved the elements for a last ciggie, standing in the porch, looking out at a clear moonlit night lighting up the snow. So still, my funnel of breath hanging in the thin air. I looked up into the crystal wonderland and spotted a shooting star, feeling dizzy trying to keep up with it. I took one last drag on the ciggie, bid farewell to 1970 and welcome to 1971 and in my head wished a Happy New Year to all those that I loved. Teeth chattering, I legged it.

CHAPTER 19
LIFE'S ABOUT SHARING

The rest of the weekend was spent trying to get over the hangover from the New Year party. I did get a phone call home when I confirmed my New Year's resolution to stop drinking, before going down to the bar for a hair of the dog or two. "Ah, life," I thought, "and all our best intentions, maybe next year".

I returned home from work on the Monday as normal, cooked some tea and had a shower and change before Vika came round at about 7pm. She had been home for New Year, wherever that was, so we kissed and wished each other, "*S novim godam.*" Vika was putting some music on the stereo while I poured out a couple of glasses of Tuborg. There was a knock on the door. I walked through, undid the latch and opened the door.

Was I dreaming? The angelic face I had pictured a million times, snuggled inside a large black woollen scarf above a long black coat. Whether I couldn't speak or wouldn't speak, unsure of what to say, I didn't speak and felt myself almost close the door. It took Larissa to break the silence. "Hello, Alan," she said softly. I still didn't respond, but stood back and beckoned her in. Perhaps my face gave away the turmoil that was taking place within, but she did cross the threshold, although with a very puzzled, if not concerned, expression. I slowly closed the door behind her and spoke. "One minute," I said, and walked back into my flat.

"Vika," I said gently, "sorry but I have a problem that I need to sort out and it would be better if you could go." She didn't look at all happy at what she was hearing and made a beeline for the door. She swung round within an instant of seeing Larissa and let fly, "No, I'm not going. Tell her to go. Who is she? What is her name?" she started to rant.

I heard the door latch and ran through; Larissa had gone. I grabbed the door and swung it open. Larissa was turning on the first landing. I ran down and touched her arm before looking deep into her eyes, "please don't go." I held her soft, woollen-gloved hand and somehow managed to walk her back into the flat and through to the kitchen, sitting her down on a stool. "Please," I said again, "wait here."

Vika was sat bolt upright on the couch, her arms folded and her face white with anger. I removed her coat and hat from the stand in the hall and walked towards her. "Please, Vika, you have to go." She fired off another verbal volley, but this time in Russian, before reverting to English. "Who is she?" I held out the coat. "Please, Vika. Please." She jumped up without any further response, snatched the coat and hat and stormed out of the flat, slamming the door shut as she went.

I took a deep breath and walked back to the kitchen, took Larissa's hand and walked her slowly into my room. Maybe some of Vika's anger had rubbed off onto me and maybe it stopped me from breaking down, my heart now pounding out of control and my stomach in knots. "Where have you been?" I asked firmly. "Chernigov," was the reply, in her usual unruffled way. "I've been working in Chernigov in the Ukraine." I put my arms around her waist and slowly, gently kissed her lips, pulled her head onto my shoulder and breathed her in. I wondered if she could feel my heart racing through her winter coat. I was shaking but managed to unbutton her coat, which she slid off her shoulders, throwing it on the bed, followed by her headscarf and gloves. She posed shyly, her dark brown hair shining, high on her head, her green eyes sparkling with that special mischievous glint, her high cheekbones and her proud mouth and jaw line held in that beautiful way. Larissa was back, the girl that I never stopped loving, not since that first extraordinary life-changing moment outside the town centre concert.

I made coffee and we sat talking about what had happened to us since our last meeting. It appeared that her college had, out of the blue, sent Larissa, along with several other students, to work in a synthetic fibre plant in Chernigov about 300 miles to the south-east of Mogilev and about 100 miles from Kiev, Ukraine's capital. She had returned on New Year's Eve, which she had spent with her family and friends. Her brother, Oleg, had told her a story about an Englishman who had been in a big fight at a dance in Gorky Park. He had said that his name was Alan and he had been asking about a girl named, Larissa. It hadn't taken much to put two and two together, and she had realised that it must have been me. I confirmed that it was me and explained my confrontation with Saba. She admitted that Saba had been her boyfriend as well as being leader of the gang. He only needed to click his fingers and I would have been dead. "Not dead," I told her, "but they certainly had given me a good kicking." She had finished with Saba around the time she met me but it had caused trouble for her and, most important, he did not know that she was away working in Chernigov. I tried to explain my situation of not knowing whether she was dead or alive, and that that alone had caused me enormous pain. At this point, she kissed me reassuringly. "I'm back now," she said. For my future piece of mind one thing I had to know was where Larissa lived. "5 Vagonnaya," she confirmed, "over the railway line, past the station." Just that information alone made me feel easier.

We talked as best I could in Russian, until Larissa realised that it was time to catch the last bus home. We stood at the bus stop, holding hands, and I arranged to meet her the following day after college. The bus came and, as people jostled to get on, we kissed briefly but sufficiently. She jumped on at the last minute and waved through the back window.

As soon as the bus disappeared I broke, unashamedly, tears flooding down my face as I stood, head and hands firmly placed on the end of the block of flats. I let out nine months of hurt as the tears dripped incessantly onto the frozen earth until I was cleansed. I walked back to the flat, with her face imprinted in my brain; nothing else mattered, I was reborn, I was in love.

I looked for Vika the next day but it was obvious that she was at college. She was a nice girl, who had been there at the right time, and she spoke some English. Although we had slept together, I still considered her more a friend than a lover. Still, you can't say, 'thank you' to somebody that you need to finish with; you can't give them a kiss and cuddle and then throw them out. Sometimes it has to be cold, clean and quick and that 'sometimes' was now.

I waited for Larissa coming out of college, standing at the end of the flats, smiling like a Cheshire cat. I saw her figure, floating majestically over the icy ground, still about half a mile away, and watched her move ever nearer as I became more and more excited.

We kissed and walked arm-in-arm back to the flat as if she had never been away. She took off her scarf and coat, revealing a blue roll-neck jumper and black skirt. "How can you look so beautiful after a day at college?" Larissa just smiled. I had jumped off the bus from work, taken off my hat and parka, and definitely looked like a tramp. I put the kettle on, "coffee?" I asked. "Yes please," was the reply. "Do you fancy a shower?" I asked tongue-in-cheek. "No, you go," she waved her hands, "I will make coffee." I was doing the Charles Atlas routine in front of the mirror when she reappeared from the kitchen. "Coffee," she announced. "Sex?" I asked casually. "What?" She put her arms round my waist, looking intrigued. "Sexy?" she asked. "No, you're sexy. Actually, I'm sexy. Sex is something else; it's you and me. Oh, what the hell! Are you hungry?" There was a loud knock on the door. "Vika," I thought to myself, sitting Larissa down on the couch and giving her a massive kiss.

I closed my room door and opened the flat door. Sure enough, it was Vika, and she gestured to come in but I didn't give her the door. "Vika, we need to talk at work, but we can't talk now." "She is here?" She pointed inside. "What is her name?" She was getting animated. "Larissa, her name is Larissa, and she's an old friend." "Tell her to go." She tried to push past. At that point my expression must have changed. "Vika, I will speak to you tomorrow at work, not now." I closed the door, turned and leant on it, praying, "Please go, Vika. Please." I heard some movement on the stairs; a key turned and someone started pushing the door. "Hello" he said. "Shit it's Parker, sorry mate." I moved away from the door. "Vika didn't seem very happy, she's just passed me on the stairs," he screwed up his face in one of those "she looked like this" sort of ways. "She's a bit upset," I cut in. "Parker, there is someone you need to meet." I opened the door to my room. "Larissa, Parker. Parker, Larissa." They shook hands. "Nice to meet you." Parker still looked surprised and Larissa nodded politely. "She doesn't speak a work of English, Park. Parker doesn't speak any Russian," I told Larissa. They both smiled. "Coffee, Park?" I asked. "No, I'm going to have a shower." He turned towards his own room. "No nude walking, showing off your weapon," I instructed him. "No problem." He glanced at Larissa and winked.

Larissa wanted to know about Vika's visit and about her in general. I tried my best to explain, at the same time keeping it as simple as possible. I was, after all, speaking Russian, and I didn't speak a word twelve months ago. It goes something like, "Vika, friend at work. Friend here – just friend – Larissa, I don't know where – nowhere – Vika friend, understand?" She smiled, her eyes wide open trying to take it in, "and now?" "Now Vika – go – finished. Okay?" She seemed all right with the explanation and my contorted arm waving. I took a long deep breath before giving her a long reassuring kiss. "*Pilmeny* anybody?" I pointed to the kitchen. "Okay," she replied. I made some tea.

I don't know how to make perfection, but now, for the first time in my life, I wanted conditions to be perfect. I was in no doubt that I was in love but I needed to show my love, I wanted to make love, but it had to be perfect. These thoughts were running through my mind, watching Larissa rolling a cigarette between her fingers, something she did every time. It seemed to have a mesmerising effect. "What?" She smiled, breaking the spell. "No, it's nothing. Why do you do that?" I tried to copy what she did. "Russian cigarettes, aah!" She waved it away, either irrelevant or too difficult to explain. "You smoke too much." "I know," she agreed, lighting her ciggie.

We picked at some food and had a couple of drinks, chatted with Parker and listened to some music. "Do you want to go to Dnieper?" I asked. "The restaurant?" "Yes," I confirmed. "When?" "Saturday night. Is it okay if we go with some friends?" I continued. "Can Olya come?" "Of course she can." It was agreed. I looked out of the balcony window, attracted by the enormous snowflakes falling gently. We walked over and stood quietly watching the thick snow lighting up the scenery, and then we kissed – lighting up my machinery.

We met the same way at the same time each evening for the rest of the week and as each day went by I sensed her understanding and acceptance of my feelings. We spoke about Russian endearments and we settled on one for her, '*Zaika*,' - translated to 'Little Rabbit.' "If only," I thought, with an ever-increasing ache in the nether regions. We hadn't completely dismissed the others; '*Krasavitsa*' (Little Beauty), '*Solnishko*' (Little Sunshine), '*Ptichka*' (Little Bird), '*Rodnulenka*' (Little Relative) - well, not quite yet. Sometimes, just to force a cuddle I would give her the lot.

Saturday evening came round and six of us met up in Steve's flat. We were meeting Larissa and Olya outside the Dnieper Hotel. There were five lads, and Steve introduced us to Vera, a nineteen-year-old blonde girl who was the spitting image of Brigitte Bardot. It's a good job she didn't speak any English, as the 'lucky, jammie bastard' comments flew repeatedly over her head. We were to find out that Vera wasn't just a looker either, she was a lovely, friendly caring girl, who spent most of her waking hours looking after her bedridden mother, something that she had done since her father had buggered off several years before.

We jumped the minibus to town and arrived before Larissa and Olya, so the gang went up to sort the table while I waited outside for the girls. After a couple of minutes, a bus pulled up and they got off and walked to the hotel arm-in-arm. We all kissed and went in. We walked up the ornate staircase to the landing, where we deposited our coats in exchange for heavy, brass numbered tags, Larissa popping all three into her handbag. She looked beautiful, in a green chiffon dress and black high heeled boots. Olya was wearing a cream dress with brown boots. We walked up the second flight of stairs and were greeted by Alexander, 'the gaffer' as we affectionately knew him. "Mr Alan." He bowed, holding out his hand. We shook and he pointed to the rest of the gang already seated and digging into starters. I waved to the quartet and they acknowledged by standing up. A quick drum roll followed by a crash of symbols saw us at our seats. It would sound big-headed, but it was like saying, "The Royalty has arrived, let the banquet begin." It was probably more to do with the fact that we had the money – lots of it! – and while we were having fun we were prepared to spend lots of it, always leaving everyone an obscene gratuity, including the orchestra. Anyway, they were always more than kind and I was glad to give a little back.

Safe to say that we had a wonderful evening; Larissa's face reflecting a side of Belarus life she hadn't seen before; a dignified, yet joyful, atmosphere as Russian and English alike cast off a week's worries and ate, drank and danced into the small hours. We were, as usual, constantly asked to join other tables, other parties in celebrations, birthdays and special occasions. Even without the gift of language we revelled in one another's company, sharing without asking, just people glad to be glad and rejoicing in the moment. I wished that politicians and faceless sabre rattlers, who frighten us to death, could see this. Probably they knew but didn't care.

I knew that the girls were happy after collecting our coats. Larissa placed her coat on the top step of the stairs, sat on it like a sledge and slid gracefully down the shiny marble, exhaling a loud "Wh-e-e-e-e-h," as she went. Olya and Vera followed her lead; all three sat on the foyer floor, laughing hysterically, the lads chanting and clapping, "More. More. More." Even Alexander joined in.

We laughed our way outside into fresh falling snow; fine dry snow, looking like mist swirling in the road lamps. I was just thinking how beautiful it was when a dirty great big snowball smacked on the back of my head and I turned to find Larissa still posing, her chucking arm up in the firing position and laughing guiltily. "That's it. War!" A huge snowball fight followed. It ended up with me being pushed into a mound of snow, jumped on and then pulled backwards by my feet, my sheepskin acting like a sack and filling with so much snow that I had to be rocked onto my feet and emptied out. We stood there exhausted, as one last defiant snowball plopped onto someone's head.

"Taxi," Deano shouted. I turned to Larissa, who was lighting a ciggie, "It's late," I pointed out, "Do you both want to come back to the flats?" The girls stood whispering furiously. Olya had to go home. "But I will come back with you." She linked her arm through mine. We put Olya into her taxi and then split into another two taxis. We climbed in with Steve and Vera. I put my arm around her shoulder and kissed her gently on the forehead.

Strange, isn't it, even when a lad loves a girl so much it hurts, he still finds it difficult to tell her? Why? It's only three little words – I love you. (*Ya tebya lublu*). I'm not saying all guys; a lot of lads might say it all the time. Some might say it but not mean it; they may have other motives. It might fit the bill, nod-nod, wink-wink. So, how would a girl know? You don't tell her, she doesn't know; you do tell her, she thinks, "Ah, he's only saying that to get me into bed." I mean, the girl could tell the boy that she loves him, then the lad could say, "That's incredible, because I love you as well." They should know anyway; they must sense how we feel. My mum knows I love her. Mind you, I've told my mum and my gran and my sister. I've told her (my sister) recently. I've never told my dad; I can imagine his face if I did. Anyway, you don't need to tell your dad, they know. That's it! That's the difference! Men are intuitive, we don't need telling, we know. So, does she love you? What sort of an answer could I put on that simple question? I suppose that blows the intuition theory out of the bloody water. I can't tell her now; we're sharing a taxi. I'll tell her later. Just supposing I had told her before she was due to leave for Chernigov; would that have made a difference? She would have known I love her. What's saying she didn't know then? Who's saying she doesn't know now? Anyway I'm certainly not getting back into the *what ifs,* they nearly drove me mad the last time.

"Alan, we're back," Larissa tugged my arm. Steven and Vera were already out of the taxi. "God, sorry, did I drop off?" I shook my head and looked at the meter, 1 ruble 70 kopeks. I gave him a five-ruble note. "Keep the change." I pushed his hand back into the cab. *Spasibo Ee Spokoynoy Nochy.* Thank you and goodnight." I mimicked some Hollywood star with a gravely voice. "Night Steve, night Vera." I tried not to shout, wrapping my arms round Larissa's waist and pulling her towards me for a long, passionate kiss. I was beginning to feel my body tingle and my manhood rise. She knew! We tiptoed up to the flat like two night thieves and I let us in.

You don't realise how cold it is outside until you come in to a warm flat. We took off our coats quietly so as not to disturb Parker and moved into my flat, closing the door. I clicked on my bedside lamp and turned back into her arms and into a long, long kiss as we fumbled with buttons and clips and zips, until we stood in our underwear. We sat slowly on the edge of the bed and I looked at the angel in front of me. I pulled back the quilt and she slid beneath it while still on my arm. I slid in alongside her. She removed her bra and knickers while I took off my underpants, and we fell into a passionate kiss, gentle at first but increasing in intensity. With her hand's gentle caress we touched and kissed like spreading blossom on a path, moving towards the moment. I was at such a height I was worried that I could finish before I had begun, but inevitably, gently, beautifully the two became one and I…broke wind!? – a real loud botty burp. "What?" We froze. "What was that?" she asked again. I couldn't speak, as if struck by lightning. Embarrassment made me stutter, "My dad does it all the time." What was I saying? What gibberish was coming out of my mouth? What foul smell was coming out of my arse? I dropped and buried my head into the pillow. Larissa started to laugh, just a little at first. I could feel her ribs moving and heard the chuckle. I looked at her and couldn't hold back; we both laughed louder and louder, we couldn't stop. "What did I say?" I asked her. "Something about your dad doing it." We carried on laughing, even choking. After a while I managed to compose myself. "Did you know that you are beautiful?" I whispered to her. She held my head and kissed me hard and long, before moving her hands down to my bottom, moving me at her rhythm, until the love I had been holding inside couldn't stay my sole property any longer. We were awake most of the night, holding one another and kissing and giggling. What a fart! Well, life's about sharing, isn't it?

Larissa had to leave at lunchtime on the Sunday. She had told her mum that she was staying with Olya, but had to get back and help out at home; she would return that evening. I walked with her to the bus stop. We saw each other every day from that time on, occasionally Larissa able to stay over at weekends and on several evenings we met up with Steve and Vera for nights out in town. Life really couldn't have been any better.

CHAPTER 20
BEHIND ENEMY LINES

Things weren't moving quickly at the Lafsan – things were now flying with three plants on the go. Not only breaking out twelve months' spares for the pilot plant, we were completing commissioning and moving to full production in Staple Fibre. Filament Yarn spinning area was in full erection and progress was being made from light denier draw-twisters for clothing yarns to heavy denier machines including beaming machines that would produce the continuous filament industrial yarns. Basically these yarns could be used for making conveyor belting, tyre cord and the like.

There was also a steel mountain of over-head tracking going up. Tracking meant only one thing, my favourite people, welders, working up in the rafters. You can always spot a welder (a good pun, that) they are covered in bruises from ten-foot barge poles. Anyway, they are a law unto themselves. They should finish their work, be stood against a post and shot. I'm sorry if that sounds a bit harsh but put it down to experience.

There was a team of us working away on the shop floor, and suddenly great big slugs of red-hot metal are falling on your head, well, on your safety helmet. We have these massive baths full of white spirit to degrease parts; you don't even smoke in the vicinity, and now a cascade of molten metal is dropping into the tanks. "Oy, you gormless bastard!" I shout up to the nutter dangling on a trapeze wire, "What are you doing?" *"Eedy ti na huy!"* he shouts back. "What? Did you hear what he said?" I turned to the Russian lads who were cowering about 10 yards away. *"Eedy ti na huy?"* that's fighting talk. "Hey, he just told me to fuck off!" I shouted to the foreman. "Come over here," he waved me away. "Find some chequer plate and cover the bath," I instructed the lads. A couple dashed off. "He'll be up there all day; I'll speak to him later," the foreman assured me. "Slap him round the head," I said, "then kick him in the balls from me. Okay?"

Still, it's nice to be going to work in daylight and coming back home in the light. We're having an early spring as well and the end of March is reasonably warm. Larissa had stayed over on the Saturday night, and on the Sunday morning I said to her, "I've never seen where you live." "If you want, I will show you but we'll have to be careful that nobody sees us. Mum and dad still don't know I'm seeing an Englishman." "We'll keep a low profile, like spies," I assured her. We were on a mission and I was going behind enemy lines.

We took the bus from our terminus at the airport to the other terminus at the Railway Station, through the far end of town. We got off the bus and walked over a bridge crossing the railway tracks and onto a rough, dirt road that ran down a gentle hill alongside the tracks. The track nearest the road was full of enormous, old steam engines, each one with a big red or white star on the front, and each one in various stages of disrepair, like a train graveyard. There were also numerous goods' wagons. About a quarter of a mile down the road we came to a fork, with a road to the left. We took the fork and Larissa visibly bowed as we passed an old wooden house on the right. She let go of my hand and pointed to the house. "My house," she whispered.

The beige coloured house was slightly raised up, a short flight of wooden steps leading up to the front door. A large black Alsatian dog was lying on the porch. Its ears pricked up. "Jack." Actually, it sounded like, "Jeck," but I knew what she meant. Larissa again whispered, "Our dog." Behind the tall wooden fence I could see a large garden area with a big apple tree in the centre. There was a wooden shed at the bottom of the garden and a hug pile of chopped logs neatly stacked on one side.

Larissa waved her hand for me to catch up and we walked along past a row of similar multi-coloured wooden cottages and down into a tree-lined valley and to a stream. "Where's the bridge?" I looked at the river, puzzled. "There were two planks," she explained, "but the kids have moved them." She knew exactly the best rocks to stand on and made the crossing look easy. I decided to do it the man's way by taking a running jump, landing short and getting my feet wet. Larissa found it very funny. Now we could hold hands again, and we walked up the track into Pechersky Park.

The park, in summer, is usually a hive of activity, like a forest with regular grassy clearings. It attracts the country revellers and picnickers but at this time of year it's quiet, with people not used to clear paths and access to the open areas. Anyway, we were enjoying the stroll turning left at the end of a hedgerow, and Larissa quickly turned in towards me. "My mum and dad," she whispered, motioning with her head. She let go of my hand and walked towards them. My eyes were distracted by a boy running alongside the hedgerow and chuckling that wonderful, "how are you going to get out of this?" chuckle. I recognised the boy. Larissa shouted, "Alan, my mama and papa." I kissed her mum, (Maria) on both cheeks and shook her dad's (Ivan's) hand, a strong hand. *"Zdravstvuyte,"* I said. Maria was a big woman, actually bigger than Ivan. She had a round, warm motherly face with a big, round, motherly body beneath a big coat and headscarf. Dad was slightly shorter and appeared a lot slimmer, with a very dark tanned looking face and eyes that looked as if they could tell a thousand stories. He had a warm smile and very strong, leathery hands. After I had exchanged pleasantries, Larissa seemed locked in some heated, yet hushed conversation with her mum and I introduced myself to the younger brother. "Alan," I told him. "I know," was his reply, "we met in Gorky Park." He smiled. It struck me that he was the boy who had helped me to get out of the dance and almost carried me single-handed back to the bus stop before telling me that Larissa was in the Ukraine. "Oleg," he confirmed. "Now you remember, 'the fight'." He started to chuckle again. "How old are you, Oleg?" I asked. "Fourteen," was his reply. I shook my head. He was only small in height but his neck and shoulders were much bigger than mine, his body tapered to a wasp-like waist. This lad did serious weight training.

By now, Larissa had skipped back towards me and we set off again, her parents checking us out as we went. I told her about Oleg in Gorky Park and asked her about his extraordinary physique. She explained that he was Belarus wrestling champion in his age group and he regularly visited Minsk to take part in competitions. She then told me that she also had an older brother, Gregory, or 'Greesha', as he was known. He was twenty-two, like me, married to Alla, a nurse, and they had a four-year-old daughter called Natasha. They had a flat at the airport, just one minute's walk from mine. Greesha also worked at the Kombinat in the heating services department.

I asked if her parents had been okay about her going out with an Englishman and she told me not to worry, "They thought that I was walking with a girlfriend," she told me starting to laugh. "Great!" I covered my face. "Dad then thought that you were a German, and that could've been more of a problem," she explained. "He was a partisan in the war and isn't keen on Germans. Don't worry, he knows now." She gave me that wicked smile. "That's a great first impression," I said sheepishly. "Don't worry, Oleg knows not to tell them about the fight in Gorky Park." She grabbed my arm and whirled me round. "Well, thank the Lord for small mercies," I summed up, giving her a sneaky kiss.

Back at the flats we met up with Parker, who was now seeing a Russian girl called Ira. "Ira, Larissa. Ira, Alan. Alan, Larissa. Oh, sorry, you already know her." Parker tried doing the intros. "Coffee anybody?" I asked. "Is it Nescafe?" Ira asked. "Bloody snob!" I shouted back, "She's only been here two minutes and she's a bloody coffee snob already."

Larissa had switched on the television; it was an ice hockey final between, Moscow Dynamo and Moscow Spartak, or as the stars of the two teams, Maltzev against Starshinov. "Come on you whites!" This was the nearest thing to a football match that you could get over here, and Bolton were having a bad time. Anyway, I would be checking up on the Wanderers next week as I was going home on leave.

CHAPTER 21
ROW YOUR BOAT

At about 10am, just an hour before our flight was due to leave, we had skies the black of night and a massive electrical storm with rain coming down like stair rods. Grant stuck his head round the bedroom door, "We can't fly lads, so hold on for a bit while we set up some transport to take you through to Minsk." As always he was very calm and concise. "Cheers, Grant," I confirmed, filling the kettle for a brew. I looked through the kitchen window over to the airport and could make out the plane sat in what was now the biggest lake in Mogilev. It (the lake) covered the entire airfield as far as the eye could see. "Have you seen it out there?" I gestured towards the windows. "Not a prayer," I thought, my five companions deep into a hand of Shoot with about 200 rubles at stake. These guys wouldn't notice if it was the end of the world, which, to be honest, it very much appeared to be. I hand-on-heart had never seen a sky as black and rain as hard as this.

The conditions didn't ease for another thirty minutes or so, when I heard a shout from downstairs, "Come on, the plane's going!" The lads just ignored the command, as if a joke. Grant stuck his head round the door, obviously out of breath. "Guys, move it, the pilot's going." "Get stuffed, Grant," was the consensus. "I'm serious. Get your bags over to the airport if you want to go home." His face said he wasn't joking and I grabbed my suitcase and hand luggage. The other lads had left their luggage in the canteen on the ground floor. We stood in a huddle, looking out at the stair rods hitting the already flooded ground and bouncing back, forming a haze at about knee-height. I draped my coat over my head, pinned it down with my shoulder bag, grabbed my suitcase and shouted, "Leg it!"

We set up a new world record that day, 'the 400 metres suitcase toting puddle run team event' and we burst into the terminal building, skidding on the wet marble floor. "Just in time," Vladimir said, waving us towards the ticket desk. "Vladimir, you are joking, aren't you? He's not really thinking of going in this, is he?" I appealed to his sensible side. "It's certainly not my decision." Vladimir looked tense. "I'm married with two children," he admitted. Quickly dispensing with the technicalities, we moved as one silent, disbelieving group to the doors of the departure desk. I looked at the plane, a twin-engined Russian version of the Douglas DC2, but instead of a nose wheel, the plane had a wheel at the back so it sat down with its nose pointing up at an angle. I scanned the airfield and not a blade of grass was visible, just water, and nothing but water.

Soon enough one of the staff opened the main doors and people filed through, their heads bowed as if walking to their execution. We splashed our way to the plane, up the steps and on board. I grabbed a window-seat on the left towards the back and sat down. My feet were wet through. I wiped away the condensation that had built up on the window and looked at the torrential rain and the lake that we were sat in. The doors were closed and the engines started, while the stewardess handed out the sticky toffees. Nobody needed reminding to fasten their seatbelts, tight!

As the plane started to taxi, the pilot swung the back of the plane from side to side, while the passengers let out deep gasps and clung on to the leather armrests. Some wag started singing, *'Row, row, row your boat gently down the stream,'* and others joined in to complete the verse. We taxied up to the main road on the left, before turning slowly, swinging the wing tip right over the wooden fence at the end of the runway, and stopping. The pilot built up the revs and I could see the rivets in the wing dancing, trying to escape and turning water droplets into a frenzied haze. My fingers had turned white, digging into the leather. He released the handbrake and we sprung forwards down the runway. 'More power', the fuselage groaned under the strain. "Come on. Come on," I whispered under my breath. "Come on." We all suddenly lurched forwards as everything went black, the windows swamped by dark brown slutchy water. The engines let out a loud gasp, a bit like a motorbike running into a lake.

The plane was hardly moving now. Surely the pilot would call it a day; maybe he would go back and try again. "Oh, no, please, don't try again." He did neither. The revs came back more than ever. "Shit!" He was going for it. I tried to clean the window from inside; I didn't want to die in the dark. On we went, and on. "Surely," I thought, "we must be at the end of the runway." I dropped my head down onto my thighs, "Go on, up, up, up." I was shouting in a deathly library, the smell of sick hitting my nostrils. In my head I could see the pilot's teeth gritted round his *papirosy* cigarette and pulling back on the joystick. It worked; we were off the ground. I looked through the window just as we disappeared into a black cloud. The torrential rain quickly cleaned the windows followed by a white flash of lightening that nearly blinded me. The plane pitched and bounced up and into the electric storm. We were being thrown about like a rag doll shaken by a mad dog.

I could see people throwing up into paper bags and plastic bags; anything that they could lay their hands on. I was suddenly aware of pain in my hands, the blood starting to return to my fingers that were trembling uncontrollably. "We're up," I said to Graham, who was still white as a sheet. "What a pilot!" I tried to jolt him into a response – there was none. His eyes stuck out like organ stops fixed on the seat back. I turned back to the window as we started to clear the storm and up into brilliant sunshine. "Every cloud!" I looked at Graham as he started to breathe again, his head falling back onto the headrest, his white fingers still locked onto the end of the armrests.

A couple of hours later we landed in Moscow and took a minibus into the city, staying the night at the Ukraina Hotel. While the marrieds hit the shops, the bachelor brigade hit the bar to exorcise the day's events. It may have taken several bottles of the hard stuff but eventually it worked and I returned to my room in a state of ignorant bliss.

Carolyn and Bill were waiting for me in the bar when I arrived at the hotel in Jersey. We were staying at the Royal Hotel in the centre of St Helier, a good-sized, slightly posh hotel but with a nice friendly atmosphere and an excellent bar with a Portuguese barman whose bar skills alone were worth the price. I certainly tested their stocks of Chivas Regal during the week; especially when Bill got a liking for it. We were getting through more than a bottle a day. The weather was great, and Carolyn looked absolutely radiant. Obviously, married life was doing her good. We hired a car and visited places like St Brelade's Bay and the wartime remains of the German concentration camp on the island, and generally had a good time.

Before returning home, I called at the bank to check my balance and withdraw a few bob to buy an expensive Seiko watch that I'd spotted in a jeweller's window. I was sure that I had seen a similar watch being worn by Jimmy Saville on TVs Top of the Pops, given away by the bright yellow face. Anyway, although it was around £80 tax-free and weighed a ton, I was having it. Coming out of the jewellers, I noticed a crowd of people spilling out onto the street from a car showroom and walked in to see what the fuss was. It was the first time I'd seen an 'E' type Jaguar and it literally knocked me off my feet. It was in a sparkling pale blue and the bonnet was lifted, revealing a twelve-cylinder engine that seemed to have the power of sexual stimulation, and all for just over £2,000, tax-free. I stood staring at the beast, considering whether or not to have one. My more mature side won, and I took one last lingering look before walking back to the Royal.

What a joy it was to have a pleasant, trouble-free flight back to Manchester, where I was promptly arrested at customs for not declaring the tax-free watch that I had packed in my suitcase. They messed me around for about an hour before realising that I was working as an expatriate outside the UK, after which they couldn't apologise enough and sent me packing with an enormous smile.

Being home is always special. Just to see mum, dad and gran is enough, and to sample some of Willie's home-made hot pots. With the help of mum, I had bought some bits and pieces for Larissa and felt comfortable that she would like them, even with the current fashion being a million miles away from that in Russia.

Before you know it I was on my way, letting them know that I would keep them up-to-date with developments on the Larissa front. I flew down to Heathrow before changing to a Japanese Airlines flight; London, Moscow, Tokyo. I had never flown JAL before and I can honestly say that it was an experience. I had my usual window seat on the last row, made up of just two seats. The other was taken by a good-looking giant of a man being well over six foot six tall with blond hair and blue eyes and in his late twenties. His name was Erik and he was Norwegian, living and working in Japan or as he explained later, drilling for oil on a rig in the Sea of Japan.

The novelty was, he spoke good Japanese and asked if I liked whisky. "Just a bit," I replied. He waited for one of the hostesses to walk down the aisle. They were wearing individual coloured kimonos and handing out slippers and fans for the journey. Erik spoke to the girl and she bowed and disappeared into the galley, returning with a tray. From the tray, she took two tall, half-pint lager glasses filled within an inch of the top with whisky and crushed ice and placed them in front of us on a coaster. She then picked up a water jug. "Water?" Erik asked. "Just a little," I replied, sarcastically. The glass was topped up to the brim. We picked up the glasses carefully so as not to spill. "Cheers." We clinked glasses, *"Na zdorovie.* Your good health," I replied. I took an inch off the top, while Erik easily quaffed half the glass in one big swig. "What do you think?" Erik asked. "I think it's half a pint of whisky," I replied. "It's good." I nodded my head. He lifted his glass and finished the contents, while I tried another mouthful.

Flying time to Moscow was around three hours fifty minutes, during which time we had eaten lunch and Erik was on his eighth half-pint of whisky. I had gone drink-for-drink with him; the only difference being that I still had three full glasses on my tray and was gagging on the one in my hand. My head was fine and we were deep in quality conversation when I decided a slash would be in order prior to landing. That's when I found out that my legs were, in fact, travelling to Toronto in completely the opposite direction, "Fu-bollocks," I think I said, trying to stand up. "Where's the toilet?" "Just there," Erik pointed to the door a yard away. "No, that way," he pointed again. "Yes, that's the way I'm going," I assured him. One of the hostesses spotted my plight and helped me into the loo, where I did my tripod impression, legs out wide and left hand firmly planted on the wall.

After bidding Erik 'God speed" and leaving him with a pint and a half of whisky, I was helped from the plane. Passport control and baggage check had never been easier; in fact, I don't remember going through at all. I tried telling the interpreter what had caused my condition. "What was the drink called?" he asked. "I think it was Big Erik's Sea of Japan Leg Jellyfier or something." Something was forcing its way back into my mouth. "I'll never drink whisky again," I concluded making a dash for the toilet.

CHAPTER 22
YES

They say that giving is good. I love to see the look of excitement on Larissa's face when she sees something so nice and so different from anything available over here. Her mannerisms, the way she holds things up, holds the clothing against her, moves her hips, then asks the question with her eyes, "How does it look?" and in return a nod and a smile says, "It's beautiful. You're beautiful." Now, she's going to try it on. Off with her blouse and skirt – dream on! I grab her round the waist and we fall onto the bed, laughing, kissing, hands and fingers touching and exploring, like raindrops, replenishing the mind and body after three weeks' drought.

I still love those moments after, when she sits on my knee, like spoons, and I can feel her trembling. I gently crane and kiss her forehead, see the sparkle in her eyes, touch her hair with my fingers, tell her how wonderfully beautiful she is, and she thanks me for the clothes. Oh, the clothes. She simply must try them on – after we've had a ciggie and a cuppa, that is.

Back at work, things were good. The Filament Yarn spinning department was working on at a pace and Ray was back on site, checking the instrumentation. Because I had a flatmate, he was sharing with one of the other guys. He promised to come round one night and see Larissa. It was good to have him back, he was a real friend and I had missed him and his enormous Cheshire cat grin.

More and more time was being spent with Steve, both at work where he was fitting out the Heavy Denier Draw-twisters, and back at the flats where Larissa had become friendly with Vera. They were a fun couple and very much our age, although Steve was about five or six years older than me. He was from Bolton and a real character and as a couple they were fun to be around.

Saturday was the 1st of May, May Day, and a big celebration in the USSR. Every year there was a big parade in town that was bedecked in communist banners and flags. We were invited to watch the parade from a reserved area in front of a small square next door to the central police station and just across the road from the Dnieper Hotel. Some of the lads, including Steve, George and Ray decided to go and we jumped on one of the special buses that were laid on, along with about sixty or so men, women and children from our community.

It was a beautiful spring day and the town was packed with people who lined the streets. I can't remember anything during my time in Russia so colourful and carefree. Having gathered in the square overlooking the river, a wall of men and women all dressed in their Sunday best walked towards us holding thousands of flags, Soviet flags, Belarussian flags, Lenin flags, big flags, little flags. They held up bunches of flowers which they threw to the watching masses, and they sang and shouted communist slogans. "Glory to our wonderful communist workers!" and the masses would reply, "Hoorah!"

The parade was split into individual factories; the tractor factory followed by the meat factory followed by the Kombinat. Somebody grabbed my arm; it was Sasha from Staple Fibre. "Mr Alan, come on." He pulled me into the parade and I recognised his gang of lads and girls. One of the lads stuck a flag in my hand. I looked up. It was a red Soviet flag with the gold hammer and sickle in the corner. "Glory to the young communists!" "Hoorah!" I shouted. I was having great fun walking along with the gang, waving my flag as the crowds took photos. We walked up the main street and the parade turned right into Lenin Square. I could see top local party members and high-ranking army officers stood on a special stand acknowledging the parade. I had a picture in my mind of Kosygin and Brezhnev looking out over Red Square at the hordes of people passing below. "Not bloody likely!" I quickly handed the flag back down the line, slapped Sasha on the arm and ran for cover into the crowd. I made my way steadily back down the main street, eventually arriving back at our cordoned-off area.

Great, isn't it, but none of the guys even knew I had gone missing; too busy taking photos and waving at the girls. Their hands full of flowers that they were liberally handing back to the prettiest revellers in exchange for kisses or sight of a pair of knickers. They all seemed intoxicated in the spirit of the day. After a couple of hours we piled back onto the bus. "Glory to the British workers!" We countered in unison, "Hoorah!" It carried on back to the Spinners Arms and deteriorated once a couple of pints had been sunk.

Larissa came round soon after 7pm shortly followed by Steve and Vera who I had invited earlier that week. Naturally I had prepared the celebratory kitchen sink curry and chips. Larissa would pick up a chip, dip it into the curry and pull her face before she got the chip into her mouth. *"Nichego,"* she would announce. *'Nichego'* means 'Nothing', 'I don't care' or 'It's not bad'. "Nice to know you're cooking's appreciated," I said. "Anyway, I can't cook anything else." That was a lie but a good cop-out when you're in a corner. "Anyway, all the lads enjoy my curries, so make a salmon butty if you don't like it." "No, I'll eat the curry, thank you." Vera took Larissa's approach by chewing the tiniest bit of chip, dipped in the curry. "Bloody hell, it won't poison you." I stuck my tongue out at her and she laughed. Steve just carried on devouring his plateful. "Screwdriver, anyone?" I had made a big bowlful of vodka, Martini Bianco, orange juice and lemonade.

Within an hour we were listening to music and playing silly games like Paper, Scissors, Stone. Two hours later we were dancing, bumping and nipping one another's bums. Three hours later we were bouncing on my bed and having a pillow fight. Larissa was staying over, as was Vera, so Larissa came up with the idea that Steve and Vera should sleep at ours. The couch folded down to make a second bed and I had spare sheets and a quilt cover. "Sorted," Larissa confirmed.

We eventually put out the lights and I cuddled up to Larissa and we kissed and kissed again then stopped, looking at one another. Steve was in like Flynn, the steam engine already picking up speed. Larissa started to giggle and I put my hand over her mouth. He, 'the engine' was up at speed now, like one of those American engines in the Wild West, with the big chimneys and tons of smoke billowing out. Christ, it was deafening, and he went on and on and on. I couldn't contain myself any longer. "Whooh-whooh!" I pulled the pretend whistle and everybody started laughing – we couldn't stop, and pillows were thrown. "Bugger me, Steve," I said. "You'll have to wait until I've finished with Vera," he replied in a flash. "You're not coming anywhere near me." I assured him. "You're not coming anywhere near me either," Larissa pulled the pillow over her head. "The train now standing at platform one…." I turned back to Larissa and we looked at each other and started to laugh again.

For all the banter nothing seemed to unsettle Steve, who thundered on all sodding night. From that night on, I couldn't look at him without laughing. I just got this picture in my mind of Vera grabbing his ears and hanging on for grim death.

It was early June and we met as usual and went up to my flat. Larissa played some music while I had a shower and changed. I sat down on the couch and put my arm around her to give her a kiss. Her eyes looked into mine and I sensed that something wasn't right. "Are you okay?" I asked her. "I have finished my exams at college," she explained. "They are sending me to work in Saratov for two years." Her voice was quiet and she looked directly into my eyes. "Where is Saratov?" I asked sensing something was not right. "It's on the Volga in Eastern Russia, about 2,000 kilometres from Mogilev." She did her best to explain. "Just a bit too far then to come home for weekends?" I tried to take the sting out of what had just been said, but it didn't work for either of us. "Why do you have to go? When do you have to go?" She thought about the questions for a while. "It is like army service," she explained. "When you finish college, you have to give the state two years of your life and they decide where you have to work. They have decided to send me to Saratov from the 1st of August." She held both my hands as she was explaining. "Surely there is something we can do?" I pleaded beginning to feel pressure in my head. "Nothing." She shook her head. "I'm sorry, Alan. I don't want to go but there is nothing anybody can do." Her voice and her eyes told me that she was telling me the truth.

Larissa didn't stay late that evening, explaining that she had to tell her parents the news. She promised to see me the following evening. After returning to the flat, I poured a glass of brandy and drank it down in one, feeling the acidity hit my stomach and start to soothe my senses. I had lost her once; I wasn't going to lose her again. I knew the very first time I saw her that she was going to be my wife, and if she was going to be my wife, I needed to marry her, and in order to marry her I had to ask her. That's what I need to do, that's what I will do. My brain raced like a roller-coaster. I had often told her how beautiful she was and showed how much I loved her, but not once had I told her that I loved her. "Does she love me? If I ask …no, when I ask, what will she say? When it comes to that, what will I say? I know how to ask a gang of Russian lads to clean up a pump or change a gear or juggle some bearings, but how do I ask Larissa to be my wife?" I sat up most of the night peering intensely up at the stars. "She isn't leaving me again, ever!"

Wednesday the 16th of June 1971 and Larissa arrived at the flat, from home, at about 7.30pm. Needless to say, I was waiting for her, showered and dressed to impress. I even brushed my hair and my teeth but my stomach was churning. I had actually doubled up in pain at work. "Dodgy food," I had explained.

I made a coffee and we sat down to talk. We ran over the same scenario that we had done the night before, me asking had anything changed, had they got it wrong, or had they changed their minds. No, they hadn't. Where was she going? What was she going to do? How long was she going for? When was she going? All the same questions with exactly the same answers. What could we do about it? Nothing. I had tried to kiss her extra-tenderly, with a bit more passion and feeling. Surely that would alter things!

It was getting late, I bit the bullet, and, in my best, most nervous broken Russian, went for it. "Will you to be my wife?" She sat upright on the edge of the sofa, stared at me with a puzzled look, and said nothing. I wasn't breathing, just waiting for the answer – none came. She seemed to shrug her shoulders and my sigh was definitely audible, my eyes pleading, but all to no avail. She had dismissed the question and I couldn't understand why. Maybe she was trying to let me down gently, without the need for a definite, "No." Oh, God!

What remained of the evening was best forgotten. Needless to say, I wasn't the world's best host; I was feeling gutted but didn't have the language or the heart to challenge the outcome. We walked to the bus stop with my chin scraping the floor, and we said goodnight courteously, she would see me tomorrow, and after this evening, that was enough.

Thursday 17th June 1971. I held her hand, led her from the door to the couch and sat down. I held her eyes in mine.

"Larissa," I said softly. "Yes," she answered. "I love you so much, will you be my wife?" Again, she sat back, holding my hands. "Yes," she whispered. "You will?" this time louder. "Yes." Even her eyes said, "Yes." I screamed with joy, jumped up, picked her up off her feet and twirled her round and round until we collapsed back on the sofa. The rest of the evening was a joyous blur; it was 'our time' and would remain 'our time', safe to say that words would not do it justice. It was pure, raw ecstasy. It was love!

As a new dawn lit up my flat, the ecstasy of the previous day had to give way to the reality of the task ahead. Larissa was going to leave Mogilev in six weeks and we needed to marry before then. I knew some Brits who were married to Russian girls; Norman and Nina, and Grant and Svetlana, but as far as I knew nobody had been married here in Mogilev. Even so, how long had it taken for them to arrange their marriages? "Probably," I thought, "more than six weeks." Well, I suppose I had better get things moving.

Before jumping the bus, I arranged a phone call home for Saturday lunchtime. My parents had to be told and I needed to know if they could come to the wedding. I managed to catch Malcolm early, before he left for his weekly directors' meeting. He shook my hand and congratulated me, before telling me I was dreaming if I thought I could arrange things before the beginning of August. He picked up the phone and spoke to the office, asking them to contact the British Embassy in Moscow and suggested I call in and talk to Grant and Dorothy immediately after work. He then asked me, in his charming manager's way, to, "Go and do some f...ing work." Of course, when asked like that, how could one refuse? My mind wasn't really on work, but I fucked off anyway.

Back at the ranch, Grant explained that there was good news and bad news and some quite memorable news. "Give us the good news first, Grant," I said, excitedly. "You have an appointment on Tuesday with the British Embassy in Moscow.

They will give you the necessary wedding licence." He now cleared his throat. "The bad news is your parents will not be able to come to the wedding if you have it in Mogilev." "Why?" I stood up and pleaded. "It's the interior," Grant explained, "not an in-tourist destination; it can't happen." "Okay," I gave in. "Oh, and just before you go," Grant concluded, "your flatmate will be going to Moscow with you." "Parker, why?" "He's getting married as well." Grant confirmed. "The sly old dog," I said, "No wonder he's never in his flat." I went back to the flat to collar the bugger.

"Hey, you, dark horse!" I knocked on Parker's door. "What?" His head appeared round the door. "What? You cunning long sod, I didn't even know that you were courting." "Ah, we're going to Moscow together for the marriage licence." Park' had twigged. "Correct, Parker." I probably sounded exasperated. "Anyway, what's the unlucky girls' name?" "Ira," he replied, "the girl you met before." "Now I remember. You sly dog!"

I was down early on the Saturday, waiting for my two o'clock call and having a chat with Gerry about my epic task. I knew he considered it most unlikely, from the laugh and slap on the back, as I dashed for the phone call. "Hiya, mum." "Son, is everything okay?" "Yes, better than that, mum. I asked Larissa to marry me and she said, 'Yes.'" "Al!... Alan is getting married," I heard her shout into the bar, followed by a loud cheer. "Oh, son." I could tell she was starting to cry. "Mum, don't get me going, I can't explain, I've never felt like this in my life." "Oh, son, we're so happy, here your dad." "Hi, Alan, it's dad." "Hi, dad. I'm getting married." "Great, great, when?" "I don't know yet, dad but it needs to be before 1st August or she will have to go and work in Siberia; well, a long way away." Things went quiet. "Son!" Mum was back on the line. "Listen, don't worry about Larissa's wedding dress, we will send one over." "Mum, I've checked and they say you can't come out." My voice started to break. "Son, don't worry, we love you so much, we'll all be with you." "I love you, mum. I wish you could be here." "Son, give Larissa all our love and tell her we'll see her when you get home." She now sounded strong and sure. "Mum, love you all. I will phone when I know more." Time was up and I replaced the phone and sat with my head swimming.

I gave Larissa a big kiss from the Hamers and told her that they would be sending the wedding dress. She sat looking at Carolyn's wedding photos and held my hand and kept looking back at me, her head shaking as if in disbelief. "How beautiful," she repeated. "What?" I asked. "Everything," she replied, "Your family, your mum, your dad, your grandma, your sister." She pointed to each one in turn. "And me?" *"Ach* you? The dress, the dress is so beautiful." She tried not to laugh. I grabbed her and kissed her all over.

CHAPTER 23
NICHOLAI THE GREAT

I told Larissa that I was going to Moscow for the marriage licence and that Parker was going with me. "Parker?" she looked stunned. "Who is he marrying?" "Ira," I said. "Ira, the girl he was with before?" "The very one," I confirmed. I didn't tell her that I was going to buy the engagement and wedding rings while I was there – wanting to keep it a surprise.

On the Monday we travelled up to Moscow with a small party returning home on leave. Volodya, or as we knew him, Vova, the interpreter, had booked a single room at the Rossia so that we - Parker and me - could grab a shower and book a meal. Anyway, it was a glorious summer's day and we were on a mission.

We grabbed a taxi from the station, which took us straight to the British Consulate. It had a prestigious location on the south bank of the river, within walking distance of Red Square and the Rossia Hotel. High, ornate, wrought iron fencing surrounded a garden-fronted large period house. Two policemen guarded the front gate and we showed our passports and went through the garden to the front door. We were greeted by a Russian guy who spoke good English. We left our passports with the guy while we went and had a cup of tea and some bourbon biscuits. An hour later we walked out, passports stamped and free to marry our Russian brides. Parker and I walked over to the river wall and shook hands before turning back and taking in the special view.

"What the hell!?" I could see a bloke about 100 yards away, collapsed on the pavement. We set off running. Needless to say, Parker got there first. We could hear him moaning but I couldn't understand how lucky he had been to collapse on a rug. Parker was trying to roll him onto his side when the guy started to fight him off. I didn't understand what he was saying but it appeared to be, "Go away and leave me alone." Parker jumped back looking completely perplexed. "I think he is saying a prayer but why isn't he facing east?" He was definitely facing Northwest. "He can face any way he wants," Parker was in full retreat. At a reasonable distance away, we stopped. "Well, you don't expect that in the centre of Moscow, do you?" Parker looked totally miffed. "I suppose not." I started to laugh, seeing the funny side. "You can't do right for doing wrong." Parker didn't get the joke.

I told him about an incident in Liverpool some years earlier. We were going to Ireland in my car – sorry, my dad's car. Anyway, we'd arrived at the docks a couple of hours early for the overnight ferry to Dublin. We decided to take a short walk along Dock Road, when we saw a young woman lying against a wall a short distance from a pub. I bent down and tried to turn her onto her side when she swung at me with her fist and spat at me. "Fuck off nobs!" she screamed in a thick Scouse accent. She kicked me with her high-heels, taking a chunk out of my leg. "You stop there love, you're all right," I said in disgust turning to the lads, "Some people!" "Sometimes," I explained to Park', "your help just isn't needed." He nodded. We walked back to the hotel to meet Vova.

After lunch, we walked over to Red Square taking in the Changing of the Guard. We called in at an old tobacco shop up a narrow cobbled street close to the fur shop where I had bought my first fur hat. The shop was famed for its selection of Cuban cigars and I bought a box of 'Romeo and Juliet' cigars that had been requested by one of our plant hierarchy. We then strolled on to the *Berioska* Shop. All goods here were sold for sterling only, but were always the best that you could get, in Russia anyway. I soon picked out a beautiful solitaire diamond ring and tried it on my little finger, which I figured would be close enough to a fit. The wedding ring was a little bit more difficult, all the rings being very similar. I eventually settled on a Russian red gold ring because of its width and its unusual reddish colour.

Park' and Vova took the mickey by humming and looking bored when I eventually got out of the shop. "What?" I said, "That's what we came for, isn't it?" "Yes" they both started to yawn. "Let's have a look at it," I said to Park'." "You get yours out first," he replied. "Okay, if you're going to be childish, we'll get them out on the train." "I can't wait for it," he confirmed. Vova looked confused. "We're going to show one another our rings," I told him. "Don't worry, it's an English thing." Vova seemed satisfied with the answer.

We looked around some of the shops before grabbing a taxi back to the station for our overnight train. Once settled in our sleeping compartment Vova unveiled our presents that he had bought. A plastic bag was pulled from his briefcase and two bottles of vodka were revealed. "Not ordinary vodka." Vova presented the bottle to me. "This is special peppered vodka," he confirmed, before disappearing down the corridor. He came back with three tea glasses and immediately opened the bottle and poured the contents equally into the glasses. We toasted one another. *"Ras, dva, tree, poechaly!"* (One, two, three, go). As if vodka isn't fiery enough, they have to put pepper into it. The fire in my stomach needed putting out. Vova pulled a loaf of black bread and a brown paper parcel containing pickled cucumbers, one of which I grabbed and bit off about one-third, chewing it frantically. Parker followed suit. I grabbed the bread and stuck a chunk under my nose, snorting in the malty smell Russian style. "Another?" asked Vova. "Later," replied Parker. "A cuppa tea please." Vova went back to put the order in. The vodka didn't only have a violent effect on my stomach; it also hit my brain like a lump hammer. "What is this stuff, Vova?" I looked closely at the label on the second bottle "It's special 70 per cent pure vodka." "It's bloody rocket fuel," you mean.

On my special request we saved the second bottle until we reached '*Gorad Geroy Smolensk*'. I hadn't forgotten my first trip down from Moscow and my conversation with the lovely Tanya the superintendent. "By the way Vova, what is *Gorad Geroy Smolensk*?" " Smolensk" he explained "The town was awarded special status during the war. It is a 'town of heroes', just like Brest on the Belarus, Polish border, where the people fought to the last man." We toasted Tanya and all the Russian Heroes before switching to red light, and climbing into our bunks.

I woke with Vova tugging on my arm. "Come on, we're coming into Orsha." "Where's Minsk?" I slurred my words, still drunk. "We're changing trains in Orsha," he pulled on my arm again. "Where's Park?" I asked. "He's having a wash," he replied. The steam from the hot tea hit my nostrils as I leant over the side of the bunk. I reached down and fished the slice of lemon out of a glass and stuck it in my mouth and chewed, "Okay, I'm awake now." I slid off the bunk, grabbed my toothbrush and wobbled to the bog. When I came back, I checked my watch, "Shit, it's only 6am," I said. "We're getting a connection on the Leningrad to Odessa train that stops in Mogilev," Vova confirmed. I took his word for it. Orsha was a small town at the centre of the railway network, a bit like Crewe in England. It was also the site of a big battle in World War II, when the Russians used their '*Katyusha*' rockets to blast the Germans.

I had almost sobered up when the Odessa train finally pulled into the station and we climbed on-board. No sleeping compartment this time; we were economy class in an open compartment, and what a gang! We'd hardly got going and already we had a party going with about ten soldiers and three girls who between them pulled out a Pandora's Box full of booze and food.

Three-parts-cut, we were deep into a mass game of *Durak* (Fool), a game of cards that was impossible to understand when you were sober. Of course, I was the fool again, finishing up with all the cards. One of the soldiers licking the last trump card and slapping it firmly on my forehead, which brought the entire compartment into a fit of laughter. All that is apart from one huge, strange-looking git who had been giving me the evil eye for about an hour. I decided to try and stare him out – not the best idea I had ever had. He uncurled himself from the constraints of his seat, and when he stood up he was too big for the carriage, his head bowed over touching the roof. At about seven-feet tall, he looked just like Herman Munster but without the bolt through his neck. He walked slowly towards me, bent down and said something. "I don't understand," I said, nervously. He repeated the question. "He wants to know if you are German." Vova butted in. *"Nyet, Anglichanin."* I confirmed looking up at him. The giant tried to stand upright and held out his shovel-like hand. I shook it and he proceeded to pat me on the head. "I think he likes you." Vova tried not to laugh and everybody sighed with relief. "Nicholai," he said. "Alan," I responded. He smiled. He waved his hands and turned. "He wants to talk to you," Vova said. "After you then." I stood up and followed Vova and Nicholai out to the opening near the doors, Vova doing the interpreting.

He told me his story and about the war. Being so big, in his teens, the Germans had used barbed wire to tie him to a post and used him as a stabbing bag before leaving him to die. He undressed and showed us the wounds. There must have been more than twenty horrendous gashes to his stomach, arms and legs, and you could still see the rips to his wrists, ankles and stomach from the barbed wire. "They couldn't kill me," he stated, tucking his shirt back into his trousers, "and when I caught them…" he grimaced, his huge hands choking the life out of fresh air. *"Anglichanin Durak,"* I showed him, slapping my head. "Not a fool," he replied, shaking my hand before giving me his pack of cards. "You will remember Nicholai," he pushed them into my hand. I felt like saying, "how could I forget," but kept quiet giving him a block of chocolate instead. It may only have been a brief encounter but I was proud to say that 'Big Nick' was my pal. He came back and joined in the festivities and we had a special round of drinks toasted to 'Nicholai the Great.'

We were into our chorus of 'Moscow Nights' when the train pulled up at a station. The place looked familiar, but what the hell, we were in full flow now. As we pulled out of the station, I looked at a factory on a hill, belching out smoke, just like the smelly old glue factory in Mogilev. "Look," I said to Parker and Vova, "that's the glue factory." Vova cursed, realising that it was the glue factory and it was Mogilev, and we were moving again. He turned white and dashed out of the carriage. About five minutes later, he shouted to us and we left the singsong and joined him. He whispered to us, "Listen, we're in big trouble." His voice was trembling. "The train doesn't stop until Bihov, about 60 kilometres away." I couldn't help it, but I started laughing. Vova just carried on "Please don't tell anybody or I will be dead." He ran his finger across his throat and I could tell he wasn't joking. "We haven't been to Bihov before." I again tried to lighten the mood. "No," he said, sternly, "and you won't be going there again," his eyes trying to tell us something. We stood there, silent for a moment, trying to take in what he was or more appropriately wasn't telling us. "Come on," he said, "we'll get a cup of tea." I let them go back to the carriage while I dropped the window and stuck my head out, taking in the warm breeze. The diesel engine chugged along at a very slow pace, perfect to take in the wonderful countryside.

A couple of hours later we slowed to a crawl and pulled into the station. We bid farewell to our travelling companions, including Nicholai, who stooped with his head through the open window until the train left. Vova sat us down on a wooden bench while he disappeared to arrange the return trip. Both Parker and I sat slouched with our heads in our hands, until awakened by a deafening roar. We thrust our fingers into our ears and I watched a MIG fighter plane blast skywards, followed by another and another. They went up almost vertically. Watching the afterburners lit up, realisation hit home. This was the Russian Air Force Base that people had rumoured about, and it was right next to the railway station. It all started to make sense – the strange black jet that we had seen hedge-hopping over the fields on our fishing trip. This was the reason we weren't allowed to visit Gomel, the town to the south-east of Mogilev that people had asked repeatedly to see. The road would have taken us through Bihov. That's why Vova was so afraid of anybody knowing that we had finished up here – it was a military Air Force base and we shouldn't know about it.

"All right, Vova?" I asked as he returned. "Come with me," he said, shepherding us down the platform and into a small office. "Sit down, and please don't say anything to anybody." He walked round the office like a caged lion until the train arrived. As we set off I strained my neck trying to see the base, without any joy; a steep bank lined with trees blocked any view.

Two hours later we arrived back in Mogilev. Vova reminded us to keep stumm about our extra curricular visit, and we crossed our hearts and hoped to die. "Just promise?" he asked. We did. Well, I did, with my fingers crossed.

CHAPTER 24
BEATLES?

I sat facing her, holding her hands. "Larissa," I said, softly, "I know I have done this before but will you be my wife?" I smiled to try and reassure her. Still there was a long pause and a quizzical look on her face. I nodded in encouragement. "Yes," was the answer. I put my hand in my pocket and pulled out a small black box, opened it and took out the ring, and slowly placed it on the third finger of her left hand. "Is it a diamond?" she asked looking confused. "Yes," I replied. She threw her arms round my neck and kissed me before sitting back with that girlish excitement staring at the ring. "It's on the wrong hand," she said. "In Russia, wedding rings go on the right hand." I gently removed the ring from her finger and replaced it on the third finger of her right hand. "It fits." She held her hand in that feminine way, fingers pointing towards the ceiling, rocking from side-to-side to make the diamond sparkle. "By the way, it isn't a wedding ring," I told her. "A wedding ring is a gold band that I give you at our wedding." "So, what is this?" She showed me the ring. "This is to show that you have agreed to marry me. It's an engagement ring." It took an awful lot of explaining about the rings because they didn't have engagement rings in Russia. Anyway, she was thrilled to bits, and whether she knew it or not, we were engaged.

She liked it so much, before I knew it I was being marched across the playground and gardens, over to her brother's flat.

I stood there beginning to feel nervous, waiting for the door to open. I had never met her older brother or his wife – what would they think of me? The door opened. It was Alla. "Come in," she said. She was only a tiny woman, but she was shapely with short blonde hair and a wonderful, kind, smiling face. She gave Larissa a hug and a kiss, and then turned to me. "Is this Alan?" she asked. "Yes, this is the Englishman I have told you about." Larissa ruffled my hair. Alla held out her arms and gave me three good splodgers. One on each cheek and one down the middle, after which she stood holding my cheeks with both hands giving me the full stare. "All in order," she said, cheekily. "Come in." Larissa followed Alla into the flat. What caught my eye was the big twin-cylinder Jawa standing in the hall.

It was very much like my flat but a little bit bigger and there was more in the room. They had a lovely glass cabinet full of crystal glasses and other knick-knacks and, not for the first time, there was a carpet on one wall. I'm sorry but I still couldn't get my head round it. Maybe if you get thrown against the wall in a fit of temper, it could soften the blow? "Where's Greesha?" Larissa asked. "I'm in here," was the reply from the kitchen. "What are you doing?" again, Larissa shouted through. "Come and see," he replied. I followed Larissa through to the kitchen. Greesha was at the kitchen table building a model aeroplane, very much like an Airfix kit that you get back home. He was carefully holding a wing to the fuselage, waiting for the glue to set. "That should be enough," letting go of the wing. He stood up, *"Gregory Ivanovitch,"* he held out his hand. "Alan Alanovitch," I replied, and took his hand and shook. He smiled and we kissed both cheeks. About an inch or so shorter than me but about twice as wide. His neck and shoulders were massive and his face much rounder than Larissa's, but with the same nose. "Drink!" ordered Greesha, and out came a bottle of vodka and some glasses plus some food, and it was just like a whirlwind had picked them up and deposited it all neatly on the dining room table. The whirlwind was called Alla.

"I've got an announcement," said Larissa. "You know that we are getting married?" "Yes, yes, yes," Greesha replied in a, 'get-on-with-it, you're holding up the drinking' way. "Well, today, Alan has asked me again and I have accepted and Alan has given me this wonderful ring as proof of our forthcoming wedding." She held her right hand up, displaying the ring. Ay, ay, ay!" Alla screamed with amazement. "Is it a diamond?" "Of course it's a diamond!" Greesha said, in his matter-of-fact way. "It's the *Anglichany* way," he confirmed. "Diamond ring, it's good." He poured out the vodka then disappeared into the kitchen and came back with a small brown bottle with a cork in the top. "Greesha, what are you doing?" Alla seemed alarmed. "It's a special occasion, isn't it?" Greesha took out four tiny shots glasses and dribbled some of the clear elixir into each glass before quickly replacing the cork and returning the bottle to the fridge. "What is it?" I asked. "Pure," was the reply, as we lifted the glasses. "To Larissa and Alan!" The rest I didn't understand but he sounded convincing. We clinked glasses and tipped the liquid down. "Wow," was the audible reaction as we all grabbed for bread. Greesha held the glass of vodka chaser, *"Do dna,"* he instructed, and downed the vodka. I followed suit, while the girls made strange gurgling noises, as if in pain. I chomped on a piece of bread. "Lemonade!" Larissa insisted. "What was that?" I found sufficient breath to ask. "Pure spirit," Greesha said nonchalantly. "Alla is a nurse," he went on. "It's the stuff they clean your arm with before the needle. It's good; it's pure spirit – absolutely pure." "It's burning a hole through my stomach." I rubbed my stomach. "And mine," Larissa backed me up. "Ah, you'll be fine," Greesha waived it away. "Eat something." He displayed the food on the table while recharging the vodka glasses.

We had a great night with Alla and Greesha and I knew we would be good friends. Greesha was a keen fisherman and said that we would definitely go on fishing trips together. He was six months younger than I was but somehow, to me, he seemed older and more grounded in a wild sort of way; probably because he was married with a four-year-old daughter called Natasha. In short he had responsibilities. I would have to be introduced to Natasha another day as she was staying at Grandmas house.

Well, we had lots to drink and plenty of good food and left at the normal time for Larissa to catch her bus home. She was so chuffed with the ring and told me that the coming weekend I would have to prepare myself for a trip to meet her parents at their home. I agreed that it was important and I had to do the proper thing and ask for their approval.

That Saturday, I had arranged to meet Larissa at the station bus stop at 11am and she was waiting for me when the bus arrived. The track down was familiar, only being a couple of months before that we have sneaked past the house, just to be caught red-handed in the park. On the way, Larissa apologised that her dad had been called away. She showed me the tiny old cinema where her dad was the projectionist. He had to stand in at Saturday matinee, showing a film for invalid children from a nearby home, where he doubled up as an electrician and caretaker.

We arrived at the house and were greeted by Jack, the dog. "Is it Jeck or Jack?" I asked. "Well, to you it's Jack but in Russia it's pronounced Jeck." Mum was waiting in the kitchen. "Mama, Alan." Larissa did the introduction. I held out my hand courteously. She did likewise and we shook hands. "The first time I saw you, I thought you were a girlfriend of Larissa's," she explained. "It happens all the time," I replied. "It's the hair. It's an English thing," I went on, "The Beatles, long hair, you know?" I felt I was rambling. "Beatles?" She dismissed it. "I love your daughter." God! Now I was rambling. She laughed. "Show him round while I'm busy," she instructed Larissa. I felt strange, uncomfortable, out of my depth. "Come on, Laura, show me around."

She showed me her room; well, hers and Oleg's room, her bed on the left with a carpet on the wall behind the bed. Oleg's bed doubled as a sofa with a table in front of the window that was dressed with lace curtains. Next door was the main living area with a couch, TV and display cabinet, plus mum and dad's bed up against the '*petchka*', or old Russian stove and house warmer-upper. The kitchen was, well, an old wooden kitchen with a small gas cooker run off bottled gas, but no running water; that came from the well on the corner. Mum was busily washing knick-knacks in a big white enamel bowl. We went into the garden that was not a garden. It was dirt, with about five or six chickens running around. The apple tree in the middle was nice, and created patterns on the ground as it swayed in the breeze. Along one side of the garden there were several rabbits in big wooden hutches. They sniffed my finger when I poked it through the wire. The last cage contained the 'daddy' - a whopper of a rabbit, brown with huge floppy ears. I was just about to stick my finger through when Larissa said; "It bites." I just managed to pull my finger away before it was chomped off. Next to the hutches was a massive mountain of chopped logs for the '*petchka*' in winter, and next to that, at the end of the garden, was the outside privy.

Why I opened the door, I don't know. God, what a pong! Oh, well, better have a pee. Up two steps and onto a wooden floor with a circular hole cut out in the centre. I had a waz trying to hold my breath. "Somebody," I thought, "has got to clean that lot out." I was just stirring it up. I turned and noticed a grab rail half way down the door. "That's clever," I thought, "allowing you to hang on while crouched, and stops people coming in by mistake." The bog was finished off with the proverbial rusty nail and several strips of Pravda. This place I thought was very definitely, an emergency only option.

Back in fresh air, I could start to breathe again. A large wooden shed was on my right. "What's in there?" "Two pigs," Larissa replied. "Pigs?" I was amazed. "Of course," said Larissa, "There is a wedding to cater for." "Oh, no, I can't go in there." "Me neither." Larissa pulled on my arm and walked me back up the garden, explaining how she had to get away from home when animals were being despatched. "How about the chickens?" I started to sit down on a chopped-off tree trunk. Larissa pulled on my arm and pointed. I noticed the axe marks on the stump and a strange dark staining to the wood. "Bloody hell, I was going to sit there." She threw her arms round me and gave me a cuddle. "You're just a big softy, aren't you?" "Yes," I admitted. She gave me a long, comforting kiss that made me feel a lot better.

We walked back into the house, where mum had set up a small buffet lunch. "What would you like to drink?" she asked. "Could I have a cup of tea?" I asked. "Tea?" She seemed amazed. "Yes, tea," Larissa backed me up and she walked through to the kitchen. I felt for my wallet and took out a photo of my mum and dad that had been taken after the war; my dad wearing his RAF uniform. I took it to her, sat at the table. She held the photo at arm's length and stared at it for ages; her eyes seemed to fill with water. "How beautiful," she said, "How beautiful your parents are." She stood up and gave me a hug, a proper mum's cuddle. I took out another photo of Carolyn, "My sister," I told her. "Carolyn?" She looked at the photos, shook her head and wiped away the moisture from her eyes. "Alan, do you want milk in your tea?" Larissa shouted from the kitchen. "No, I'll have it Russian style," I shouted back. Maria opened a drawer and took out a photo album just as Larissa was arriving with the tea. "Mum, no, not the old photos." Too late, the album was on the table.

We sat for an hour or more, flicking through old photos of Maria and Ivan, and *Babushka Sarah*, who we had to visit at her house out in the country. There were photos of Larissa as a girl at school, that mum and I found very amusing, while Laura tried to turn the pages to save her embarrassment. We talked about the times as a young girl when Larissa suffered with Rheumatic Fever and was unable to walk for several months. *Babushka Arena*, her dad's mother, was part gypsy and was thought of as a 'White Witch'. She had dressed Larissa's legs with a special potion wrapped in a tight bandage, and shortly afterwards she was able to walk again. Larissa also told me about being a tomboy; she used to spend her time playing with the boys and getting up to mischief. She had a bad scar on her leg where she had ripped a chunk of flesh out at the side of her knee on a large nail before sticking the flesh back in the wound where it had grown back. I told them about my mum and dad and about the shop we had and the pub where we now lived. I told them that my dad had been a prisoner of war after his plane had been shot down, how he had been in a German prisoner of war camp in Kleipeda in Lithuania, and how he had nearly died on a forced march through Poland. Larissa's father had been a partisan and was one of the first fighters into Berlin, and his name was on the Reistag wall. Eventually, it was time to leave, but I felt enriched by the afternoon getting to know her mum. I left with Larissa, after a big kiss and cuddle from Maria, and we walked back to the bus stop, Laura promising to see me on the Sunday evening.

CHAPTER 25
A HERD OF ELEPHANTS

The following weekend, we had the British Ambassador to the Soviet Union visiting our community, along with around a dozen news writers and photographers. Arriving on the Friday, we held a party in the Spinners Arms to welcome them to site. On the Saturday, we arranged to play them at football, the match taking place at the Locomotive Stadium, not far from the railway station and only five minutes walk from Larissa's house.

I was playing my usual Right Back position and had already crippled my quota for the day when somebody gave me the ball. I set off on a mazy run the full length of the field, only to finish up hitting my shot over the bar. The temperature was around 35°C, but more than that, the humidity was – difficult to explain really – just bloody humid! It was like running in liquid molasses – whatever that is. Anyway, I'm led to believe that it's sticky – I know that from the joke: *'A tanker full of molasses overturned today. Police asked motorists to stick to the inside lane.'* So, after the almost world-beating run, I simply couldn't breathe and had to be helped off the pitch. I say helped but I was dragged off and not screaming. Carefully I was left draped over a wooden bench, where eventually I managed to throw up.

Well, the general consensus was that I wasn't looking after myself properly and I should start to take more care. "I'm getting enough fluids," I countered in my defence. "Maybe," I thought, "the *Samogonka*, peppered vodka and pure spirit was starting to have an effect." Speaking of peppered, our team got slaughtered about 5-1. Mind you come the evening down in the Spinners we got even. Our team battered theirs in the 'boat race' drinking contest.

The following day, we formed a joint team that played a special Mogilev town team in the main stadium in front of a crowd of about 2,000 people. With just a shade of good fortune we won the game 1-0, one of the journalists scoring a blinder in the last five minutes. After the match, we were all presented with special commemorative trophies before going back to the pub for a drink and a sing-song.

With around two weeks to go before D-Day, Larissa arrived one evening to say that she had called at the Registry Office or *Dom Stchastia* (House of Happiness) in Mogilev, where they had agreed Saturday, 31st July at 3pm for the wedding, but only providing that we could secure authorisation from the local authorities at the Town Hall, or *Dom Sovietov*, as it was known locally.

The following morning, I informed Malcolm of the proposed date for the wedding. "Let Grant know," he said, "We'll have to find you fresh digs." "God, I'd never given it a thought." I sat on the edge of his desk and scratched my head. "Well, once you're married you can't be sleeping in a single bed, with Parker as a flatmate, can you?" "No, I suppose not." "Well, tell Grant to get it sorted." Malcolm always had this way of making things sound easy. "What about a stag night?" He dropped another time bomb. "It can only be this weekend, Friday night?" My mind was doing cartwheels now. "Friday night sounds good." Malcolm agreed. "Better tell the lads, hadn't you?" "Wilco, boss." I set off to inform the guys. I turned back. "Oh, boss, any chance of a honeymoon?" I gave him the full puppy eyes and droopy gob. "Alan, don't worry, you take Monday off." He started to chuckle. "Malcolm, you're too kind." "Go on, bugger off before I change my mind." I left.

Grant confirmed the following Tuesday for my move to a new flat. "Next flight of stairs on the fourth floor. It's being vacated by a family going home on the Monday." "You'd better arrange for Pickfords then" I suggested. "We'll borrow a wheelbarrow from the Kombinat," Grant countered. "One suitcase, a stereo, some records, and a pouffe full of dirty socks, it can't be that difficult, can it? By the way, how are you fixed for lads' night this Friday?" "With you lot? Not a chance." He looked terrified. "I'll bring Sveta round for a drink after your wedding." We shook on it.

I made my call home the following evening and told mum about the proposed date for the wedding. She had another little sob before explaining that Peter and Aileen were collecting the wedding dress that weekend, before returning to Mogilev next Monday. "Perfect timing," I told her. She said that they would all be with me in spirit and to give Larissa an extra kiss from them, along with her parents. She also made me promise to phone home on the Sunday after the wedding, along with Larissa. Again, I promised before we were cut off. "Finish. Finish," the operator cut in.

Friday night and the party is in full swing. There's a flat full of people, including Greesha, who walked across and is having a great time showing the gang the finer arts of Russian vodka drinking. Oh, and he's already won the Mogilev All-in Arm Wrestling Championships 1971.

It's a beautiful summer evening so I'm out on the balcony with George, who I have just asked to be my Best Man. We're shaking on it; that special shake where you grab one another's arm just below the elbow and squeeze. I think it must make the agreement or arrangement that bit more special. "Just one thing, Alan," George looked a little puzzled, "why me?" "That's a bloody good question," I thought. I couldn't say it was because Steve was back in the UK on leave. Anyway, Steve was not really the Best Man type. George, on the other hand, was – well, George. He was the rock in a group of madmen; great fun and a terrific sense of humour but seemingly more grounded and steady, the sort of guy you would go to war with. "Because I think you are the Best Man," I assured him. He gave me a hug. "Don't get me going," I said in conclusion.

I'm drinking my umpteenth tall glass of Screwdriver, without the orange. The orange is great going down but after a couple of gallons of the stuff, you suffer with tremendous indigestion – well, at least I do. I think there's a bit of skulduggery going on as well, because everybody seems too keen on getting my drinks and I'm starting to get some unusual after-tastes in my mouth, some very hot flushes working their way up from my stomach. Not to worry, I feel sensational. "George, before I forget, Larissa would like Vera to be her Best Woman, or whatever they are." " She should be thrilled to bits. Anyway, she will probably have asked her already tonight." George put his hand on my shoulder. "I don't see how; Larissa's at home tonight," I assured him. "No, they're having a party round at Deano's flat." He gave me a playful push. He may have pushed Dr Jekyll but, believe me, Mr Hyde was out of the traps in a flash and he pushed George back, hard. I turned and threw my drink, glass as well, down into the garden below. I had this sudden pain between my temples.

You could say 'I was found but now I was lost', and I drove my way through the bodies in the flat. I was temporarily halted by Greesha, who must have seen the madness in my eyes. Anyway, he picked me up bodily and hoisted me over his head and pressed me up to the ceiling, just like a sack of feathers, up and down about four or five times, while everybody cheered. Eventually he set me down, right way up. I marched towards the kitchen. George was coming the other way, holding two glasses of the evil potion. He held one out to me. Without saying a word I punched him on the chin with my fist, knocking him off his feet. It was a miracle. He sat on the floor, still holding out the two glasses. "I didn't spill a drop," he exclaimed, checking the floor around him.

Heading steadily downstairs and along the flats I turned into the last entrance and up to the third floor. There was music and girls' laughter coming from Deano's flat. I hammered on the door and heard some shouting. I started to kick the door. Vera opened the door slightly, "Alan, what do you want?" she said, softly. "Where's Larissa?" I shouted back, and started to push the door open. "No, no, Alan." Some of the other girls pushed back. I kicked at the door, "Where's Larissa!?" Deano pushed past the girls and opened the door. "What are you—?" I cut him off short pulling him out onto the landing. My right foot tore deep into his chest propelling him down the flight of stairs. The door behind me slammed closed and I heard screaming, "He's gone mad. Alan's gone mad." I hammered on the door again before turning and walking back downstairs. "What are you doing?" Deano asked, wiping his face and checking his limbs. I walked past him without replying and marched back out of the flats. As I emerged, I could see blokes spilling out of my entrance and fights kicking off, people running in all directions. I spotted George, and made a beeline. Before I got there, he disappeared into the men's toilets, so I ran in. Things got very sketchy now, because the next thing I remember was a smack in the gob, ending up lying on the concrete floor with George on top of me. He grabbed my hair and drove my head into the concrete. Needless to say, I blacked out.

I woke up around dawn, with my clothes piled on the floor at the side of my bed. "Perfect," I thought, as the stench of puke hit my nostrils. I had thrown up all over the clothes. My head! What was wrong with my head? I touched the back of my head with my fingers – no blood, at least I couldn't feel any, but it was bloody sore. It had something to do with Larissa, but just what had happened? I started to remember the fighting, when suddenly my stomach kicked back.

The next time I woke up, I was looking at a familiar face, with thick black eyebrows. "Alan. Alan." It was Malcolm, shaking me. "Alan!" "For fuck sake, I can hear you." Obviously I didn't say it, or at least I hope I didn't. "Malcolm, good morning." I sat up in bed. "Alan, you'd better get up and have a shower," he said calmly. "You have a lot of sorting out to do," he nodded, knowingly. "Shit, yes," I agreed. "Sorry about the mess." I indicated to the sick-splattered clothing on the floor. "It's the last time I'll put you to bed," he added, opening the balcony doors fully and walking through onto the balcony. "Quick" I thought, "into the shower," as I ran for it. "Bollocks, he's going to sack me. I hope I didn't punch him." I had a strange recollection of seeing him in the public toilets downstairs.

I started to scream for the water to warm up, giving it every swear word I knew, including Russian. I gave up and jumped in cold, rubbing at myself like a maniac, dropping the soap and kicking at it like a Welsh fly half. "Bastard!" "What?" I heard Malcolm shout. "Nothing Malcolm it's the soap. I dropped the soap." I heard the door go and some conversation. I grabbed a towel and started to rub furiously, before wrapping it round me and brushing my teeth. Why is it only once you've showered, that you realise that you have been run over by a herd of elephants. Knives started to bite into every nook and cranny as I tried to tiptoe back into my flat. "Good morning." I could just make out George under the crazy hair, burst lip and black eye. "How are you this morning?" he asked. "Great," I coughed, trying to hold onto my towel. "Erm, Malcolm saved your life last night." Malcolm took over. "I had to drag him off you; he was slamming your head into the toilet floor." Malcolm pointed at my head. "Ah, I was sure that I had seen you last night." Malcolm cut off the small talk "Listen," he now looked stern, "there was a lot went on last night and we've had complaints, but I'll sort those out," he pointed to himself. "Your problem," now he pointed at me, "your problem is Laura." He fought for his words. "If you really want a wedding, you had better go and make the peace – if that's possible." Now George piped up, "She's over at her brother's. I have just been across and she wouldn't let me in." His voice was desperate. "How's Deano?" I asked. "Don't worry about Deano," Malcolm assured me, "get dressed and go and save your marriage; if you want to get married that is." "Thanks Malcolm, I'm going now." "And?" "And I'm sorry about last night." "Go on, piss off." He grabbed George's arm and they left me to it.

I knocked gently on the door and Alla eventually opened it. She smiled, while shaking her head, "Oy, oy, oy." She stared at me with sensitive eyes. "What is he doing here!?" Larissa shouted from the living room. "He's a maniac, just a drunken maniac!" I stuck my head round the door and looked at her, my eyes appealing for some compassion. *"Durak. Durak,"* she repeated. "What the hell were you doing?" She pointed at me, "Look at your face. Are you mad?" I stood there with my head bowed, I didn't have an answer, I didn't have an excuse, I didn't have anything. I felt like stripping bare, that was all I had, and even that wasn't much. "Just look at him," she pointed towards the kitchen, "Greesha," she ordered, "Greesha, come out here!" Greesha's battered face emerged round the kitchen door. I mean battered, cut to shreds, with a big black, nasty-looking circular scar over his right eye. He looked at my cuts and bruises and started to laugh. I couldn't hold back and burst into laughter. "Oh, typical! Two *Duraky*!" Larissa, exasperated, walked into the kitchen with Alla. Greesha walked towards me and we embraced in the centre of the lounge. This was more than a hug; it had meaning, a man thing. *"Brat,"* (brother) he whispered in my ear. *"Brat,"* I whispered back. We embraced even stronger, eventually slapping one another's back in a mark of submission. I knew instantly that I was now family and, more than that, I had a friend for life.

While Greesha set a table for breakfast and Alla cooked the ham and eggs, I apologised to Larissa, trying to explain about my drinks being mixed and being upset and shocked at the news of her being in the flats. I had to take several lectures before we could embrace and kiss some of the hurt away. We sat down over breakfast and hairs of the dog, and discussed what had happened to Greesha. He had followed me downstairs, where somebody had stubbed a big cigar out just above his eye. He had hit the guy just once, the bloke doing a pirouette before collapsing unconscious in the gardens.

After returning home he had tried to go to work on his motorbike. Because he was drunk, he had set off across the airfield and then over some rough waste-ground where he had fallen off, losing his shoe. The bike wouldn't restart and he finished up pushing it all the way home. We moved from the table and slouched into the comfy chairs, yawning in unison. "Typical." Larissa looked at us both, before picking up a cushion and battering me with it. "Home," she pointed, "we need to tidy up."

Larissa pulled me across the void between the blocks of flats, but at least she was holding my hand and I took comfort from that. I knew that she was angry but we were together. In a fit of drunken madness, I had done my absolute idiotic best to wreck things and yet she was still holding my hand, making things better, and now she was going to enter a bomb zone.

I opened the door to unveil the wreckage and even I was stunned. "What a tip," I said. She didn't disagree, just started clearing, white-faced, grudgingly, but doing it, nevertheless. I tried to hold her but she pushed me away, *"Durak,"* barely audible. I tried to help but merely seemed to follow her round the flat like a naughty puppy looking for a pat on the head as proof of forgiveness. None came. When the flat was eventually repaired, Laura said she was going home. I walked with her to the bus stop. "Will you come back tonight and stay over?" I asked her. "No," she answered, definitely. "I will see you tomorrow." She suggested I apologise to Deano and everybody else that had been caught up in the riot. She looked appealingly into my eyes. "We are supposed to be getting married and you are running round and kicking people." She shook her head. "Make things right and maybe we will get married. Okay?" I grabbed her and held her close. "I love you." I spoke gently, holding her eyes in mine. "We'll see." She turned and climbed on the bus. I walked back to the flat sheepishly, deep in thought. "Better go and apologise." I started right away.

CHAPTER 26
BULLDOZERS & TRACTORS

On the Tuesday evening, Peter called round at the flat. Just arriving back from leave and as promised he was carrying Larissa's wedding dress. I, of course, wasn't allowed to see it, so it was handed straight to Larissa to take home. She was in tears and she hadn't even seen the thing. "How am I going to thank them?" she asked, tears splashing on the cardboard box. "Easy," I said, "we're going to phone home on Sunday 1st August, then you can thank them for the dress, say, 'Hello, mum and dad' and wish them both happy birthday." "What, both of them on the same day?" "Yes, both on the day after our wedding; unusual, isn't it?"

I met Larissa outside the Dnieper on the Wednesday morning and we walked round to the *Dom Sovietov*. This was a real town hall with a huge ten-storey austere exterior and enormous heavy wooden doors that squeaked when they were opened. "Bloody unforgiving if you get your thumb caught in one of these buggers!" Larissa didn't understand.

The girl stood behind the reception desk told us to sit down. "We haven't said who we want to see yet," Larissa whispered in my ear. We sat for about five minutes before the girl barked out something in Russian, and Larissa jumped up and walked to the desk. "We're upstairs." The sound of our shoes on the marble floor, echoed off the high ceilings.

This place was old and cold. We walked up a flight of marble steps, round on a landing and onto the second flight of stairs. This time, we had a dark red carpet, which continued onto the third floor corridor. "Class," Larissa again whispered. A door squeaked open, "Haunted house class," I confirmed. We arrived at another desk. This time an older woman greeted us in the usual official way, "What?" Larissa took out a piece of paper from her handbag and handed it to the woman, who gave us both a good down her nose stare. "Sit down." She pointed to a line of four wooden chairs. The place was deathly, "a cross," I thought, "between a humongous library and a morgue."

After about twenty minutes, the old woman walked across and asked us to follow her along the corridor to the last pair of double doors. She turned the large brass door knob and pushed the door open. We walked through into this huge room with a beautiful old carpet and heavy red curtains trimmed with gold, held back with gold tassels. There was a beautiful chandelier above an enormous dark wooden desk, and on the wall behind the desk was a big portrait of Lenin. Behind the desk sat a middle-aged woman. She stood up as we approached.

The woman was only small but very smart in her dark grey suit and open-necked white blouse. "Sit down." Her smile was enhanced by the brightest red lipstick that lit up in the shafts of sunshine pouring into the room. "Now, how can we help you?" She looked at Larissa. We sat down and held hands, both shaking nervously. "We would like permission to get married this Saturday 31st July." Larissa held her gaze. "What? This Saturday? Why so soon?" The official sat back in her chair looking astounded. "Alan is an English specialist working at the Kombinat and we need to get married before I am sent to work in Saratov for two years." "And when do you go to Saratov," she asked. "On Sunday 1st August," Larissa appealed with her eyes. The woman sat thinking for an age.

She looked down at some papers on her desk and she looked long and hard at Larissa before her eyes caught mine. I hadn't opened my mouth but my eyes frantically appealed to her. We squoze one another's hands and looked at each other before she spoke. She smiled a warm understanding smile. "It will be," she announced, simply. Larissa quickly questioned her, "We can get married?" "Yes, you can get married." She stood up and looked at us both. "Wait back at the desk for the papers," she concluded. "Thank you. Thank you," we both said. She nodded her head before we turned and left.

I closed the door with a thud and we embraced in the corridor, letting out a loud squeal. The door opened and the woman looked at us mid-kiss. She smiled knowingly and held out her hand, pointing towards the desk. She walked in front of us and spoke to the woman behind the desk, while we sat down, gripping tightly with our hands. "Goodbye and good luck," she said quietly, before returning to her office.

We collected the documents before hurrying downstairs and out onto the main square where we broke into a skip, like young children who had just broken up for summer holidays. It was like being set free; we were getting married. I wanted to shout out loud that this girl, who was holding my hand, was going to be my wife. I didn't; content that we knew.

We walked down the block and I turned into the third entrance. "Where are you going?" Larissa asked. "Surprise," I told her, pulling her inside and up the steps, stopping at the fourth landing. I took a key from my pocket and opened the door. Larissa stood and stared at me. I bent down and swept her off her feet. "What are you doing?" she pleaded. "Just in case I forget later," I said softly, walking into the flat. I nudged the bedroom door handle open with my elbow, pushed the door open with my foot, entered and laid her gently on the bed. "Your new bed," I told her, before sitting down and kissing her. I sat up and started to unbutton her blouse. "No, no, no." She grabbed my hand. "Not until we are married." "What?" My eyes opened wide and my jaw fell open. Larissa smiled. "Not until Saturday night. I promised my mother, anyway I want to see our flat." She skipped off into the kitchen. "Down boy," I ordered the engine room. "It's just like ours, apart from the washing machine." "Yes." I sounded really interested. She opened the toilet and bathroom doors, "Hmm," before moving onto the lounge. "It's bigger." She walked to the windows, onto the balcony. "There's no bed," I explained, "that's why it looks bigger." "Come on; let's get your stuff round." Larissa set off back to my flat.

I grabbed my case that I had already packed, and Larissa tried to pick up the pouffe, only to drop it again. "What's in here?" she asked. "Er, socks." I knew that I was going to be embarrassed; in fact, I knew I was going to get my arse kicked. "Socks and, erm, underpants; well, woolly thermals, you know, long johns." I tried to show her, pulling up an invisible pair. She rolled the pouffe over and started to undo the lacing. "Shit, now I'm in trouble." After about fifteen pairs of stinky socks, came a pair of admiralty weight long johns, which she held up against herself. "Long johns?" I nodded in agreement. She wasn't amused and stuffed the dirty clobber back into the pouffe. "You're washing these." She kicked the pouffe. "Yes," I nodded sheepishly. She gathered my records together in a bag and set off with those.

About an hour later, we were done and I returned my old flat key to Grant, in the office, before going back to Larissa in our new home. We chatted about the arrangements for the Saturday, over a coffee. Greesha had agreed to host the wedding reception, having more room in his flat; it also made sense, with the close proximity to our flat, which would make it easier for my workmates and their wives. We still couldn't believe that things had been arranged so quickly, but what the heck now, we were just so happy that we had everything to look forward to.

"What will we do when the work finishes?" Larissa gave me that searching look. "We will go back home to England,"

I said matter-of-fact-like. "To England? Why can't we live here?" "Now, there's a question," I thought to myself, trying not to look perplexed. "How could I work here?" Surely she understands that. "Why not? You can speak Russian, so you can get a job at the Lafsan." "It would be too difficult. Anyway, you'll enjoy England, and my mum and dad will love you to bits." I was trying too hard. "I'll think about it, but my mum and dad won't be very happy." Aha, Laura is playing the same family game. "I thought you knew we would be going back home?" "Well, I didn't." "We will talk about it again." "Hmm," was her final word. "Hmm," was mine, but I didn't say it. I take that back. Her final word was a big sloppy kiss, pinning me down on the sofa. She stopped kissing me, obviously feeling my reaction, and gave me one of her mischievous smiles, tinged with a touch of guilt. "Sorry, am I—?" I cut her off. "Yes, you bloody well are."

It soon disintegrated into one of those bulldozer tractor moments, just like children. I should know; as kids, I always finished up as a bulldozer. Sounds good, doesn't it, big and strong? But bulldozers can only push; tractors, on the other hand, can go over the top of things as well as being able to push. Carolyn, my older sister, was bigger than me and somehow always chose to be the tractor. "Strange," I always thought. No wonder mum and dad wondered why I was growing up looking like a bruised banana. But that was then and this is now, my turn to be the tractor; all elbows and knees, and before long, Larissa was mashed into the carpet....not! Hamer was again tractored and bulldozed to pulp. Things weren't like that as a kid, when I was Finger, Thumb or Icky champion; well, our team was. Now, that's a game. Can you think of another game where the sole purpose is to break the opposition's backs? There are some brilliant minds in Bolton. Oh, yes, and one or two badly-deformed backs.

The best thing about losing is that you are the one that has to be kissed better and nursed back to full health. I only wish the nursing could be more comprehensive, but we were under instruction; or at least she was. As we walked down to the bus stop; Larissa pointed to the Spinners Arms. "I will be able to go in there next week," she started giggling. "Yes, you will, and we can go into the sin bin." "What is the sin bin?" "I'll show you next week." I winked and she nipped me again. After her bus had rounded the corner, I turned and did my Popeye walk sound effects as well, all the way home. Just two more days. Two days!

CHAPTER 27
A WEDDING TO REMEMBER?

Saturday 31st of July, I woke up late. Sorry, I woke up early but I got up late, lying in bed thinking about, well, just about everything, Larissa, her family, my family at home, thinking about the day ahead, and the ceremony. What do I say? Actually, what are they going to ask me? Do I say, *"Da,"* or *"Ya budu,"* (Yes, or I will). I could relax and watch at my sister's wedding but that seemed complicated and they were speaking English. I thought back to the day we met and the things that had happened since, as a tune runs incessantly through my head. It's *'The Long and Winding Road'* by the Beatles. It's strange how music comes into my head and repeats over and over and again. Anyway, I love this song, even though it has a habit of making me feel sad. Somehow the lyrics allow you to make up your own ending, and I certainly wasn't going to be sad today. "Stop bloody daydreaming, get up and get ready!"

"Best Man calling," George shouted from the hall. "Come in, pal." I stood checking my suit. "Bloody hell, it smells like an Old Spice convention in here." His substantial nose stuck around the door. "If it does, it's you. I use the other stuff, you know the green muck." "Ah, yes," George broke in. "Yes, that green muck you splash all over, Larissa likes it, doesn't she?" "What?" "That green sh…." " Just think if Ray had been using it, she might have been marrying him." "What!?"

George had gone into the kitchen. "Shall I do a pot of tea?" He shouted again. "Feel free," I confirmed, pulling up my strides.

George reappeared with a tray containing a pot of tea and two cups. "Don't bloody hit me this time." He feigned a duck as he passed me. "Ha, ha, very good. Anyway, I'm saving it for later when you're doing the speeches; if you say the wrong thing, that is." "I can say anything I want in English. They won't know, will they?" "No, but I will and I can translate." George thought for a while. "Bastard." He was always very articulate. "Nice suit." George felt the lapels. "It should be, it cost a fortune," I said. "It's an Aults special, an Odermark, made in Austria." "Where's Aults?" "What? Where's Aults? Are you kidding? The best gent's outfitters in the north and you don't know where it is?" George thought for a moment. "No," he replied softy. "Don't tell me, it's down the lane, over the Jiglin Bridge, past granny's house, on the left." Now he was being silly. "Not far off actually, it's on the right." "That's if you're coming from town," he countered, "I was coming from the station." "Correct." I patted him on the shoulder. "Are you ready?" he asked. "Yes, are the taxis here?" "I'll go and have a look." George disappeared down the stairs.

After about fifteen minutes, George came back with Vera. "Are we ready?" "Ready and waiting." I walked onto the landing and closed the door. "Key." I tapped my pocket. "Ring!" George shouted. "It's here." I took it out of my pocket and gave it to George. "Do I keep it?" he asked. "How the hell do I know?" A thought hit me. "Vera, who has the ring, me or George?" "I don't know. Oh, Alan," she looked at me with big brown eyes, "how beautiful you are." She kissed me on both cheeks. "Oh, you smell beautiful too," she continued. "Green shit," George informed her. "Green sheet?" Vera tried to copy. "No, no, don't worry Vera, he's joking. I'll hit him later." I clenched my fist and showed her what would happen. "Alan, your suit is beautiful. What colour is it?" "Plum." "What colour?" "Plum." I didn't have a clue what it was in

Russian. "Anyway Vera, you're the one that looks beautiful." She was wearing a tight-fitting white dress, with white high heels. Not that it really mattered with Vera, she could have worn a clapped out pair of curtains she would still have got wolf whistles. George was wearing a smart dark grey suit. I looked him up and down. "You look like you're going to a bloody funeral." His reply was short and to the point, and brought a slap from Vera. "Come on kids, off we go." We set of downstairs and into a lovely warm summer's day, with quite a strong wind blowing. The sort of day when you realise you should have had your hair cut. At the end of the block, two taxis waited. I felt a little disappointed that nobody was waving me off. Hopefully, some of them would get to town later.

Twenty minutes later, we arrived at Larissa's. I asked Vera to go into the house and see if she was ready. "I thought it was unlucky to see the wedding dress?" I asked George. "I think so, in England anyway." "Am I supposed to close my eyes, or something?" George climbed out of the taxi. "Come on, they want us to go in." He shut the taxi door.

We walked into the garden that was full of people I didn't know. Just then mum appeared through the crowd and gave me a big hug. She stood me upright at arm's length, said something nondescript, and disappeared back into the house. As I gazed through the fence at group of people gathering around the taxis mum came back. She was holding a big, white lace bow, which she proceeded to pin onto my lapel with a safety pin. *"Prekrasno,"* (Beautiful) she said, starting to cry. "Mama, what is it?" I asked courteously. "Its tradition," she sobbed, "from the country." "Mmm, lovely." George pinched my cheek. "Bog off, it's tradition," I said. Just as I said it, everything went quiet and George gave me a nudge.

Larissa was stood on the porch in her wedding dress. My mind flashed back to that first glimpse of her standing in the doorway of the School of Foreign Languages. Everybody around me said exactly what I was thinking. Her beauty was breathtaking, her dress and veil were stunning, and her pride shone like a beacon. Her father stood at her side, eyes filling. As she made her way down the steps, two little children, a boy and a girl, held the back of her lace train. I just wished my parents could be here to see her.

I opened the taxi door for Larissa and she climbed in, the children carefully folding her train before handing it to her. I walked round the other side and opened the door for the kids to jump in, before I sat in the front seat. George, Vera and Oleg climbed into the other taxi and we tried to set of, waving to family and friends.

The taxi only moved a couple of yards before stopping. A crowd of about fifty people had blocked the road and were stood chanting, *"Gorko. Gorko. Gorko!"* while clapping rhythmically. Larissa wound down the back window and her dad handed her a carrier bag full of sweets. "Here." She passed the toffees to me. "Get out and throw them to the people." "What are they shouting?" I asked her. *"Gorko,"* it means 'bitter'. You have to sweeten our way by giving them sweets. "Why didn't I think?" I said, sarcastically. I climbed out of the taxi and handed out the sweets, stopping before I got back to the car. I unwrapped a toffee and put it into my mouth. "Mmm." I stuck up my thumb, "Sweet." I climbed back in as the crowd moved to the side and allowed us passage.

"How are your mum and dad getting down?" "They're not," she replied. "They're taking a taxi straight to Greesha's." "Why?" "They have to get the food for the reception." "Okay," I thought, "don't ask questions, it must be the Russian way."

We drove into the centre of town, past Lenin Square, and next left was a small park with grass, flowers and silver birch trees. The taxi had difficulty turning into the road, there were people everywhere, hundreds of them. Slowly, the car moved through the crowd and pulled up outside the Registry Office. I jumped out and let the children out before walking round and opening Larissa's door. She climbed out as people jostled for position. "What's going on?" I asked Larissa. "I've never seen anything like it," she replied. We looked for George, Vera and Oleg, and saw Oleg pushing his way through the crowd, laughing. "What the hell's going on?" George looked round the square and started laughing.

We walked straight into a big reception lounge with background music and bouquets of flowers everywhere. Greesha was there, along with Larissa's relatives and lots of my friends. There was a photographer who asked us to pose for photographs, and Ray was dashing about taking a cine film.

Within a couple of minutes, two large sliding doors slid open, revealing the marriage hall, and we were beckoned through by a smart, attractive woman who stood behind a small wooden desk. We walked slowly through and took our positions in front of the desk, George standing on my right and Vera to Larissa's left. The woman smiled and started to recite something but I honestly didn't understand a word. She held out her hand towards me. "Frederick Alan Hamer ..." I immediately saw a look of puzzlement on Larissa's face. I nodded slightly, thinking, "Yes, it's me." "Do you take Larissa Ivanovna Strotskaya to be your lawful wedded wife?" Larissa gave me a gentle nudge. *"Da,"* I replied. *"Koltso?" "Da"* "Ring?" I whispered, turning to George. "Ring?" George fumbled in his pocket and pulled out the ring. I took it and turned, held Larissa's right hand and gently slipped the ring on her third finger, alongside her engagement ring. Then I took a breath. "Larissa Ivanovna Strotskaya, do you take Frederick Alan Hamer to be your lawful wedded husband?" Don't get me wrong but I am actually guessing as to what she said exactly, but I took it to be that. *"Da,"* Larissa replied, before turning to Vera and taking the ring. She held my right hand and placed it on my third finger. We stood holding hands and holding our breath. "On behalf of the Belarussian Soviet Socialist Republic, I now pronounce you husband and wife." After a pause, she smiled. "You may now kiss the bride." Vera lifted Larissa's veil back onto her head and I took hold of her and kissed her gently, while camera bulbs popped behind us. Starting to giggle we turned back to face the official. She said a few words, I think wishing us future happiness, before inviting us to sign the wedding book on the end of the table. We all signed, including George and Vera, before thanking the official and walking back into the reception lounge where we were positioned in front of one wall flanked by flower arrangements.

One of the children presented Larissa with a huge bunch of flowers before another lady came forward with a tray containing glasses of champagne and a box of chocolates. "How's Mrs Hamer?" I asked Larissa, with a mouthful of chockie. "I'm good, Frederick" she started to laugh. I gave her a kiss. "Alan," I insisted. "Alan, you need to dance" George grabbed my arm. "I'll hold your drink." The music had changed to a waltz. We walked into the centre of the room and started to dance, and simultaneously everybody started to laugh. The two children were still hanging onto the back of Larissa's dress. One of the women took hold of their hands and took them to one side. "A waltz," Larissa said, "One, two, together." I carried on with the Hamer shuffle. Fortunately, others had taken the floor.

Twenty-three I may have been but I was still a kid. I knew this because I felt giddy, like a boy again, on my first Christmas morning. The only difference was I now felt secure, safe that this girl of nineteen would protect me, would be at my side and keep me safe. As the dance finished, the kissing began, everybody congratulating us and saying how beautiful Larissa was. "She's mine." I pulled her towards me, my arm around her waist.

We walked back out into the sunshine and into the crowd, which had grown even bigger. It looked as if half the population of Mogilev was here. We found a spot on the grass where the photographer could take some photos. "They want to see us kiss," Larissa whispered in my ear. She didn't need to ask twice and I put my arms around her and gave her a long, passionate kiss that was greeted with a round of applause. "I think it's the dress," she said, as we looked at one another. "I think it's the beauty in it," I confirmed.

Larissa, Vera, George and I climbed back into the taxi and we slowly manoeuvred our way through the applauding sea of well wishers. *"Ploshad Lenina,"* Larissa told the driver, and we turned right and back to Lenin square. I didn't need to ask. "It's custom to thank the state," Larissa explained. "We will only be ten minutes." We walked to the foot of Lenin's statue and Larissa carefully placed her bouquet of flowers on the top step, before stepping back and holding my hand. The more I looked up at Lenin, the more he reminded me of my grandfather; taking away the beard, of course. He looked a kind man. "Fred," I said, pointing up, "Fred Lenin." Larissa wasn't amused. "Vladimir Ilich Lenin," she corrected me. "He looks like my grandpa, so I'll call him 'Fred.'" "You are Fred." Larissa took my arm and George and Vera started laughing. "Fred," they pointed at me. "Alan." I had the last word.

Fifteen minutes later, we pulled up at Greesha's flat to a welcoming party waiting outside. Music was coming from a neighbour's balcony. Larissa's mum and dad emerged from the flat, her mum holding a tray covered with a white linen cloth on which was a loaf of brown bread, a pot containing salt, and two glasses of vodka. Larissa's father spoke. "The core of your life together, bread, salt and drink. Be happy together. Love one another and never forget your family and your homeland." We sprinkled some salt on chunks of bread, drank the vodka and ate the bread. We were then allowed into the reception and allowed to give mum and dad a kiss and a cuddle.

Greesha's flat was for two people, so to walk into his living room and find a banquet set up for about thirty people was, well, extraordinary. A top table was set up in front of the window, with three legs coming off it. There must have been a dozen dinner tables, covered in white linen cloths, plates, cutlery and mountains of food, including two pigs, six chickens, and there could even have been a rabbit stew as well as a field-full of potatoes cooked up in different guises, and a mountain of salad and *smetana*. We walked through to the kitchen, to find Alla, Tamara and Maria slaving away over a hot stove. Next to the fridge was a mountain of booze, both vodka and wine. "Enough," I thought, "to get the Household Cavalry pissed, including the horses." "Sit down. Sit down," Papa Ivan shouted to all the guests. Larissa and I were invited to sit down first, followed by George and Vera, family and friends who grabbed seats willy-nilly.

Dad was the first to speak, followed by a toast, followed by a round of, *"Gorko, gorko,"* where I had to throw sweets to everyone, followed by the Best Man's speech, two minutes in English, followed by drinks. I think Vera said a few words, followed by drinks, another round of, *"Gorko,"* followed by a toast before I stood up to make a speech and realised I was already drunk. I thanked everybody, from Larissa's mum to Procol Harem; they all got a mention. I told them all how much I loved Larissa and, of course, that deserved a drink, so we had another one. We then had a quick, *"Gorko,"* before mum came in with a big pan full of fried eggs. She stood in the middle of the room and asked me to pay for an egg. I pulled out a ten ruble note and put it on the table. Maria picked up the note, spat on one side and stuck the note to her forehead, before displaying it to guests who groaned. "Is that how much you think she is worth?" Larissa whispered in my ear. I again found my wallet and pulled out another twenty rubles and handed them to Maria. This time she spat on the two 10s and stuck them on her shoulders like army epaulettes, before again displaying them to a disappointed crowd. "Bollocks," I thought, "give her the lot," as I emptied my wallet of about one hundred and twenty rubles and held it out for her. She took the money and thrust it into the air to mass applause. Maria then deposited an egg on each plate, which we ate before having another glass of vodka.

After the mass queue for the toilet, most people moved outside to the dance, music blasting from a balcony stereo. We were doing very nicely, when I got the call from Greesha. "Alan, I have a very important man you must meet. He is a big boss from the Kombinat." He pointed to the next entrance.

"Alan, no drinking," Larissa insisted, before releasing me into Greesha's care. "No, I won't. I'm drunk already," I assured her, shaking my head.

The door was opened and a big, middle-aged man invited us into his living room. "Uri, Alan. Alan, Uri, my manager from work." We shook hands and sat down at a large dining table laid out with some food and a bottle of vodka already opened. Uri poured the vodka into three large glasses and he toasted Larissa and myself on our marriage.

I told him that I worked with Tchaikovsky in Staple Fibre and with Eershov and Kondratov in Filament Yarn. He said he knew them very well, while pouring out a bottle of something strange. "What is this one?" I asked, staring at the label. "Ah, this is very special liquor," he assured me. "No, I can't drink any more." I put my hand over the glass. "Alan, you must drink this one and then we will leave. It will make your stomach feel very good." Greesha started to rub his stomach. Uri was telling me about women who wanted to take control and how you must always agree, but men must be men. I picked up the glass, *"Ras, dva, tree, Poechaly,"* and slotted the full glass of gook in one. It tasted like foul poisonous glue. I'd never had a glass of Araldite before. Greesha thanked him for his hospitality and we left, stumbling down the stairs.

I couldn't believe it, the dance was still going on and people were going round and round and round. Larissa was dancing with Malcolm and not paying any attention to me at all as I stood on the steps, waiting. All the time, the music played and she went round and round. "My turn." I grabbed Malcolm's arm. "Alan, you're drunk," Larissa barked at me. "C'mon Malc, my turn." Malcolm relented and I quickly grabbed Larissa and started to twirl. "Alan," she stopped, "You've ripped my dress." "Sorry, I must've caught it with my foot." I was stooping over her arm and mumbling, before forcing myself upright and giving her one of those idiotic tell-tale, 'look at me, I'm pissed' smiles. "That's it." She grabbed my arm and led me back into the reception. "No more vodka for Alan," she announced. I sat down, holding up my hands in complete approval. Too much more about the celebrations, I don't remember, other than George slipping something in my glass.

Somehow, I must have wandered off, probably during a ciggy break, and got back to our flat, got in and locked the door behind me. Anyway, I remember waking up on the sofa. There was a loud bang as the door frame flew off and the door crashed open. I vaguely remember Larissa giving me a few choice words before giving up on me.

I woke up at about 4am and stumbled for the bog. On the way back I noticed Larissa sleeping peacefully in bed, so decided to go and disturb her by planting a big noisy kiss on her forehead. "What time is it?" she asked yawning. "Don't know," I replied. "What are you doing?" she asked, rubbing her eyes. "I'm hungry," I said, "I could murder a pan of chips." "Chips, now?" "Yes." She climbed out of bed with an air of resignation. "Chips? I must be going mad!" I walked back to the couch and sat down.

Larissa woke me up, placed a cushion on my thighs and put a plate full of chips on the cushion. She handed me a fork and put the salt, pepper and vinegar on the arm of the couch. "Bread?" she asked. "No thanks, that's great," I confirmed, already stuffing a fork full of chips in. She came through and sat down next to me with a cup of coffee. "Why wouldn't you let me in last night?" Her voice was soft and calm. "Sorry, but I didn't hear you." "You didn't hear me? We were banging for ages." "Sorry, I didn't hear," I repeated. " The lads had to smash the door to get me in." She sounded completely exasperated. "Yes, I can see. I'm sorry." The chips were starting to make me feel better. "Oh, God, I love chips."

I woke up with my head nestled against her stomach, looking along the plane of her legs, towards her knees. Her left arm was draped across my chest. I yawned and put my hand to my forehead. My head was pounding and I didn't like the tune. I slowly climbed off the sofa and walked past the rubble behind the door and on to the loo.

A hot shower and a brush at the peggies made me feel almost human. Larissa had put the kettle on and was showering, while I got dressed. "Well, that was different," I said, as she walked back into the bedroom. "What was different?" She looked, with those expressive eyes. "You were drunk, weren't you?" "It wasn't me; it was Greesha and his boss." She cut me short, "Oh, yes, they forced you to drink, didn't they?" Her eyes again appealed for the truth. "I know," I had to agree. "It wasn't that I drank, it was what I drank, and I honestly don't know what it was, perhaps Greesha knows." "I think you need to apologise to Malcolm," again giving me the stare. "Not again. What did I do this time?" "You looked very angry when we were dancing and you grabbed his arm and pulled him. You were not very nice." "I'll apologise." I held up my hand. "And you'll apologise to me." Now she looked serious. I walked towards her and gave her a big squeeze. "I'm sorry." I looked into her eyes. "And you should be. Now, let's forget it." She had the last word. There are times when you want to say more, times when you need to say more and times when you should get down on your knees and beg. This was a time to take the mild admonishment on the chin, count your blessings and do as you are told.

Larissa finished putting on her make-up, put on a nice cream dress and we walked back over to Greesha's for day two. Cheers greeted us when we arrived, about twenty-or-so revellers, already digging into freshly plated food and certainly not knocking back their first drink of the day. We settled down to a full Russian breakfast, washed down with a lovely cup of tea. "Yes, tea!" I had to be firm. "Why tea, not vodka?" everybody, apart from Larissa, asked. "Tea, coffee, lemonade, Coke, it doesn't matter as long as there's no alcohol in it." People looked at me as though I had gone mad.

The day was a blur really, eat, drink and dance. People seemed to arrive in shifts. We had to go back to the flats to take the phone call home. On the way, we passed a gang of friends walking over to Greesha's. On the way back, we bumped into 'Big Dave' carrying his wife back home – she was completely non compus… "Good day, Dave?" "Great," was his reply. I know of the feeding of the 5,000 and this was a long way short of that, but there was some sort of small miracle happening here. How so few can cater for so many, with so little must be a miracle, and how they manage to keep it up for so long, is another. However they did it, they did it, and we were all the better for it. It was a wedding to remember – I think!

The call home was special, being the first chance my parents had to speak to Larissa, and her to them. Even though she didn't speak a word of English, she did manage to thank them for the dress and wish them 'Happy Birthday'. We left mum in tears and wonderfully happy, as we were. We made a conscious decision to leave early that evening, even though I had the Monday off work. We decided to leave the party in full swing, preferring to spend some time together alone, married – something that we had missed the night before. Yes, tonight, we decided to get naked and dance alone.

I suppose I should say that we lived happily ever after and of course, we did, but there would be one or two noticeable little hiccups; oh, yes, and one massive belch, along the way. We made the most of our Monday honeymoon, barely surfacing from the pleasures of warm, clean linen and a 'Do Not disturb' sign on the patched up door. "Speaking of honeymoons," she said, "Grant's Svetlana has asked me if I fancy a trip to Batumi." "Where is Batumi?" "It's on the Black Sea in Georgia. There are famous Botanical Gardens there." "Sounds nice, when do you want to go?" "Next week, I think." She now looked as if a tentative probe was getting somewhere. "Why not?" I said calmly. "I will probably be working twenty-four-hour shifts, and that won't be any fun." "I'll speak to Sveta and let you know." She gave me a special kiss. "Good grief," I thought, "this is going to be expensive."

CHAPTER 28
CHICHEVICHY

Larissa and Svetlana arranged their visit to Batumi, leaving Mogilev by train the following Wednesday. Before that, we obviously had to invite the family round for Sunday dinner and christen the new flat. For once, we were going to eat English style.

They all came round, mum, dad, Greesha, Alla, Oleg, Tamara and Lyonya, Larissa's aunt and uncle plus Vera, Steve and George. Both grandmas lived too far out to make it. Mum headed straight for the kitchen to check on the progress and generally have a good nosy. We were preparing smoked salmon and prawns served with a dressed salad. This was to be followed by a full Sunday lunch of roast chicken and a ham joint, with roasted potatoes, green beans, carrot and turnip and Big Al's special stuffing, with gravy. For afters, we had Black Forest Gateau and/or Dundee Cake, plus fresh fruit salad and double cream. Last, but not least, was the cheese and crackers, the centrepiece being a large wedge of Stilton that had cost a fortune.

As I walked into the kitchen, mum was chucking the Stilton into the bin. "Mum, what are you doing?" "It's bad. Look at it. It'll make you ill." She cringed as she pointed at the bin. I bent down and retrieved the delicacy. She slapped me on the back, hard. *"Durak,* look at it!" She snatched it from my hand. "Look!" She held the cheese right in front of my eyes "it will make you ill." She removed the lid from the bin and propelled it in with feeling. Larissa came into the kitchen. "What's all this shouting about?" Both mum and I tried to get our case before the judge first. Mum won. "He was trying to serve poisonous cheese." "Which cheese?" Larissa butted in. "The special Stilton," I pointed to the bin. "Mum, that's how you buy it. It's supposed to be like that," she tried to explain. "No, no, no. It's mouldy, bluey green, it's bad." I dropped my hands onto my thighs as a sign of resignation and started to laugh. Mum gave me another whack before joining in the laughter. We spread our arms and gave one another a hug, still in fits of laughter. "Come on, children." Larissa tried to move us out of the kitchen. "Get from under my feet." She could move me but wasn't moving mum. "Alan, go and show the lads how to work the stereo, they want to put some Russian music on." "Okay boss, leave it to me." "Drinks anyone? Ah, drinks everyone." It was Tuborg all round.

Tamara was mum's younger sister and to be honest didn't look like Maria at all, being very slim, even stick-like, and she was taller. Lyonya was slightly shorter than Tamara but a lot stockier with that typical male weathered look, and when he smiled, which was often, he displayed several bright, gold-capped teeth.

The whole family seemed warm-hearted, easy-going and up for a good time; the guys always up for a good drink. I decided the time was appropriate to try a glass of malt whisky, you know, the sort that you smell, sip and savour. Well, this was going to get the Russian treatment – lift and neck. I went back into the kitchen to grab a bottle of lemonade; just in time to see mum chopping up the spring onions. It's easy. Place the spring onions on a block, take a sharp knife and cut away the green stems from the white onion bulbs. Now, this is the good bit, the Russian bit. Scrape the onion heads into a bin alongside the finest Stilton cheese, close the lid and chop up the green onion stems into tiny pieces and sprinkle liberally over smoked salmon, prawns and salad. "What? Am I going balmy?" "What now?" Larissa turned from the cooker. "Just look in the bin," I said quietly. *"Luk"* (onions). "No, you look, we eat those." "No," mum joined in. "All the taste is in the green shoots," Larissa assured me. I rolled my eyes, "Okay!" Before going back and checking that everybody had a drink, I had one last snipe, "I'm carving the meat, mum will throw it in the bin and serve the bones." Mum chased me with a knife. She loved me to death.

The meal turned out fine, being a mixture of English Sunday lunch meets Russian dig-in and suit yourself buffet. All this interspersed with toasts and choruses of Moscow Nights, which we changed to Mogilev Nights, *'Mogilevskie Vechera',* and my all time favourite, Black Eyes, *'Ochi Chornie'*. I had my own words, picked up from the Russian guys at work. They were always guaranteed a laugh. They got me another hefty slap from mum.

As at all parties, dad got drunk and was first to fall asleep on the couch sending Z's up like there was no tomorrow. Mum got me in a bear hug and refused to let go, saying that I was her sunshine, her beauty. She smothered me in kisses. I made a joke about it, apologising for the cheese and onions, which just made her cuddle me more.

Larissa said after the party, that her mum loved me more than she did her, which I simply waved away. She put her arms round my neck. "She loves you so much because she knows how much you love her daughter." We kissed tenderly at the end of a different and very enjoyable day.

For some time the hard-core fishing guys had been planning to visit the biggest lake in the area, called *Chichevichy*. Because it was such a big lake and about 60 miles away on the *Bobruisk* road, we decided to spend a weekend camping there. So I persuaded the lads, Larissa being in Batumi, that there was no time like the present. I went home and explained to Larissa. "Why not?" She was in full agreement. When the cat's away the lads are out acting like boy scouts – well these lads are anyway.

On the Friday night, Larissa phoned to say that they had arrived in Batumi the day before. They had spent all day walking round the famous botanical gardens. However, there was something freakish in the weather down there and it rains most days, so were going to take a train to Suhumi, where supposedly it never rains. Well, that's girls for you. Set off with the best intentions, botanical gardens and all that, and jack it in within a day to go and lie on a beach in the sunshine. "Do you want me to bring you anything back?" Larissa asked before hanging up. "No....well, maybe a wave in a bottle," I said. "What?" "No, it's okay *Zaika*, just enjoy yourself and look after one another."

So, Saturday morning at the crack of dawn, the four intrepid campers were off. The minibus took us out about an hour and a half drive to the south-west. We crossed the edge of the lake where it was fed by the river Drut, and carried on for another five minutes, before turning left on a rough, sandy track. We bounced along for about ten minutes or so, cutting through a forest of huge pine trees. There was a grass clearing of about 30 square yards at the side of the lake where there was a small drop off to a clear, sandy beach.

We quickly unloaded all the tackle and arranged for someone to collect us about 5pm on the Sunday. We had two tents; Pete and myself would kip in one, Dave and Jonty in the other. Next job was to set up a camp fire so that we could get the cuppas going. It didn't take four, so I volunteered to check the lake, the depth and such. "No better way," I thought, "than strip off and dive in." The lot came off, apart from my elasticated golls, just in case I stood on something sharp. I waded out to a drop-off about 10 yards out, before diving in. I swam out about another 15 yards before diving. At 8-10 feet down, I was into branches, big branches of a big tree. I came back to the surface for air. "How deep is it there?" Pete shouted. "Too deep to know, there are big trees down here." I swam around for a bit, diving down, only to find a steep drop-off about 15 yards from the shore. I swam back to the ledge and found my feet. "It's bloody deep out there. Has the kettle boiled yet?"

I heard a noise, a droning noise, getting louder, and within seconds an enormous flying thing was attacking me. "Watch out, Al, it's a Stuka." The bugger dive-bombed me again, flying round and round. I dived back into the water and held my breath for ages before popping back up and again finding my feet. Rubbing my eyes I started to walk towards the shore. "Shit," it attacked me again. "Run!" Peter shouted from the bank. "What is it?" I was panicking. "I think it's looking for a perch," Jonty shouted mid hysterical laughter. "Yeah, and it's not the fishy one," I shouted back. I grabbed a stick and started waving it round like a Whirling Durbish. "It's having you for breakfast, Dave laughed. The thing tried to land on my leg and I decided to tell it to sod off, in Russian, while running round the tents, bollock-naked. If anybody had seen me, they would probably have thought it was some strange English ritual.

Anyway, the Russian worked, we thought, and I towelled down before regaining my dignity. I found a decent spot for a slash up by the trees, before walking back to camp. "What the bloody hell?" The exclamation came out as a whisper so as not to disturb the creature, now sunbathing on the back of the tent. The guys shot round and stood silently staring at the monster. I got closer. "It's like a housefly," I said, "but the same size as a sparrow." "I don't know about Stuka, it's more like a Lancaster bloody bomber," Jonty chipped in. "Leave it alone." Dave waved us away. Pete gave the Anglo-Saxon one last bash but to no avail; the winged monster was sunbathing and that was that.

We decided to have a go at fishing and in no time at all had completely forgotten about the Lord of the Flies. A couple of the lads were spinning for pike, while Peter and myself were sat looking out at our floats and catching fish. Only small at first, roach and perch were being deposited into a keep net. After about an hour of heavy feeding, Peter connected with something substantially bigger. He battled with the fish for over ten minutes and I surmised that it must have wrapped around a branch. Eventually the fish tired, and Peter hauled it ashore. "It's a dustbin lid," I shouted. "It's the biggest bream I've ever seen," Pete grappled to pick up the monster. I stood up to get a closer look. "Maybe we've arrived in Giant Land," I said. "Man-eating flies, dustbin lid size fish." We took photos of the fish, which the lads estimated to be well over 10lbs, before returning it to the lake, far too big to fit into the keep net. We caught many more fish, including other bream, but nothing to match Peter's monster.

We fished on through the baking heat and come teatime we had a net full of fish. I suppose it was then I asked the most stupid question of all. "So, what's for tea?" "Er, fish soup!" Jonty answered, with just a hint of sarcasm. The next time I looked, we had Jonty perched next to a cut-off tree stump, calmly decapitating fish with his Swiss army penknife. "What the hell are you doing?" I shouted at him. "What?" "For God's sake, give them a bang on the bonce first." "Why? They can't feel anything," he said, completely unfazed. "Here," I said, handing him a small hammer. "When I'm not looking, give it a gentle tap on the head, then cut it off."

Before long, a big, black cooking pot was bubbling away full of spuds, onions, carrots and fish, including the heads. The only bits that didn't go in the soup or stew were the fins and guts. Jonty added a packet of his secret potion, "Special fish soup herbs," he said. I don't know what was in it but it was magnificent, a culinary masterpiece, with fresh bread, butter and washed down with a can of beer. With the backdrop of the lake in all its glory, this was unbeatable.

I had only just finished my first bowl when an old looking Russian guy paddled his log canoe up the lake. After giving him a wave, he changed course; paddled his unstable looking craft to the bank and climbed out. We shook hands before inviting him over for a bowl of soup. He took one look at the soup, *"Oocha,"* he stated. *"Oocha,"* fish soup, he repeated. *"Oocha,"* we agreed. We opened a bottle of vodka and poured it into four cups and a glass, handing the old man the glass. *"Do dna,"* was the cry, and the vodka was despatched.

After the evening meal, we decided to play cards. *"Durak,"* the man suggested. He told us that he lived a couple of kilometres down the lake, near the end that was dammed to provide drinking water. At least that's what we thought he said. After beating us at cards, and with a block of Cadbury's Fruit and Nut safely stored in his pocket, he set off back down the lake, waving his paddle in salute.

We sat and fished on, as the sun dropped down well behind the giant pines at our backs, casting an amazing orangey dappled light over the vast expanse of water in front of us. The silence and remoteness giving total peace and time to recollect and just enjoy nature. When the light faded, we banked our rods, washed in warm lake water and retired to our sleeping bags. After about an hour trying to get comfortable, I eventually dropped off.

As dawn's early light pierced through the vent flaps I got up quietly, trying not to disturb Peter, and crawled out on all fours. Jonty was already up, chunnering to himself. He spotted me and waved his hand for me to join him on the beach. "Take a look at this," he whispered. The keep net, or what was left of it, was lying out of the water; a gaping hole down one side, with little bits of fish scattered everywhere. "What do you think made these tracks?" He pointed to a trail of several large paw prints in the sand. "A bear?" I asked, astounded at the size of the depth of the prints. "I don't think there are any wild bears here, are there?" "I don't know, wolves then?" "They could be, but they must be big." He scratched his head. "I'm glad they found a fish supper." I picked up the remains of the keep net. "They could have eaten us."

Dave and Peter were undecided as to whether we had been visited by the three bears or a gang of well-fed, overweight wolves. "Look at that." Dave pointed across the lake. A fish eagle was trying desperately to lift a big fish out of the water. It skimmed the top of the water at first, unable to gain height, but somehow, inch by inch it lifted the fish. It turned in a wide arc and set off down the lake with its capture. "Food for the kids this morning," Jonty quipped. "Amazing," I stuttered, "I've never seen an eagle before." What an unbelievable sight it was - simply breathtaking!

The rest of the day was spent lazily catching fish, skinny-dipping in the warm water, sunbathing, and just as I did as a child, always keeping one eye open for the flying monsters and eagles. In the afternoon, we packed up the tents and were ready when the taxi arrived right on the dot. We piled the tackle into the boot and set off for home. Four Red Indians, large on life and heads full of *Chichevich*y. It was a wonderful experience to see Belarus at its untamed, majestic best.

Kombinat days were busy, the Filament Yarn building now full of Drawtwister machines at various stages of erection, while the spinning room was well into commissioning. Something strange happened though at certain times of the day; one minute manic, with workers everywhere busying themselves, the next minute quiet, almost ghostly. Where were people disappearing to? I decided to ask one of the Russian lads.

He tugged my sleeve and put his finger over his mouth. I followed him to a rough concrete stairway, and up we went, emerging through a door onto the roof. I couldn't believe my eyes; it was Blackpool beach without the donkeys. There were people everywhere, talking, sunbathing, laughing and eating, and that was the small area I could see. I walked towards the centre of the roof and looked around. "Bloody hell, is anybody doing any work?" He once again put his finger over his lips, "Shh." We walked back down onto the shop floor.

The only other thing of any note was word of a small riot by the remaining convicts working on the services building behind Filament Yarn. It appeared that some of the Russian girls had been teasing the men, lifting their dresses and showing them what they were missing. The men had retaliated, at first throwing stones at the girls before attacking some of the guards and charging the wire fence. "Amazing," one of the lads commented, "what sight of the Bearded Haddock will do to some men." "That says it all," I agreed following a fit of laughter.

I made a phone call home the following Sunday lunch. I jokingly told my mum that my wife had already left me, but really told her how good things had been since the wedding. Dad came on the phone. "Al, we've got Hami in the bar, and he's bringing the British swimming team out to Minsk in a couple of weeks." "That sounds good." My ears pricked up. "He wants to know if you and Larissa can get to Minsk for the weekend and meet up with him. "Tell Hamilton we would love to but I will need to chat with the office to make sure we can go." I agreed to phone the following weekend and confirm one way or another. Grant requested the necessary travel permit and everything was agreed, so long as my wife and, of course, his wife too, eventually decided to come home. My mistake, I had obviously given her way too much money.

CHAPTER 29
RELAX - IT'S MARK SPITZ

What is it with pain that you constantly complain and yet do absolutely sod all about it? I've been getting gut ache for over a year and, all right, I've seen the Harley Street doctor who visits. He put me on a course of tablets for a peptic ulcer and still no improvement. It hasn't bothered me this week though … no, this week it's been outranked by toothache. Every day it has got worse and now I'm going mad. Mad enough to book an appointment with the local dentist. "Are you sure?" Grant asked. "Does it really hurt that much? When's your next holiday?" He just kept throwing them at me with a big toothy grin. "Cheers Grant; make me feel better why don't you?"

A trip to the dentist with Mr Touse? A bit like going to a funeral with Tommy Copper – somehow the chemistry isn't quite right, but I suppose he did his best to take my mind off things. We were taken straight through into a long, narrow room with at least ten dentists' chairs in a line down the room. The room was painted dentist white and smelled heavily of insanity. I looked along the walls for straight jackets.

"Sit down please," Mr Touse interpreted, pointing to a chair about halfway down the line. About three chairs away, was a big, middle-aged guy, obviously having a tooth out. You didn't have to be clever to realise this – the dentist holding an enormous pair of mole grips in his right hand. He placed his left hand on the patient's forehead, his right knee up in the bloke's groin, and started pulling. The man grunted continuously until the tooth came away; the dentist dropping it into an enamel bowl, before going back for the next one.

"Good morning." A dentist placed his hand on my shoulder. "Mr Touse, can you tell him my tooth isn't aching anymore? Actually I think I'd like to go home." "Ah, ha, Mr Hamer, you are very funny." "What's the problem?" The dentist felt left out. "Toothache." I pointed to the tooth. "Top back." Somebody please explain to me why dentists have to pick up a sharp, pointed, metal thingy and stick it into every nook and cranny in your mouth. Even when your teeth are perfect, by now they are aching – bloody great puncture holes everywhere. Your mouth must resemble a colander. I see myself in the bar tonight taking my first mouthful of beer, and before I can get it down my neck it starts pouring down my chin. "Dentist?" someone asks. "Yep," I reply. A pal of mine once said you should take a firm grip of the dentist's balls and ask, "We're not going to hurt one another, are we?" No, I'm going to sit here petrified, like the big guy further down, trusting that he's going to make things better.

"Arrgh!" Eventually, he's found the tooth. "That's the one," he said quietly. "Jesus wept," I thought. "He must be a genius as well; he's found the tooth." Tousey confirms the find. "Come here, Tousey," I think to myself, "I'll grab your balls instead."

Now he's got the drill. "What about the anaesthetic?" Too late, he's drilling. If he's after oil, he's going the wrong way. My fingers are ripping the leather pads off the wooden chair but still he drills deeper and deeper. "Rinse your mouth," Mr Touse translates, but my fingers won't grip the glass and half the liquid drops down my front before I spit into a big pot. I look to my left and the other dentist is still pulling teeth, while the bloke continues to grunt and snuffle.

My dentist places an enamel bowl on a small table to my right. I looked into the bowl; there were about two dozen broken fuses lying in it. They looked like the metal end off a thirteen-amp fuse with a two-inch wire protruding from the centre. The dentist took out one of the wires and started to slowly screw it up into my tooth. As he went up, so did I, lifting myself up in the chair, my arms taut, like hydraulic rams. The dentist stopped. "Relax," Mr Touse barked out the translation. "Relax?" My head racked in pain. He continued to screw up the nerve before suddenly jerking the wire down and depositing it in another tray. This process, he repeated about twenty times, with the occasional rinse. The dentist then placed some sort of swab into the cavity before filling the tooth. I, in turn, started to breathe again. Mr Touse translated. "The dentist has put arsenic into the tooth to kill the nerves, and he's put in a temporary filling. If the filling comes out, you must return immediately; otherwise he will see you in four days." "Can we go now?" I urged. "It must be getting dark." I jumped out of the chair without looking at the dentist and legged it towards the door.

I was low on conversation on the way back to the flat and, for once, Tousey stayed quiet; probably understanding that I was within an inch of ripping someone's head off.

There lies another quandary – why is it that women don't understand the meaning of pain when related to a man? Larissa seemed keen to know how I had gone on, and yet when I tried to relay just what the dentist had done and how excruciatingly painful it had been, she simply didn't understand; more interested in wanting to see the temporary filling, poking at it with her finger. "You would make a good dentist," I told her. "You could do with one of those pointed, metal thingies to practice poking with." She gave me one of those looks. "Coffee?" she asked. "Go on then," I replied.

I did go back on the Friday morning and received exactly the same treatment, more drilling, more wire-screwing and, of course, more pain. Although I have to admit that whatever sort of poison he had packed my tooth with, it certainly had some effect in reducing the feeling. Anyway, he finished off with a filling and I actually found a way of thanking him, before getting out of the place; vowing never to return.

I returned home from work to find that Larissa was busy packing our suitcase, ready for our trip to Minsk. The taxi was due at 6.30pm, which just gave me sufficient time for the three S's, before throwing a shirt and a pair of jeans in a case. We arrived at the Yubilanaya Hotel just after 9pm and quickly checked in before going down to the restaurant for something to eat. After we had eaten, we moved to the bar for about an hour, before retiring to bed for an early night.

We met Hamilton at about 10.30am in the reception. Typical swimming type was Hami. Good looking, mouth full of pearly white teeth and a Great Britain Team Coach blazer. He gave us team GB badges, before boarding the Great Britain team coach at about 11am for a short trip to the pool. Hami asked if we wanted to see the competitors' changing-rooms and took me through the men's room while one of the interpreters took Larissa through the ladies' room; meeting up at the side of the pool. We were then escorted to a block of seats on the far side of the pool.

What we hadn't realised, but what soon became very apparent, was the competition was the USSR -v- Great Britain -v-USA. We should really have noticed the posters with the three flags on them, and we now certainly noticed the special bunting displayed around the pool.

We sat with the competitors from all three countries and I couldn't help but notice the big guy who plonked himself down next to me. I gave him a quick stare, before looking at Larissa. "Mark Spitz." I tried the old cotton mill language – all mouth and very little sound, but with absolutely no effect other than complete puzzlement. "What?" She asked, just that bit too loudly. I tried the left-hand index finger across the chest point. "Mark Spitz," I whispered. Larissa shrugged her shoulders; I gave up and turned towards him. He was staring straight at me. "Okay?" I asked. "Yeah," he replied, still giving me the quizzical eye, as if thinking, "who the bloody hell are you?" Expecting the question, I quickly looked away, thinking up a question of my own. "Looking at me pal, or chewing a brick?" I didn't know what it meant, but as kids, it was regularly used as a threat. Bloody hell, I was sitting next to Mark Spitz.

Eventually, he gave up his place, very probably having to go and swim, and Larissa was completely none the wiser. I have to say, once he sat down my day was ruined. I hadn't a clue who was swimming for whom; who had won which race – nothing – just bloody Mark Spitz sat next to me. I wonder if he went away, saying to his friends, "Guess who I sat next to?" "We don't know, Mark. Who were you sat next to?" "This gormless-looking English twit, who kept pointing and whispering to his missus."

I think the USA won from the USSR and we were third. I do believe we won the men's breaststroke and just maybe the long-distance race. That's the race where they swim up and down for about half an hour and finish up going different ways so nobody really knows who's won; other than those who have won – and maybe they get confused.

Back at the hotel, we sat having a drink with Hami and thanked him for a wonderful day. He promised to pass on our love and kisses to mum and dad. I let Larissa give him the kisses to be transported home, deciding to shake his hand in the customary, manly fashion. Larissa seemed blissfully ignorant to most all that had happened. "Mark who?" "Oh, forget it. Only seven gold medals at the last Olympics, and the greatest swimmer that ever..." I had to think about the translation for a while... "Swam!"

CHAPTER 30
WEDDING PHOTOS – KGB STYLE

I was beavering away as normal when Grant arrived on site with Malcolm. "Alan, you need to go to town with Grant to answer some questions about the wedding. Don't worry about the work; I'll get someone to cover." I must have looked puzzled. "I've got a taxi waiting." Grant set off towards the main doors and I followed. "The KGB need to speak to you about something," he said, quietly. "They phoned the office this morning and were quite insistent that you call at the Head Office in town today." "What's it all about?" I asked now feeling quite intrigued. "I don't know, other than they were confirming that you had recently been married." He looked as puzzled as I felt.

The KGB Headquarters was an anonymous looking building housing various council departments. It was situated on *Ul.Leninskaya* off Lenin Square. KGB or *Komitet Gosudarstvennoy Besopasnosty* simply meant The Committee for State Protection. Grant was asked to sit down by a uniformed policeman at the front desk. I was escorted by another uniformed man, down a long corridor and into a big and very dark room, where I was asked to sit on a wooden chair in front of a blacked-out window. The man then left the room, pulling the door to, but not shutting it.

The sliver of light through the crack in the door was the only light in the room. Eventually my eyes adjusted and I could make out a large desk, with the obligatory portrait of Lenin on the wall behind it. The room was very similar in size to that of the town hall official we had visited before our marriage, except here there was no light, no carpet on the floor and no curtains. In fact, looking closer, apart from the desk, the portrait and a number of filing cabinets along the wall, there was nothing at all in the room. I had plenty of time to look as well, being in there for at least thirty minutes listening to people walking up and down the corridor outside; seeing their shadows as they passed the door. Every shadow sent a chill down my spine. "What do you expect?" I asked myself, "It's the bloody KGB."

Sure enough, the door eventually swung open and a large military man, wearing a peaked hat, walked into the room, closed the door and sat down. He clicked on his desk lamp – one of those special interrogation lamps on a spring-folding arm that they always have in spy films. He removed his hat and placed it on the empty desk. The lamp illuminated the crimson star on the front of his hat. The star was gilded with the Soviet Hammer and Sickle. The officer didn't speak, instead appearing to study some papers in a folder that he took from the desk drawer. He tilted the lamp until it made me squint. "You're name?" he ordered, in Russian. "Alan Hamer," I replied. "Hamer, uh?" He then started to lecture me, on God knows what, that went on forever. I did manage to pick out some bits like 'wedding' and 'photographs' and 'private' and 'police', but the bulk of it was complete nonsense; or maybe I'd just switched off. *"Anglichanin,* I don't understand," I told him, in Russian. "What? You're English?" "Yes," I replied. He stood up and marched out of the office.

A couple of minutes later he returned, switching on the light as he opened the door. Grant came in behind him and sat down to my right. The officer again started talking and Grant translated. The officer wanted to know about the wedding photographer – it appeared that this photographer had been naughty and had done our wedding photos as a privateer, trying to earn a few shillings on the side and obviously someone had grassed him. Anyway, the top and bottom of it was that they thought that I was Russian and involved with the photographer.

What then transpired was that they now knew that I was English and it was me that had been married; and it was me that wasn't going to have any wedding photos. Grant tried his best, but the photos had been seized and would not be available to go into a wedding album for us. They said that they were sorry for the mistake and the outcome, but there was nothing that they could do. I left the KGB Headquarters in the clear while totally mystified and obviously the loser.

Larissa was less than pleased when I told her about the day's events. "We've already paid him 200 rubles," she said, pulling her own hair. "I will go to town tomorrow and sort it out," she carried on. "Go where?" I asked. "To the photographers," she insisted. "The photos should be beautiful and they cost us a fortune." She was incensed. It called for a big cuddle.

I knew when I arrived home the following day and Larissa had a face like thunder. "What's wrong?" I asked. "He isn't there anymore, he has disappeared. His shop has disappeared - nothing there - it's empty - locked up." "Whoa, slow down," I said. "There's no wedding photos, there's nothing," she carried on, now breaking into tears. I put my arms around her. "Don't worry, Zaika, Ray has a cine film and we can get some photos done this weekend and you never know, something might turn up with the other photos." I didn't know then, but they didn't show, they were gone forever; probably in a grey KGB folder in a dark office.

We travelled to town on the Saturday morning and met the rest of the Strotskys' outside the Dnieper Hotel. We walked en mass to the photographers situated on the other side of the road just before the theatre. In my eyes, there's formal and there's formal, and these photos were formal - formal, plus a bit more formal than that. I always thought that wedding or family photos were supposed to be happy, show a few smiles, obviously not here. No, here you had to be formal, no smile, austere, flaming downright glum looking. I suppose if that is how people are brought up to react when being photographed, then you have to accept and understand. But it did look odd. He didn't even say 'cheese'. What sort of photographer is that? I nicknamed us 'The Glums.' Well, at least we might get these. I decided not to mention the KGB just in case it hexed the proceedings.

From the photographers, we grabbed the bus to the station before walking to Larissa's house; having a quick change when we got there. Mum had set up a long table down the centre of Larissa's old bedroom and we were soon full of food and good cheer. The highlight was definitely dad pulling out the piano accordion and giving us a right royal knees-up with lots of Cossack style whistling and foot slapping. I hadn't had so much fun for years. Even when the vodka got hold, I was allowed to go next door for a nap before rejoining the party, which carried on until very late. It also gave me a chance to meet some members of the family I hadn't seen before – aunts, uncles, cousins, plus friends and neighbours. They all joined in and made it an evening to remember.

The next day was about having a good lie-in, followed by breakfast, a massive bowl of chicken soup; followed by a walk to clear the head and let off some steam, if you get my drift. When we arrived back, Oleg decided to have a ride on Greesha's motorbike; so I had to ride pillion. He was still only sixteen, and it showed; finding every ditch and pothole to ride through. We were only out for about ten minutes and I arrived back totally knackered and amazed I was still in one piece.

The following Sunday, we called at the bazaar to pick up some bits and pieces for a picnic in *Pechersky Park*. I stood on the road at the entrance to the market, waiting for Larissa who had gone back for something. There was a drunken bloke who was hanging onto a telegraph pole trying to pluck up courage to let go. Eventually, he did let go, leaning forward, targeting the next pole. Three steps – wavered; another step – realisation he wasn't going to make it. His head went up as he swivelled on his soft inebriated ankles; his head dropped. He was off again. Hands outstretched, he grabbed the pole, and yes, he had made it back to where he started. Larissa grabbed my arm. "How funny was that?" I asked. *"Durak,"* she said, "you should know." "Hey, I've never been that bad – well, not for a while anyway, and certainly not on a Sunday morning."

We arrived at mum's house just before lunch, and quickly set off for the park with mum, dad, Greesha, Alla and their young daughter Natasha, Oleg, Lyonya, Tamara and their three children, Lena, Natasha and Igor. The day was sunny but heavy and humid, and dad had assured me that winter was just around the corner and we would soon be getting out the fur hats. It seemed a million miles away to me, but I didn't argue with an expert. I chose to follow Larissa's path across the stream; Oleg jumping it as if it wasn't there. We walked into the woods for about twenty minutes before finding a nice clearing to settle down to some food and drinks.

You name it, we had it: chicken, ham, smoked sausage, smoked fish, salted fish, eggs, salad, kitchen sink – the lot! We also had beer, vodka, wine and lemonade to drink. What more do you need, except maybe a king-size bed.

I was quickly getting the hang of drinking Russian style. It's very simple really, being all about food intake– you drink, then eat. And it's not just any food; you have to eat some oily foods like fish and *smetana* or cottage cheese. This, I am told, lines your stomach and allows you to drink loads of booze. Well, the Russian guys should know, they are professionals at it. Anyway, you never get stuck for advice; the lads certainly telling you to lift your glass, while the girls constantly tell you to eat whatever it is that they have stuck in your hand. It's quite exhausting really.

So, it's late afternoon and I've got a face like a fire bucket, and it's not just from the sun. We packed up, and are plodding our merry way home when Oleg bumps into some of his friends and we stop for a chat; followed by an impromptu wrestling match. The sky had quickly changed from blue to this weird, sinister yellowy grey colour and there isn't a breath of wind. We could hear a roaring noise, feint at first, but getting louder; like a giant wave crashing up a beach. Then I saw a wall of dust about 6 feet high, moving towards us. Mum shouted something and everybody formed a rugby scrum, holding one another, bent over. Hailstones started to hit us, the size of small golf balls, crashing on our backs, stinging as they hit. Harder and harder they hit, and the noise was deafening. Some of the lads made a run for the trees. "Bad idea," I thought, as a bolt of lightning strikes nearby with a deafening crack of thunder. As quick as it came, it went, and we watched it move; the cloud of dust wandering on in the direction of mum's house. We all stood up, soaked to the skin and covered in muck; doing that tiptoe thing in the sodden grass. "Come on," ordered mum, "let's go home."

"Come on, get your clothes off," mum held out a big towel. I stripped off down to my underpants. "Come on, don't be shy." I waved my finger at her and made a grab for the towel, but missed. "I know you, you just want to see my willy." I stood there, holding onto my dignity. Mum laughed, before whacking me with the towel. I made a grab with one hand and tugged it away from her, quickly wrapping it around my waist. "Naughty mama," I said. She just carried on laughing. "Somebody put the kettle on," I shouted, "winter's just arrived."

We climbed into bed that night and I lay with my arm around Larissa, thinking. Only now I was thinking in Russian, not English. It was then that I realised that Mogilev was becoming more and more like home to me. It will always be my home – I have family here, haven't I? The thought gave me a warm feeling, a sense of belonging – it felt good.

Ivan and Maria had a plot of land, a bit like an allotment but bigger, and about ten kilometers away from their home. Now that we were getting the autumn showers, it was time to get the potatoes in before winter struck. First thing Saturday morning, we met up at mum's and travelled mob-handed to the field.

Already there was dad with a big, rather old looking carthorse, hooked up to a wooden plough. He had already ploughed a couple of furrows in the field and we shared out the buckets, rolled up our sleeves and started digging up spuds. There's something rewarding about scrabbling about in the soil, particularly when you're pulling up the king of all foods, 'The Spud' or, as they are known over here, *'Kartoshka'*. And what do you do with spuds? – You make chips. And what do chips do? – They make you very happy. Natural then, digging for potatoes would make you very happy. Certainly for a while it does, until the repetitiveness kicks in, allied to the aches, pains and cramps, then it just becomes hard work. The only break I got is when I found a frog and chased Larissa round the field with it.

After lunch, Greesha asked if I wanted a go at ploughing. "No problem," I said, "I'll have a go at owt." He showed me how to hold the plough. While holding the horse's reins, he ploughed a furrow halfway down the field, then stopped. "Okay, you have a go," he said. I took the reins and gave the horse the start noise, slapping the reins down on its back. The horse jolted forward and caught me off balance throwing my weight onto the ploughs handles. The plough came out of the furrow and started to skim along the grass; at which point the horse went faster and I found myself holding onto the plough, looking more like I was driving a dog sled. "Whoa, whoa, bloody whoa!" I hung onto the reins and tried to dig in my heels. No chance! I was being dragged along on my arse, while Greesha shouted out instructions in Russian. Eventually, the horse got tired of dragging me and stood looking round at me with those big questioning eyes. "What are you looking at" I pointed at the horse, "you great useless, stupid sod! That's telling it," I thought. I was pulling myself up, using the plough, when the daft bugger took another pace forward, pitching me forward; my left hand skidding on a big lump of shit. "Shit!" I shouted. Greesha grabbed the reins. "I've got the horse," he said. "You can keep the bloody horse," I replied desperately trying to wipe the shit off my hand. "Don't worry," said Greesha, "it's only shit." "I know what it is, Greesha. Ah, you plough, I'll pick." "Okay." I think he could see that I was slightly pissed off. I walked past the horse. "Bloody stupid Russian nag." I gave it the stare and nodded. No reaction from the horse, none at all. I couldn't believe it; absolutely no visible sign of remorse at all. "Ah well" I thought, "horses can be like that."

I love animals, but horses are different to other animals. I remember a girlfriend at school, her name was Christine, and Christine loved horses. Most weekends, she used to spend at a stable, and now and then I would ride my bike over to see her and help out. One day, a pony escaped from the yard just as the horses were being boxed for the night. "Hamer to the rescue," I had said. The pony was only small so it would be no match for me, would it? I crept up on the horse – or so I thought – and grabbed it round the neck, linking my hands on the other side. The pony started walking away, so I walked alongside, trying to turn it round. The horse now picked up pace, and although I was running, I was losing my grip around the neck; now holding a handful of mane at the pony's shoulder. As I slipped back, the pony kicked to the side and connected with my right thigh; launching me over a wooden fence and completely knocking me out; only coming round when they turned a hosepipe on me. Fortunately, I didn't suffer any broken bones, but undoubtedly I have been as mad as a wasp ever since. Unlike humans, I have surmised horses kick first and don't bother asking questions later. It's at times like these when I can call upon the old Hamer motto, 'If at first you don't succeed, sod it'.

Back home, we celebrated the annual spud-pick with a party, with lots to eat and drink. The toils of the day, mixed with the alcohol, made me very drunk very quickly and I had to ask Larissa why Russians drank so much. "There's a story," she said, "about a collective farm where people were drinking heavily, resulting in very little work being done, and ultimately a large shortfall on the quotas. The elders called a meeting to outline plans to have a month without any alcohol at all." "Sounds a good idea to me," I said. "Yes," she continued, "they decided to celebrate the plan by having a party... where they all got drunk!" "Now I understand," I confirmed, too drunk to understand - "let's have another drink."

Back at work, we had two new Italian blokes working on site; Phillipo and Millado, I think they were called. They didn't speak a word of English, but were some sort of ceramic bobbin specialists. Actually, I hadn't got a clue what the hell they did, other than talk a lot and wave their hands about. Anyway, they were good fun and livened lunchtimes up a treat. I speak Italian – well one line anyway: *"Ey pericaloso sporo jesse."* I remember it being written on a brass plate above the train window. It may not have been that - but when spoken, it sounded something like that. We were travelling by rail on a school holiday to Lake Garda, three lads and twenty-eight girls. What a bloody holiday that was! Especially when you factor in the weather; electric storms hitting the area every other night. Well, as you know girls aren't keen on thunder and lightning, are they? They need to seek refuge with the boys, and being nice boys, we were always willing to comfort and console. So kind were we, it got us into trouble with the teachers – something I could never understand. Anyway, I shared my knowledge of Italian with the 'new boys' and they acknowledged it with blank faces and shrugged shoulders. "Good try," George slapped my back, "at least it's shut them up for a couple of minutes." A couple of weeks later, we were saying *"Arrivederci Romans"* and the lads were flying back home before the big freeze arrived.

CHAPTER 31
UGLY OLYA FROM ORSHA

A nice fresh layer of snow had fallen during the day and it lights up in the bus headlights; everybody chatting about work and the night ahead. Now that Larissa has received her visa we can look forward to three weeks leave back in the UK.

"Hiya, luvy," I panted, out of breath from the dash upstairs. "What's for tea?" "*Pilmania* and chips, your favourite," she answers, pushing me towards the bathroom. "Go and shower." "Do I smell?" I asked flippantly. "No, that's because you shower."

After tea we settled down to a night in watching television; absolutely riveted by the news, that was followed by the Soviet Union weather forecast. Why they have to read out the forecast across seven time zones and in January, remains a mystery to me. Why not just say it's bloody freezing, and leave it at that? Just what the difference is between minus 8°C and minus 38°C, is lost on me, but I suppose if you had to walk 5 miles to work every day it would make a difference. It pays to switch off before midnight when the national anthem is played. We decided to have an early night, partly because I am suffering with a stomach-ache and I have run out of tablets for the ulcer.

An hour later and I am still not asleep. In fact, my stomach is hurting so much that I'm sat on the edge of the bed, bent forward with my head resting on the bedroom wall, and now I have started to gently butt the wall. Larissa woke up. "Are you all right?" She started to rub my back. "My stomach's playing up." I tried to sit up, taking a deep breath. The pain hit me again and I thudded my head into the wall. "Luvy, I have a problem." I forced out the words. "I'm getting an ambulance." Larissa jumped up and put on her dressing gown. I didn't argue, I didn't have the strength. She went down to the dezurnaya's office, knocked her up, and phoned from there.

Larissa hadn't been back long when I heard the door open and an emergency doctor and nurse walked into the bedroom. "Lie down," the nurse said, easing me back onto the bed while the doctor asked about the problem. He felt around my stomach, and Larissa explained about my problem with the peptic ulcer. The nurse rolled me on my side and whacked a needle into my bum before sterilising it with the pure spirit. I almost told them that I had drunk the stuff, but thought better of it; now wasn't the time. The doctor explained that after about fifteen minutes the pain should ease off and told me to request more tablets from back home. Larissa offered them a cup of Nescafe and I could hear them talking in the kitchen for a while before they checked on me again and left.

The injection was definitely working and Larissa climbed back into bed and soon after fell asleep; her arm still draped over my stomach. I tried to get to sleep but lay there for about an hour, during which time the pain started to get stronger. I knelt on the bed, desperately trying to fathom out what was going on before deciding to butt the wall again. It didn't help and I gave Larissa a shake. "Luvy, it's even worse than before," I said through tightly gritted teeth. I heard the door open as she again sought help. "The ambulance is on its way," she said arriving back. "Try to relax they won't be long."

Ambulances are Volga estate cars, each manned with a doctor and nurse who can assess and treat patients in their homes. This time the doctor was a woman. "Lie back," she said pushing her fingers deep into my stomach. "Where is the pain?" "Everywhere," I said, exhausted. She pushed her fingers in again before letting go quickly. I let out a gasp. "Appendix," she said confidently. "We need to be quick."

We soon arrived at the hospital, just over the main bridge, and I was escorted in by the nurse, stopping momentarily at reception. I was taken up a flight of stairs, along the ward to the far end where there was a small room partitioned off from the main ward. It contained a single bed with a wooden chair on one side and a small wooden bedside table on the other. "Get undressed." The nurse left the room and reappeared with a white linen smock. I stood doubled over in my underpants. "Take them off," she instructed. I took off the kites and quickly put on the smock, the nurse tying the bows down the back. "Sit on the bed, please," she said, and left. This time she came back with a syringe in a stainless steel tray. She gave me a jab in my left arm and left without a word. It was only as I saw her head disappear down the ward that I could start to moan; the pain now unbearable. "It won't be long now," I kept telling myself, "Not long now."

"Come on," the nurse barked. No wonder I hadn't seen her, she was only about four foot tall, thin as a toothpick and looked about ninety years old, with this ridiculously silly white baggy hat. I'm not saying that she was the ugliest woman I'd ever seen, but she sure as hell looked like her. "Come on," she waved impatiently. I managed to get to my feet and followed her into another small room with a low black leather bed. The old girl spread a rubber sheet on the bed. "Lie down," she pointed at the bed. I lay down as flat as I could; my body shaking with the pain. She calmly lifted the smock up from the bottom and draped it round my chest. "So," she said, studying my undercarriage.

Just then, around half-a-dozen young nurses filed into the room, trying desperately not to laugh. "Students," the old nurse decreed. In pain I might have been, but I could still feel myself shrinking physically as well as mentally. The nurse held up an enamel mug and a shaving brush, and very liberally applied a mountain of shaving foam to my nether regions while pinching the end of my willy with her thumb and forefinger. The girls were now in full giggle mode, trying to cover their mouths with their hands; their faces turning blood red. I clocked the one on the end waving frantically to somebody outside. The door opened and three girls, not in uniform, crept into the room. "Get out!" The nurse jumped up and waved her right hand towards the trio, splatting a dollop of shaving cream on the glass. The girls shot out of the room before turning and pressing their noses onto the window and peering in. "Oh God, no," I thought to myself as the nurse started digging into the mound of cream, feeling for my manhood. By now, it was like looking for a hundred and thousand in a Knickerbocker Glory. "Please God, let me die now," I mumbled to myself. Even the girls couldn't look anymore; doubled up with tears rolling down their cheeks.

My embarrassment was quelled somewhat when the nurse pulled a cut-throat razor from her pocket, opened it and started to hone the blade on a large leather strop attached to the bed. "Hold the tray," she ordered one of the nurses, who tried desperately to control herself. She did so, after a long wicked stare from the older nurse. "Ugly Olya from Orsha," I muttered through the pain. The nurse started shaving from just below my belly button, slopping the cream vigorously into the tray after every stroke. Eventually, she bared a path to the business end and finally located my John Thomas, or more appropriately, JT. Gripping it firmly, she pulled as if to say, "Gotcha." She now quickly navigated her way round the base and it was done. The nurse finished off with some damp gauze; cleaning off any loose hair and shaving cream before covering me up with the smock.

The student nurses now started to file out of the room. "Okay then girls, seen enough?" I whispered. I'll bet tomorrow everybody in Mogilev knows that Englishmen only have little willies. Oh, well, that's definitely the worst over with. "Follow me, please," Olya beckoned me with her hand, and I forced myself up off the bed and, head bowed, shuffled along behind her across the ward into the operating theatre. "Lie on the bed, please," she pointed to the operating table on the left-hand side of the room. I shuffled across to the table that was around waist height with one central steel leg. I tried manfully to climb onto the bed, but in my current state couldn't manage it. I turned to look at a group of nurses and two men dressed in white overalls talking in the corner of the room. One of the men acknowledged my look. "Get on," he shouted. At this point, I must have lost my temper. "You get on the fucker," I said back, pain ripping my guts apart. It was then that I noticed the three four-inch leather straps hanging down the side of the operating table, wondering what they were for. I placed my hands on the table and jumped, grabbing hold of the far side. Teeth firmly clenched, I pulled myself up before rolling on my back and collapsing in pain, sweat pumping out of my forehead and running off my face.

One of the nurses walked over to the side of the bed, leant over me, grabbed the buckle end of the strap and fastened it firmly onto my chest. "Do you think I'm going to fall off?" I tried the question without response. She repeated the operation twice more; one strap across the top of my thighs and one over my ankles. Then she walked around the table and secured my left hand tight to the bed before placing my right hand under the back of my head. The nurse finished off by inserting a metal bar into the side of the table and turned it across my chest. Over the bar, she placed a small white towel. I felt like asking what the hell was going on but I didn't; my eyes scanning the room for some indication of what was happening next.

A nurse, along with one of the men, positioned themselves either side of my head. The rest of the crew gathered lower down; one of the nurses daubing something very cold over my stomach. The nurse handed the surgeon a syringe and he duly stuck it into my stomach. He handed the needle back to the nurse, who handed him a scalpel, and he cut me while I held my breath. Although I felt the slow deliberate cut, it was just a cut and I've been cut before. What came next was completely different from anything I have felt before or since. They started to apply clamps, each one feeling as if somebody had a pair of nutcrackers around my balls. After the first set of clamps, the surgeon started to cut deeper, and now I'm praying out loud. The doctor at my end assures the surgeon that I'm okay and he continues to cut and clamp, while I bite on my lips. I groaned with the pain, and the nurse wiped my forehead with a cold, damp cloth. The torture went on for a further fifteen minutes or so before they released the clamps and started to stitch me up again.

No description can explain the pain that I felt during that fifteen or so minutes - safe to say that even today I go cold recalling the memory. After they have covered me in sticky orange goo, the surgeon walks to my side and tells me that I am very lucky, but everything is okay. I suppose I should have said thank you, but I couldn't speak, my lips stuck together with the congealed blood. I think he knew I wasn't a happy chappy.

At least they didn't ask me to walk back to my bed. This time I hitched a lift from a passing stretcher. The rest of the night felt like an eternity, unable to sleep, going over and over in my head the night's fun and games. I must have nodded off eventually, because I remember waking up with stomach ache. "Funny that," I thought. Maybe it was God's way of getting me back for my wedding night.

At the crack of dawn, Ugly Olya wheeled in a trolley. She first primed the needle, before jabbing it into my arm and depositing a load of battery acid. I thanked her, *"Spacibo,"* I said, giving her the eyes. *"Pazalusta* (It's a pleasure)," she replied. She helped me sit up in bed; fluffing my pillows before placing a large bowl in my lap. *"Manka,* eat," she said firmly.

"No, I've had it before," I replied. "Eat." She picked up the spoon and stuck it into my mouth. I started to choke. *"Manky"* I said, "it's semolina - frog spawn!" She started to refill the spoon. "Toilet," I said, "I need a toilet," suddenly realising I was bursting for a pee. She placed the bowl on the table, and I fully expected her to bring one of those bed bowls. Instead, she pointed down the ward. "Toilet that way." she said gruffly. I must have let out a loud sigh, because she gave me a puzzled look. She shrugged her shoulders before telling me again to eat the *Manka*.

I dropped my feet towards the floor and forced myself up to a sitting position. This action alone took the wind out of me and I could feel my wound pulling. After sitting for a minute, I pushed myself onto my feet. Now to find the bog. I set off gingerly out of my room and down the ward. I must have looked strange in my white smock, obviously with my bare arse hanging out at the back, doubled up, my two hands holding my insides firmly in.

After about ten minutes, I finally arrived at the gents' toilet. I knew this because it had a plaque outside with a matchstick man on it. Sure enough, next door was a plaque with a matchstick woman on it. Just as I placed my hand on the door, it swung open and an old woman stood there with the sort of bow legs that literally couldn't stop a pig in a back alley. She prodded me in the chest. "Ladies next door," she pointed. "I know it's ladies next door; so why are you in the bloody gents?" I thought it, but forgot to say it. So, I've got long hair and I'm doubled up in pain but really. *"Ya Anglichanin,"* I said in my deepest, gravelly voice, while pushing past her. It was then that the smell hit me. Several patients stood in a group at the far end, near an open window. They were smoking their *Belamorsky Canals* (Russian fags). The air was acrid blue and mixed with the choking stench of urine I felt like passing out; desperately trying not to cough. Over to my right was a small storeroom with the door wide open. Obviously, that's where the cleaner lives, the one that thought I was a girl. "Good morning," I said shuffling past the smokers. "Good morning," they replied, looking dumbfounded. To the right was a step in front of a large steel trough. The step was soaking wet. And me with bare feet. "Balls to it." I stepped up and winced as I did. "Ahh," having a pee never felt so good. My eyes were taken by a figure on my right, dressed in white. I looked at his eyes. Good grief, it was the surgeon, a newspaper hiding the rest of his face. He was crouched in an open bog having a dump! My eyes fell to the bottom of the paper and I was looking at a big pair of Betty Swallocks perched between a pair of hairy legs; his white, baggy pants hanging round his ankles. I nearly ruptured my stitches when he farted. I set off back, before I caught sight of the follow through. I hoped he washed his hands before he operated on me, and thinking about it, sat back on my bed waiting for my feet to dry. Where the hell was his nob? Maybe I surmised he was looking at something naughty. Did Pravda have a 'Page *Tree*'?

I kept looking at the *Manka* but couldn't work up the courage to eat it. If I'd been thinking clearly, I'd have taken it to the toilet and ditched it down the hole, but my brain still wasn't functioning properly. It had shut down probably to cope with the ravages of the night before. I lay back and swung my feet in.

I thought I was having a vision; Larissa was stood at the end of the bed with Alla. I rubbed my eyes, and Larissa and Alla were stood at the end of the bed. Alla was dressed in her nurse's uniform. "What's happened to your mouth?" Larissa stared at me. "I was hungry so I ate it. It's better than the *Manka*." I pointed to the bowl of frog spawn. "So, go on, how are you?" She kissed my cheek and sat down on the bed. "I'm good - I'm alive - that's good," I replied sarcastically. "Why, what happened?" She had that look on her face as if she was expecting some fantastic story. "Nothing, they just strapped me down and did the operation. It was easy really." Her eyes were glued to mine, watching every flicker. "They told Alla that you made a lot of noise," now she probed with her eyes. "They probably told Alla that I had a little dick." Alla held her face in her hands and started to laugh. Anyway, I was on a roll now but Larissa cut in first, "They said that you were shouting." "I was not bloody shouting." Larissa hushed me by putting her hand over my mouth. "I was not shouting, I was praying out loud," I tried to whisper. "Anyway, who would tell Alla that you had a little dick?" She was good at that, changing the subject just to confuse me. "Who? The nurses - the young girls training to be barbers - cut hair - shave people - work in bloody slaughter houses - I don't know!" Alla hadn't stopped laughing and holding her head or saying, "My God," since she came in. Now she decided to chip in. "Nobody has said anything, apart from one of the doctors who said that you weren't very happy during the operation." "Alla, in England they put people to sleep for an operation, not just tie them down and butcher them." She sat down and held my hand.

"So, have you seen Ugly Olya from Orsha?" I looked at Alla. "Who?" "The old nurse that shaved me," I explained. "Ah, you mean Nastya? She is lovely." "No, you're right, that's her name, Nasty." Larissa held up a bag. "I've brought you some things in - pyjamas." She dropped them on the bed. "Slippers; we borrowed Greesha's," she showed me. "Too late; smell my feet," I pointed, but simply got a firm slap on the leg. "Toothbrush, toothpaste, razor, brush, all in here." She tucked a bag under the bedside table. "I've made you some sandwiches, chicken ham and tomato." "Luvy, how long do you think I'm staying?" Alla chipped in; "You'll be here two or three days, that's all." "No, listen. If I can walk to the toilet this morning, then I can go home and lie in bed." "Only the doctor can say when you can go home." "So, tell him I want to go home today." Alla shook her head. As usual, Larissa had the final word. "Forget about going home today, but we will talk to the doctor; maybe tomorrow. Anyway, we have to go.

Alla sneaked me in because she is on duty. We will see you tomorrow Okay?" She leant forward to give me a kiss. She stopped and gave my bottom lip a prod with her fingernail. "Aw," I winced as the nail dug in. "Baby," she said, before kissing my cheek. Alla kissed my other cheek, through the laugher. "Here, take the *Manka* with you." Larissa took it from me and left, blowing me a kiss as she went.

I was woken up during the night, a girl or young woman screaming the place down. The noise was coming from the operating theatre and I couldn't help thinking that she must be strapped down having her appendix out. I wondered if I had been shouting after all. She's probably screaming at him to wash his bloody hands, or maybe she's having her lucy shaved, with all the student doctors watching. "Huh, the lousy bastards could have given me a knock."

Once the girl had stopped, I managed to fall asleep again; waking up to Olya's trolley and a nice big steaming bowl of *Manka*. "Eat," she ordered. "And a very good morning to you too," I said in English. She turned on her dithery old legs and gave me the nicest smile, while waving her index finger at me, like you would to a naughty boy. "Oh, God," I thought, "Alla's told her." I tried to smile back but the guilty feeling made the smile disintegrate, and the kacky, skaggy mess of a mouth didn't help either.

In the afternoon, the doctor came to see me, checking my scar that I hadn't yet seen. He thought it looked good. I thought it looked horrendous. He did, however, have some good news. "You can go home," he said. "Brilliant." I grabbed his hand and shook it. Olya, or Nastya, whatever her name was, walked over and kissed me on the cheek. "Eat your *Manka*," she pointed at the dish. If I couldn't smile with my mouth, I smiled with my eyes. "Thank you," I said. She looked at me before turning and pinching my little toe between her thumb and forefinger as she left, shouting at somebody in the main ward.

The best thing about an operation is definitely the convalescing; sitting or lying watching telly while your wife runs around looking after your every need. I was getting into the television lark, snuggled up to my wife on the couch. "What's on tonight?" I asked. "Cartoons," she replied. "Oh, my favourite, Crocodile Gayna and his pal Chiborazka." I actually knew the song:

"Ya egrayu na garmoshke oo prohozick na vidoo, k sozaleniyu den rozdieniya tolko raz v godoo!"

How sad is that? Basically, the crocodile is singing in front of passers-by, the song saying how sad it is that you only get one birthday each year. Larissa joined in with me and then gave me a kiss on the head, just like you would with a child. I snuggled up for more kisses. After Gayna, the ice hockey was on; CSKA Moscow playing Leningrad. CSKA, the army team, won the game and stayed top of the league. What could be better than this? "Bring my pipe and slippers, lass!"

CHAPTER 32
BLACK & WHITE PLEASE

Looking out through plane windows always has the same effect, helping to release my brain, allowing it to wander and float between the clouds. Well one thing was for sure - they, my family that is, had fallen in love with Larissa. I chuckled thinking about the waitress; "black or white?" She asked everyone before serving their coffee. Larissa had been watching her approach. "Black and white please," she announced before the girl could ask. Yes and she had re-named the kitchen; it was now the kitchroom. "Well you have bedroom, bathroom, living room, why not kitchroom?" I had to agree, it made perfect sense. "Kitchroom it is." Loads of shopping, loads of presents... "Luvy, fasten your seat belt." Larissa was nudging my arm, "Moscow."

March followed February and April followed March; just like back home really, and we soon had to get geared up for the big day, May Day. Greesha had been selected to walk in the big parade and, in turn, invited me to go along. We jumped on a bus to town and met up with a number of his friends in Soviet Square. Fortunately, he had the flag and I tucked in alongside him. We had the usual loudspeaker announcements, "Glory to the wonderful Soviet Synthetic Fibre workers!" "Hurrah!" we all shouted. This time I decided to do the full loop, although I did keep my head down passing the dignitaries on the big stand in Lenin Square. I waved at Fred Lenin as I passed by and I'm sure he winked back at me.

An hour or so later we arrived back where we started and decided to walk down the hill towards the bridge. Greesha caught me by surprise when he spotted a lorry full of his mates and started to run. The wagon slowed down in the heavy traffic and Greesha managed to jump on the back; his mates pulling him up and in. I was still about 10 yards behind when the lorry started to speed up. "Quick," he shouted, hanging over the tailgate, his hand stretched back. I was running as fast as I could when he grabbed my hand and pulled; my leg crashing against a big metal tow frame. He somehow managed to haul me over the back and head first into the open trailer. There must have been thirty or so lads and girls packed into the back and I could only manage to get one foot grounded; the bad leg trapped between several bodies and the back of the wagon, as we started to pick up speed. At the front was a guy holding the biggest flag of Lenin I have ever seen. The flag was a burgundy coloured velvet material with a gold embroidered head of Lenin in the middle and gold tassels all around the edges. Now, the truck moving faster, the end of the flag was whipping my face. Even when I tried to duck, it was pounding the top of my head. "Glory to Soviet women's large breasts!" the lads chanted. "Hurrah!" was the reply. The girls obviously felt left out. "Glory to Soviet men's big dicks!" "Hurrah!" Even though I was being pummelled, I was starting to enjoy this. Ah, well, all good things must come to an end, and somebody shouted for the truck to stop at the junction of Gagarin and Shmidt where we decided to jump out. My right leg had gone numb and my left leg was broken with blood running down; so when I hit the deck my legs folded. I did my parachute roll; finishing up on my back, waving to the gang as they drove off.

"Quick, there's a bus coming!" Greesha shouted, grabbing my arms and part dragging me over the kerb. "Thanks for that, brother," I said hanging onto him, trying to stand unaided. I pulled up my jeans revealing a nasty looking gash on my shin. "Hah, you'll live." He dismissed it as insignificant and started off towards the flats. "Come on, we need a drink," he shouted as I tried to keep up the pace. We went straight back to his place, where Alla and Larissa were preparing for the afternoon feast. "Did you have a nice time?" Larissa asked. "Smashing," I pointed to my leg. "Don't poke it," as she targeted the wound with her finger. "Oh!" she held back from saying it and marched into the kitchen; reappearing with some smelly stingy stuff on a piece of gauze. "It's fine!" She pulled my jeans' leg down. *"Do dna!"* was the cry, and I forgot all about it.

A couple of weeks later we were invited round to Lyonya and Tamara's flat about half a mile away on Gagarin Street. They had a big ground floor flat that led out onto a large gardened square with swings for the kids and round seating areas for the grown-ups. The reason for going had been kept quiet but I was soon taken into the kitchen to see the reason for the secrecy. On the cooker was an enormous pan with the lid upside down; then sealed around the edges with some sort of white muslin strips. On top of the lid was another pan containing cold water that was constantly emptied and refilled. A strange smell percolated from within. I pinched my nose. They pointed to the window that was sealed. "To stop the smell from getting out," Tamara whispered. We stood back as the pan lid was removed; the foul-smelling liquid gently simmering. Standing in the liquid was a tripod affair with a ring on the top, and sitting on the ring was a glass bowl containing some cloudy looking liquid. She took out the bowl and replaced it carefully with an empty one before re-sealing the lid. "Now," she struck a match and lit the liquid. It burned with a feint blue flame. "It's ready." The flame was extinguished. *"Samogonka!"* "Thank God for that - I thought it was nitro-glycerine. So, that's how you make home brewed vodka?" It was passed through a funnel into a bottle, then immediately out of the bottle and into a number of glasses.

"Drink!" Tamara instructed. I always do what I'm told and necked the potion. The grimace must have given it away and Tamara started to slap my back. "Wow," I gasped. "Is it good?" "I don't know yet," I replied, fighting for breath. "You try it." They did and came to a unanimous agreement that it was good. "And if I had fallen over?" "Then it wouldn't have been good." They agreed. She told me that they had made it from sugar with yeast added, but that you could also make it from potatoes and yeast.

After our second glass we went outside for a fag break. A crowd of lads sat in the centre of the garden playing cards. Suddenly, everybody started to run as two police motorcycle combinations raced onto the square. The policemen grabbed one tall lad; probably around the same age as me, and started to beat him mercilessly with their white truncheons. People started shouting abuse at the police from balconies, and a woman ran across to his aid but was unceremoniously pushed away. After they had beaten him to a pulp, they picked him up by his arms and legs and dumped him in the side-car; one of the policemen sitting on top of him with his legs hanging down over the side. They rode off with their capture while women screamed and waved their arms in the air. "What on earth was all that about?" I turned to Greesha who had come outside for a look. "Gambling." He rubbed his thumb and forefinger together. "Money," he whispered. "Men play for money and then somebody can finish up getting stabbed." He went on, "somebody must have phoned the police; so they take one to make an example of him." "Bloody hell, some example," I concluded.

CHAPTER 33
LEAVING ON A JET PLANE

Every day now I see a plant that is coming to fruition. Actually this plant is already bearing fruit and what was once a dark and dismal pit is now a clean, bright place of work; thousands of people producing high quality yarn. When we have time to stop and think about what we have achieved together, you have to feel pride. We have been comrades and we have been a community; like a miniature Great Britain, living and working together. People drawn from all backgrounds, taken from our homes and transported behind the iron curtain to an alien place with an alien climate. We have worked together, played together, even fought together, but it was together. Children have been educated and wives have been…wives.

Now that the costing boys are moving in to do the sums, a large number of us have been given our final travel date; 30th June, 1972. Larissa seems comfortable with our move back to the UK, probably the love she received on our visit playing a large part in that. We have to be mindful though of her family; she is, after all, their little girl, the special one. Hopefully, they realise just how much I love her and my commitment to ensure that she is happy and, in turn, that they are happy. One last thing that they reminded us of is a visit to see *Babushka Sarah* out in the country.

We left the bus at the edge of town and set off walking along a rough track. After about ten minutes the track ran out and we carried on across a large field of waist-high grass. It was a beautiful fresh June day and as we cut our way through the grass, clouds of white butterflies took flight. The children set off, chasing them, waving their hands in the air and laughing. At the end of the field was a railway embankment that we climbed crossing the single track. We stood on the line and Greesha pointed to a tiny village in the distance. "*Babushka's* village," he announced. Our party, around sixteen strong, ploughed on.

About 20 minutes later we came into the village. A central dirt road separated two rows of old wooden houses; probably I estimated a total of twenty, each one different but all with shoulder-high wooden fences. *Babushka's* house was next to the last house on the left. We entered through the front gate and walked to the back of the house. There was a large open yard and garden with several chickens and a rickety old wooden barn. Behind the barn was a very big orchard and gardens that seemed to go on into the distance. Maria waved for us to go into the house, Larissa taking my hand. "Come on," she said, "let's go and meet granny." Moving inside from bright sunshine the house was dark. My eyes soon adjusted as we moved from the small 'L' shaped kitchen into the living room. The room was old, quaint and spotlessly clean, with pure white lace curtains and tablecloth and the statutory burgundy and gold woven rug on the left-hand wall. "*Babushka*, this is Alan," mum introduced me. She stood up from her chair; an old lady of grandmother proportions, with grey, wavy hair and a warm friendly face. She checked me out with her eyes before holding out her hands, grasping my arms and administering three kisses before enveloping me in a meaningful cuddle. "*Anglichanin, da?*" she asked. "*Da Babushka*, it's lovely to meet you," I replied. "And where's my little girl?" She held her arms out for Larissa, who duly obliged. "Sit down, sit down," and her subjects obeyed. "So Alan, do you love her?" She looked me in the eyes. Larissa squeezed my hand. "Yes, I love her very much," I told her. She sat silently for a moment. "Then so be it," she concluded with a smile. "I should have been at your wedding but I have the cow," she pointed towards the barn. Mum joined in, "She has to milk the cow twice a day," she explained. *Babushka* stood up, "Come on children, you should be outside in the sunshine. Larissa, show Alan our orchard. Maria, you can help with the food." *Babushka* had spoken and we duly obliged.

Larissa showed me the orchard including her apple tree; already showing tiny green apples. At the far end was a field full of potatoes, and it made me wonder how she managed to look after all this. We walked back after getting a shout from the house. I was presented with an enamel mug full of milk. "Drink," *Babushka* told me. The milk was warm; I looked at it quizzically. "Straight from the cow," she explained, "the very best for your health." I drank it down in one, not wishing to offend. "Okay, now you can drink vodka," she said.

We ate wonderfully, we drank and sang heartily and we talked intimately about an old lady and her memories. More important, she wanted to know about my family and me and about England and my work and whether we were going to have children and would they speak Russian, and we laughed. I walked with her to the well at the far end of the village. I carried two buckets of water back and wondered how she managed during a Russian winter. The more I looked at her the more I saw Larissa in her. She was a kind looking old lady, yet strong and proud; gratefully accepting her lot and happy in her family.

We stayed that night, sleeping in any nook and cranny, and left the following day with a solemn promise to Sarah that I would bring her back home to visit her. "Now, you go and look after one another," she said, tears rolling down her cheeks. The embrace moved me emotionally, and I felt sad to say goodbye, but say *do svidanya* we did. As we walked back across the field, my mind wandered as I sucked in the fresh air. This was Belarus and this is how I wanted to remember it.

The leaving was strangely like a carnival. Two buses parked outside the flats waiting to transport around sixty people to Minsk on their final trip home. Hundreds of people flocked around the buses, including the entire Strotsky clan. Mum had been crying when she arrived and now she was trying to convince Larissa that she should take two huge silk cushions that she had made; Larissa desperately trying to explain that we didn't have room. I looked at mum with the two cushions, one under each arm and tears flooding down her face. I tried to console her putting my arms around her neck and kissing the tears from her face.

Music is blasting from the flats - John Denver is singing, *'I'm leaving on a jet plane, don't know when I'll be back again, oh, babe, I hate to go'.* I turned to dad, Ivan, man of iron and man of few words; his eyes blood red. He grabbed me and crushed me in his arms. "Son," he rasped, wiping the tears from his face. *"Papa,"* I replied, trying to hold back the emotion. I knew that I couldn't break down now; I had to be strong, for Larissa. We moved from person to person, hugging and kissing, and I waved to them all after seeing Larissa onto the bus.

The crowd cheered and waved as Mr Touse sounded the final *"poechaly."* As the bus pulled away we strained our necks for our last fleeting glimpse of our home. I put my arm around Larissa and kissed her better.

We leave Mogilev and head out onto the open road and I'm looking out through the bus window. I'm trying to reflect on time that has passed so quickly. As I looked up into a beautiful summer sky I can vividly remember, seemingly not five minutes ago, arriving here cold and miserable; everything looked grey. After a time, you learn to understand that it isn't about colour, or anything we are programmed to think. It's about people and feelings, touching and communicating, understanding and even misunderstanding. It was about falling in love. That's why I would miss the place so much.

Mogilev had given me something special, yes, memories to last a lifetime, but much more than that. I had set off to the Soviet Union a snotty-nosed kid from Bolton and now, three years on, I was returning from Mogilev still a snotty-nosed lad from Bolton; still gazing up in to the sky and daydreaming. The big difference was that now I had a future; she was here, tucked under my arm, warm and beautiful. Larissa lifted her head and looked at me with those glorious green eyes. I kissed her forehead and she snuggled deep into my chest. "Thank you Mogilev for the best three years, no, the best *'Tree God'* of my life."

CHAPTER 34
FRUIT & NUT

Westminster Bridge Road, Lambeth on the 8th floor I nodded politely to a secretary hurrying in the opposite direction. The lino covered corridor squeaked, echoing my thoughts. Three years away and a job completed. I sat in the cavernous and now shabby waiting room thinking over my time away. After today's de-briefing at head office I could return to Bolton to get on with the rest of my life.

"Come in Alan." Somehow the Leamington Spa accent never sat right with his grizzled tough nut looks. "Flash tie Ronnie" I poked a finger at it. "M.C.C. tie, heathen Bolton fan." Ronnie was in his late forties and built like a brick outhouse, with a wrinkled sun-baked face and greying crew cut. "Get a move on and I could make Lords for the afternoon session." Sheldon was at his desk busy signing off some documents. "Grab a pew Alan." His eyes flashed momentarily over his half moon reading glasses that sat precariously on the tip of his puffin-like nose. Sheldon was the boss, 'the gaffer' but you wouldn't have known. He looked as if he had been locked up for several years without food or light. Even his suit looked as if it had been pulled off a tramp; the shoulders covered in dandruff and dead hair. Still I couldn't take my eyes off his nose; holding my breath waiting for the glasses to slide into the abyss. "Feel free to talk; I'll only be a minute." His eyes momentarily caught my stare. I started to breath again and quickly looked around the room.

"Nice new Axminster, but apart from that the only difference is the missing portrait of Fred." "Fred....who?" Ronnie couldn't resist the invitation. "Fred Lenin of course; he's quite big out there." "Her majesty," he pointed to the huge portrait hung behind Sheldons' desk, "The Queen." I stood up and bowed. "So Alan how was the project?" Sheldon took off his glasses, rubbed his weary looking eyes and sat back in his big leather chair. "Arrrm, it seemed to go quite well at our end, but you tell me." "Close the curtains Ronnie and hit the lights."

"I never knew they had a paddle for a tale...and that's where it lives?" We sat looking at a close up of a beaver just before it dived into the basement of its lakeside log cabin. *Click*, went the shutter. " Black, my favourite colour; now that's a score. *Click.* "Wonderful work with the fuel silos." *Click.* "Hangers and MIG's parked up; a nice blend of military and civil. *Click.* "Even one in flight, the Concorde guys are loving that shot." "That was slightly more difficult," I announced; "timing was everything, and I thought it was a bomber." "The driver?" Sheldon asked. "Boris, couldn't have been better; a fresh pike and fruit and nut for desert, what more could anybody want?" "And the other shots?" "Up a tree, I couldn't believe my luck. The telescopic was genius, a disgorger screwed into the fishing scales; thank the guys in 'props'." After a few more *clicks,* "Lights Ronnie and bring in some tea." Ronnie hit the switch.

"So what about Sheep's Head?" I asked breaking into a stifled chuckle. "Spur of the moment thing; a quick in and out. We needed to get hold of the schematics from the new tank depot behind the tractor factory. We collected him at Heathrow." "What a character, he deserves an Oscar." "By the way how was *Dedushka Petya* and his bloody clapped out BSA?" Sheldon sounded as if he was asking about a long lost friend. "Now that's a long story; I didn't actually see him." "What?" He sat upright in his chair. "He sent his grand-kids;

two young tearaway girls. He probably knew they would give me a hard time; one of the girls was wild." "Go on!" "They drove the bike into a sodding lake and the schematics were nearly a goner." "Where were they?" "Tucked down her boots." Now I was laughing. "Stupid old bugger's getting a liability." Sheldon banged the desk with his fist. "He's happy enough I suppose; they stripped me of a bag full of BSA spare parts along with his chockie bar. Anyway how did he get the BSA?" "Now that is a long story."

"Milk, Mr Tree God?" Now Sheldon forced a smile. "Please," I replied somewhat embarrassed at the name. "So, go on, where did the novel sign off come from?" "Obviously from the tree you climbed to get the photos." Ronnie butted in. "No actually from the translation 'three years'- '*Tree Goda.*' It was the first thing that connected when I landed." Ronnie now looked bored while Sheldon shook his head.

"Anything good from Nicholai?" Having dunked a couple of bourbons, I tried to move the meeting along. "Amazing what you can get out of a pack of cards, but that needn't bother you." "And *Dyadya Volodya,* by the way I nearly died when I saw that log canoe. Did 'props' send it out?" "Would you have preferred a speed boat?" "Well maybe a rowing boat." "He sent some nice pictures of the dam and details of the hydro-electrics."

Now he stood up and slowly circumnavigated his desk before leaning against the front, towering over me like a stick insect. "So, Alan… what went wrong?" He decided to pick at what was left of his decaying teeth. "What went wrong? I fell in love…is that wrong? Sorry but that's something we can't control….isn't it?" I could see Sheldons eyes narrowing. "You can control loosing your fucking mind!" He threw a piece of rotted tooth at me. "Oh, blame it on the fruit and nut, anyway I stuck it out." He lifted a folder from his desk. "Could do better it says at the bottom of your report." "That's from 'ops'? No bloody wonder, Denzel's a school teacher for Christ's sake;

he writes that on all his reports." "Alan, in the trade we call these 'bullet points'. Alcoholic - married - damaged goods - finished - shall I go on?" "Hang on a bit, I swarmed up a bloody big tree in a pair of wellies for you to take pictures of friggin aeroplanes. I was more interested in the beaver building its house if you must know!" There was a deathly silence and Sheldon looked shocked at the outburst. "Thank you Alan." He stiffened before walking back to his chair and sitting down. "So you're happy enough sodding off back to Bolton and playing happy families?" "Just watch me; you won't see my arse for a cloud of dust." "Then I think you should collect your chocolate and piss off before I get Ronnie to dump you in the river...on his way to the cricket of course." For a split second I thought I saw Sheldon smile. "My pleasure boss." Ronnie cracked his knuckles. "Don't worry Alan, we'll keep in touch." I think that was meant to be Sheldon's final word. I let out a sigh and walked towards the door that Ronnie held open. "Before I go did you find out who 'Red Leader' was?" Sheldon waved his hand towards Ronnie who duly closed the door. "The stuff you took from KGB H/Q was basically crap; however one name did pop up too many times to ignore. It would appear that 'Red Controller' was a certain Alexander Touse." I was just about to open my mouth when Sheldon finished off. "Don't tell me, you thought it was him all along." "Actually boss," I couldn't stop myself from laughing. "I thought it all fitted too neatly, but it just goes to show." I slid two fingers into my top pocket and pulled out a playing card. "Do you know what *Touse* means in English?" Sheldon sat back in his chair and pondered the question. "Tousey gave me this card as a memento, but the significance never struck me." I spat on the back of the card before slapping it on my forehead revealing the ace of spades. "*Durak*...fool, is that what he is telling me?" I peeled the card off my head, wiped the saliva on my jacket and held it out for Sheldon. "So go on, *Touse!*" Sheldon grew impatient. I pointed to the card. "Ace! Simple. *Touse* means

Ace. It never struck me until now." I turned towards the door before stopping. I felt in my inside jacket pocket and pulled out a block of Cadburys Fruit and Nut and tossed it to Sheldon. Surprised, he grabbed the gift with both hands. "What's this?" He started to remove the wrapper. " Mr.Touse's not so little black book," I disclosed proudly. "How the f…?" "Don't ask, but I think it's going to be worth more than you can fit inside a block of fruit and nut." I held his gaze for long enough. "That is a box of Cadburys Milk Tray all tied up with a nice red bow; and just so you know Sheldon, my lady loves milk tray." I winked. "Happy reading."

THE END...NO SORRY, THE BEGINNING...

ABOUT THE AUTHOR

Alan Hamer was born in Bolton, Lancashire in 1948. He has been happily married for over 35 years and has 2 grown up children. Alan enjoys fishing and supporting his local football team Bolton Wanderers. *TREE GOD: Behind the Iron Curtain* is his first novel.